ABOUT THE AUTHOR

Daniel Grant is a writer and television news producer in London.

He lives in Godalming in Surrey with his wife Alison.

Sex Lessons is his debut novel.

Get the latest updates at

www.danielgrantonline.com

SEX LESSONS

DANIEL GRANT

Published by YouWriteOn.com, 2011

© Copyright 2011 Daniel Grant

Cover by John Chandler at Chandler Book Design

First Edition

The author has asserted their moral right under the Copyright, Designs and Patents Act, 1988, to be identifiedas the author of this work.

All Rights reserved. No part of this publication may be reproduced, copied, stored in a retrieval system, or transmitted, in any form or by any means, without the prior written consent of the copyright holder, nor be otherwise circulated in any form of binding or cover other than that in which it is published and without a similar condition being imposed on the subsequent purchaser.

All characters in this publication are fictious and any resemblance to real persons, living or dead, is purely coincidental

A CIP catalogue record for this title is available from the British Library.

ISBN 978-1-908147-65-3

For Feeney

PART 1

ONE – THE PREDICAMENT

I stare at the pill. It knows my dilemma. I should just go ahead and take it. Save myself the hassle, but something inside prevents me. My feet feel nail-gunned to the floor. I gaze at the glass of water next to the sink. I could put the pill back in the cupboard and not take it this time. Might be fine. So hit-and-miss though. I hate that I rely on these things. It went okay the last time. Granted, I was drunk and we didn't actually do it but things did happen where they should. Wonder what they did in the Middle Ages with these sorts of problems? Who knows? Why am I thinking this? You're going to have to do something soon James because you've been in here for five minutes and she's already getting suspicious. I can hear the question in her mind. 'What's he doing in there?' It's a good question. What am I doing? Okay, come on. To pill or not to pill? I guess that is the-

SEX LESSONS

'James, are you okay?' Her muffled voice drifts through the door. Damn, I thought I had more time. Better reassure her, better say something.

'Yeah fine, be out in two secs.' Good. Sounded genuine, not too much panic in my voice.

'Get that cute arse out here,' she calls back. I glance at the walk-in shower. Not sure I could get away with another shower in the space of fifteen minutes. Decision time.

The pill sits, watching me, indifferent to my dilemma. I take it between my fingers, examining it. Quickly, I open the bathroom cabinet and place it back in the packet. I take a deep breath, making sure not to catch my eyes again in the mirror, turn around and open the door.

She's been up to something because as soon as I step out into the bedroom, she turns. She's on her hands and knees on top of the bed and looks at me with a guilty stare, like I just caught her. Then her eyes relax and the slightest of smiles creeps across her striking face. She's wearing white lingerie, expensive by the look of it. Doesn't matter, it's not going to help this scenario.

'Here he is,' she says. Jenny's a stunner. Long brown hair, almost down to her waist. Glistening green eyes. Long eyelashes, full lips. My eyes move downwards. She's small, maybe five-five, but her curves and cotton-soft skin give her a lovely hourglass figure. Her legs are smooth and sleek. Her breasts...now that I see them in this light they look like implants, but what the hell.

DANIEL GRANT

I walk over and kiss her on the neck. She turns around and drapes her arms over my shoulders, pulling me in closer. Her lips caress mine. Her hips are like hand warmers on my fingertips. Her tongue plays and dances inside my mouth. Feels like there's a teenage house party going on inside my chest. She smells so good, it aches. Everything appears perfect, doesn't it? However, in about two minutes it's going to go horribly wrong. I want to stop it, prevent the impending storm somehow but it's out of my hands. My mind churns negative thoughts like a washing machine cycling up for a spin. All the possible catastrophes-in-waiting. I'm starting to panic, it's been too long, there's nothing going on in places there should be. Her fingers wander playfully down my chest. I close my eyes. She reaches under my boxers and slightly withdraws her lips from mine.

'You okay?' she whispers.

'Yeah,' I stumble. Got to do something. I move quickly, grabbing her arse and turning her over so she's lying on her front. I might have caught her off guard because she makes a little squeal. I need to stall, that's all. Buy myself some time before the downpour. I kiss the smooth arch in her back and move downwards, my tongue twisting and turning. I pull her legs apart and position my head between them. She starts to moan. My attention checks in on the little guy, he's either out to lunch or on an extended holiday. I hope it's somewhere warm. Damnit, I knew I should have taken the pill, what the hell was I thinking? It was right there. I could try to extricate myself. Take it now? Don't think I'd get away with it though, too many questions. Jenny's breathing has become fast; she is writhing under my touch, her face pressed into the pillow. I can't see a way out of this. She grabs the brass railing and presses her forehead down into the sheets.

My eyes glance over to the bed table, an unopened condom lies on top. The creased foil makes it look like it's been in my wallet far too long. I hate condoms. Some men moan about a male pill, I would take it and shake your hand for selling it to me. I might even do a little skip out of the pharmacy.

Jenny's close now, her breathing is out of control. So's her moaning. My tongue is starting to ache; it wants her to hurry up. My mind, on the other hand, wants to keep things exactly as they are. It knows as soon as this bit's over I head straight to jail. No passing 'Go', no two hundred pounds. She cries out.

'Right there, OH GODDDD!' It occurs to me she's making such a racket, the neighbours probably can't sleep. Fuck 'em, they keep a cuckoo clock up against the adjacent wall to my bedroom and it wakes me up every single night.

'Oh, oh!' She sounds like a porn star and writhes left then right almost trying to move me away with her thighs. The moaning suddenly stops, silence descends. Her hips quiver and I start to slow down. Only seconds remain now.

DANIEL GRANT

Any last requests? I reluctantly move up next to her, like a messenger with bad news for the Queen. She rolls over; the back of her hand now resting over her forehead. Her eyes close, there's a slight glisten to her skin. I watch her lips, barely open. She pants quietly.

Suddenly she turns to me, a big smile on her face. Her eyes sparkle in what little light there is, almost as if she had been crying.

'That was great,' she says. I smile back but it's fake, my mind is racing all over the place. Negative thoughts unleashed. The panic is real and upon me. I know what's about to happen. I know everything that happens from now until the end but have little choice but to watch it unfold before me. She moves her hands down to my groin. 'Let's see if you like this,' she whispers into my ear, biting my lobe gently. It tickles, I shrug my shoulder involuntary at the sensation. She starts to rub. Her hands are warm but it's not going to work. My heart is beating so hard against my chest, it hurts to breathe. Come on, damn you. Please!

Wait. Hold on. What's this? A feeling, some...sensation. Keep going I say to him, with as much encouragement as I can muster. I feel him start to rise; her hand glides more easily. She kisses me, her tongue finding mine once again. My palms move along her hips. Could this really be okay? Perhaps this might work after all. She moves her hand faster and faster, ripples of pleasure swell through me. Just keep it up, do

SEX LESSONS

not let go James. If I'm going to proceed to the next stage, I need to do it fast.

I move her so she lies on her back. She gazes at me, her eyes piercing my soul like a pencil through Clingfilm. I pretend not to notice. Can't deal with that. Good boy, you're doing so well. I position myself between her legs.

'Wait, the thing-' She tries to grab the condom but it's too far away. I'd forgotten all about it.

'I got it,' I say, taking it and peeling off the foil. But even as I do, I feel the energy ebbing away. God no. Come on little man. Be quick, get it on. I scramble around and pinch the top, desperately trying to unfurl it. I'm losing rigidity, damnit, come on.

'Do you want me to do-,' she asks.

'No!' I interrupt too fast. She looks at me, her eyes betraying a flash of concern. I yank the rubber down and quickly try to position myself. She lies back but the smile has gone from her face. I try to enter her but it's a battle lost. He is no longer there. In spirit or body. I try anyway. Anything to keep this going. He won't go in and the rubber is starting to slip off. Everything stops for a split-second as I take in what's unfolding before me. Jenny stares at me with sympathetic eyes. She's been here before. She knows how this goes. I want to cry. Scream. To run out. Never see her again. The shame feels like a hydraulic press forcing itself down on my chest. Despair and dejection gallop through me.

DANIEL GRANT

Reality hits play and this unfortunate scene resumes towards its inevitable conclusion. I slide off slowly and lay next to her. We stare at the ceiling. I listen to her thoughts, swaying and sighing with disappointment like a sea breeze. She starts telling me how it doesn't matter, it's happened to her many times before. I barely hear her, consumed by my own self-pity. My eyes stare out into the darkness. I should have taken the pill like normal. Not try to be a hero.

So here I lay, talking to you in my head; the beautiful Jenny laying naked next to me, trying to make me feel better about it all. I'm almost certain we will never see each other again after tonight. Not that it matters to be honest. I don't need any further embarrassment. I have the memory now anyway. Another souvenir of my failure.

TWO - PRESS HERE FOR ASSISTANCE

When I wake up, Jenny is gone. So weird how that happens; they get up, dress and leave and I don't hear a thing. The front door sticks as well so you'd think I'd hear a slam or something.

My apartment's in a swish part of Rotherhithe, East London near the Thames. The bedroom alone is bigger than the Canning Town two bedroom terrace I grew up in. It has natural wood floors and its own fireplace.

I clamber out of bed and wander into the kitchen looking like something from Village of the Damned. The kitchen is huge, six hobs and an oven bigger than my washing machine. It's ultramodern and kitted out with the latest gadgets, half of which I have no idea how to use. The whole place looks like a show house from the Ideal Home Exhibition.

Jenny's left me a note. It sits on the table, my name on the front, enticing me to open it. I try to resist but curiosity compels me to pick it up and rip it open. She has neat, girly handwriting.

It reads, 'James, I just want to say how much fun I had last night and although things ended prematurely (ouch!) it would be great to catch up again soon. Sorry to leave without saying goodbye but I have an early meeting. Give me a call sometime or come and visit me in accounts. Luv Jenny.'

Note to self, never go out with someone you work with. Maybe you're thinking that's not too bad. She seems like she's still interested. Maybe it's not all doom and gloom. Yeah? Well you know what I say to that? Bollocks. She's being polite about a horrible situation which I made worse by my Oscar-worthy wallowing. Seriously, what party girl wants that crap? I'm sure she likes me and if I wanted, I have no doubt we could be friends, but seriously, what's the point? Every time I saw her would just remind me of my shortcomings. No pun intended. Fuck it, coffee will make me feel better. I walk over to the sink and swipe a mug. It has a picture of a yellow happy face on it. I start searching for the cafetière; I can't find it. This sucks. I could have sworn I stuck it in the dishwasher yesterday. Sorry about this, I can't do anything until I've had a cup of coffee. Then something hits me. I walk back to Jenny's letter and rescan it. 'P.S. I think I accidentally broke your coffee pot this morning, sorry.'

SEX LESSONS

Well that's brilliant. I check the bin, the metal plunger peeks out, pleading with me to save it. I slam the lid shut in disgust. That settles it, definitely not being friends now. If I'd known this was going to happen I would have sent her packing with a quick snog and a boob-feel.

Miserably, I fish out a black suit and pull it on. I feel it's a day for mourning. Stitched in to the inside jacket pocket is my name, in case I forget who I am. I glance at myself in the mirrored wardrobe. I grab my keys and walk out. Today is going to be shit but at least I look good.

'How long have you had this problem?' Doctor Moore sits across from me. His thick frames, scrawny hair and large crooked nose are distracting, as is his incoherent C&A twinset. I stare at him and consider my response. I need to get private health insurance, not keep fucking about with the NHS like this. The doctor's office is a cramped affair with just enough room for two people. On the walls are nineteen-eighties posters of human anatomy and a yellow box for discarding needles. The stench of bleach and industrial Glade sits under my nostrils. This guy's in desperate need of a Feng Shui consultant. I think I may have a number in my wallet.

'Since I was a teenager. Can you just write the prescription?' He looks over his glasses at me.

DANIEL GRANT

'Mr. Kennedy, I am here to help you. I know sometimes these things are difficult for men to talk about-'

'Look, it's not personal but I've done this so many times and every time I come in here, there's a new guy sitting in the chair.' He stares at me, waiting. 'Look, I've got a date tomorrow night, I need the pills. Are you going to prescribe them or do I need to talk to another doctor?' I lied about the date by the way. I would have been seeing Jenny but, well you know the story there. He sighs heavily, a faint whiff of garlic on his breath.

'No, I will not and I shall make a note on your record that no one else do so either.' Anger races through me.

'For fuck sake-' I start to say but he carries on with his condescending speech.

'You have a problem and I don't think it's necessarily a physical one. You need to see a psychologist and sort it out...' The doctor is trying to help, I can see that, he's not a bad man. At this stage, however, rationalisation has donned fake glasses, packed its bags and fled the country leaving anger flooding my arteries to bursting point. Before I even realise what I'm doing, the door is open and I'm out, storming down the corridor. The elderly woman on reception gives me a confused glance as I rush past, papers on the desk flying up behind me.

'Hey!' she calls, her croaky old-woman voice barely registering. I stop, turn around and bend down to help her pick them up.

SEX LESSONS

'Thank you,' she says. I nod. Then, anger resumed, I stomp through the automatic double doors and out into the fresh air.

Fucking doctors. Seriously, it's not like I'm asking for a new heart or a Lumbar Puncture, just a few blue pills and a pat on the back for asking nicely.

I get to my car. It's a metallic black Merc, a world away from the clapped-out nineteen seventies Cortina I used to drive about town in. My parents had generously saved up and bought me the tampon-white Ford for my eighteenth birthday. I was chuffed because money was scarce and for them to go out of their way like that was pretty amazing. Especially after convincing myself they didn't really like me all that much. My friends, however considered it a babe-repellent and most days I had to park it a good five minutes walk from the school.

I slam the door behind me. The rage is still inside but it's starting to subside now. Soon I'll be in regret mode and I don't want to be anywhere near Doctor Moore when I get there. I start the engine. It hums beautifully, awaiting my command. I shift into drive and pull away, replaying what Moore had said.

'You have a problem Mr. Kennedy and I don't think it's necessarily a physical one.' Not physical, whatever you say doc. I don't need to see a fucking shrink. Talk about what? That back in sixth form, Susie Green copped off with

DANIEL GRANT

someone else? Susie Green. Haven't thought about her in a while.

I drive to my office. I work for United Bank in the City and it's more than a little tedious. And before you say anything, not all bankers are dicks. Okay, some definitely are, I'll point out the gold plated ones as we go. But look, I'm good at what I do and they pay me a ridiculous amount of money. My job consists of basically managing a small investment team which tries to guess which way the market will go so that United can make money even if the market falls. Confused? Yeah, well I told you this shit was tedious. I started as a trainee here about eight years ago. One day the guy who was teaching me allowed me to trade on my own. On that day, I made United over two hundred grand. The boss gave me a car (on hire-purchase) and a new job with an expense account. I was twenty two. I don't trade myself anymore, I just have to make sure my little unit doesn't fuck up.

I walk through the massive glass entrance with 'United Bank' etched in big letters above it. The reception takes up what should have been the first three floors. You need binoculars to see the ceiling. The security guys are trying to control a bunch of Japanese clients, all of whom need ID tags. I swipe my card and the glass door swings open. I enter one of the eight glass lifts, leaving the echoes of unfamiliar language behind me.

The lift starts to accelerate at stomach-wrenching speed. Floors race by faster and faster.

SEX LESSONS

I wouldn't exactly call my building a skyscraper but it's colossal. Don't ask me what the people on all these levels do, I've no idea. Somewhere in there is the team I manage. I only ever see them when they need a bollocking. I reach the twenty-seventh floor and step out. The open-plan office is one of those great twentieth century inventions. The people in my office are, in general, a good laugh. We like to hang out after work socially, drinking till we're stupid. You'll meet some of them later. Ah okay, see this fat guy in the glass office to the right that looks like he took a hockey puck to the face, he's the big boss. Mike Cartwell. You know how I was talking about arseholes? Well this guy is the king of them all. The imperial arsehole.

Here's my desk, near the centre of the room. It has no less than six flat-screen monitors which are linked to the exchanges and pricing info from Bloomberg. It also has two phones with a mini-exchange so I can talk to traders from other companies and an empty packet of crisps, sorry about that. Hang on, that's Smokey Bacon flavour, I don't even like Smokey Bacon. Someone's been messing about with my desk. I examine the computer and desktop carefully. Nothing seems out of place. Maybe it was someone from my team I yelled at last week. It happens so regularly, it's remarkable there's not a contract out on me. I consider the implications as I sit down and log in. I take out my FT Employment supplement and position it open on my desk. Always good to remind my boss how indispensible I am. Which I can confirm, by the way, I am not. I also get friends to call me up pretending to be headhunters. All just part of the game.

Even though I don't actually sit with my team I can see what they're all doing on my terminal here. Like big brother. Sometimes I send them cryptic messages, just to fuck with them. See here, all these numbers on the monitor I don't mind if they're red or green as long as my team has bet on the correct colour otherwise it's a bad conversation.

This floor has three glass offices at the front for the bigwigs like fuckwit Mike. The unfortunate thing about open plans are everyone can hear and see everyone else. Poppy, the girl who sits at the desk opposite me, is such a loudmouth. She's got big, chubby cheeks, has constant childcare issues and friends who are always splitting up from their husbands. Thank God she isn't on my team. I don't know her that well but I can confirm she is a giant pain in the arse.

'Morning James,' Poppy says, yawning. Christ, how many fillings? It's like looking inside the Terminator's mouth. Wouldn't want to be standing behind her at airport security.

'Hi Poppy, you're looking fetching today. Fantastic suit.'

'Really?'

'Yeah, very cool,' I say, nodding. She glances down at her jacket.

SEX LESSONS

'Oh. Thanks.'

'You're welcome.' I feel dirty but what the hell, the comment hit the spot. A small, imperceptible smile has crept across her cold lips.

I'm working on moving desks to one near the window. Some of the cubicles have fantastic views of the Tower of London and the Thames. Normally sat over there, in one of those pews I mentioned is-

'Nice to see you finally made it in.' Mark Pasty stands next my desk.

'I had to stop and say hi to your mum,' I retort, 'she kept me longer than I was expecting.' Mark shoots a cynical smile and shakes my hand.

'She can be like that. Just be gentle, she's getting on a bit,' he replies. Mark has the dubious honour of being my best mate even if he does look like George Michael's spitting image puppet. He also has the most ridiculous second name, Pasty. Oh, and don't bother trying to come up with ribs on it, he's heard them all. It's ironic really because he's half Greek, has olive skin and is the least pasty person I've ever met. Mark turned twenty-nine just last week. I suppose he's handsome in a preppy, posh sort of way. He makes more money than me and enjoys reminding me of it. Although he appears okay at the moment, he's still getting over Jess. They were engaged until last week then she broke it off. I'm still not sure why, he hasn't mentioned it and I don't want to pry. I know he was sleeping with Paula though, our sex-crazed Argentinean trainee. She resigned last Friday, giving no reason.

'What's with the suit? You going to a funeral?' Mark asks.

'No, I fancied wearing it. Looks sharp though, doesn't it?' I say, extending an arm to show off the cuffs.

Darren Hargreaves walks passed. I don't know him that well but I do know he has the biggest forehead of anyone I've ever seen.

'Hey guys. Nice suit James? Big interview?' Darren asks. Mark turns to me, a smile as big as the moon.

'No, I just felt like wearing it, that okay?' I snap back. Darren looks suitably surprised at my outburst.

'Sure, yeah, looks good.' He walks away. I glance at Mark who's still grinning.

'Don't you have work to do or something?' I ask.

'Yeah. Yeah I do,' Mark replies chuckling, 'hey, we still watching England lose on Saturday?'

'Mate, until I met you I didn't know Greece even had a football team.' Between you and me, I did know. Didn't they like invent sport or something?

'Wager then. Say, two hundred for England to lose,' he says, pretending it means nothing. I know he loves these little bets.

'All right, seems like a waste of money though. For you I mean,' I reply, turning my computer on. Mark looks away.

SEX LESSONS

'What do we have here?' he asks, staring over towards the reception desk.

'What?' I reply, trying to sound nonchalant. I can't see over my computer monitor. He walks two steps away from me, still absorbed.

'Oh brother,' he says, still staring. I can't resist any more, I stand up and look over to see what he is gaping at. The subject of his attention is, I quickly realise, the most beautiful woman I have ever laid eyes on. Mike 'arsehole' Cartwell is showing her around. He points to his office then to the trading floor, explaining things as they saunter slowly towards a conference suite. She has long blonde hair, late twenties maybe. She's wearing one of those tight, power woman suits. One button holds the jacket in place and it looks like it's struggling. My collar starts to feel tight around my neck, I loosen my tie.

'Jesus,' is all I can fumble out. I glance at Mark who is equally entranced. 'Who is that?' I ask, more to God than anyone. We stand transfixed; sensory input all but shut down. The sun shines through her hair giving her a strangely religious backlit glow.

She gives a polite laugh to Cartwell, her teeth blinding all who gaze upon them. Cartwell's such a penis. He got where he is not through hard work, but because he plays golf with the Chief Executive. Man I want to punch that guy. Cartwell leads the beauty into his office and shuts the door. Everyone returns to work.

'So who is she?' I ask Mark again.

'How the hell do I know?'

'Well you'd better find out. Soon. There'll be other players,' I say. He takes this on-board and nods slowly.

'I'm on it,' he says, walking away with determined purpose.

SEX LESSONS

THREE – REGRETS

I arrive back at my apartment around eight; I hate winter in England. It's freezing and the sun fucked off hours ago. I remove my clothes and walk into the bathroom, the tiles feel cold beneath my feet. I stare at myself in the mirror.

Like a slap across the face, I'm suddenly right back with Jenny last night. Almost as if making a new choice now would make a difference to everything that happened since. I open the cabinet, take the last blue pill out of the packet and examine it between my fingers.

'Where were you?' I say, a slight accusation in my voice. The pill, apparently not liking my tone suddenly slips from my grip and drops into the toilet. 'Shit!' I immediately thrust my hand down the bowl, fishing around for it. My fingers touch nothing but porcelain and icy water. I yank my arm back and peer into the toilet bowl. Gone. Disaster. Instinctively I put a hand to my forehead and, feeling its chill, realise it's the hand I just went fishing with. 'FUCK!'

I walk back to the sink, throw water over my face and begin soaping my arm. I glance back at myself in the mirror. My last option is now on its way through the London sewage system. Good one James.

I hit the tap on the walk-in shower. A jet of hot water blasts from the head. I stand beneath it. Feels good, the water surging over me. My mind begins drifting back to last night. I know I shouldn't dwell but I can't help it. Her fragrance as we kissed. The look on her face, the moment she realised what was happening. Sympathy and disappointment. Pity fixed in her eyes. My heart races as image after image hits me in full HD clarity. I turn, facing directly into the powered water; it hurts as it hits my eyes. The water shoots up my nose and inside my mouth. I cough, splutter and step away, shutting the water off. I place my hands on the wall, my arrested pose. I stare down at the floor, listening to the drips slapping the tiles. The water gurgles down the drain. How can I fix this? You probably caught on this is not the first time. In fact, it happens with depressing regularity. That's why I started taking the pills, an attempt at some stability in my life. It was working as well, until now. Think positive, James. All the events of your life have brought you here. What was it that started it though? Something from my past. Susie Green, perhaps. My mind keeps wandering back to her...

SEX LESSONS

FOUR – FEELING GREEN

Susie was seriously gorgeous, how I'd managed to bag her as my first girlfriend I have no idea. Long brown hair, big eyes and a smile that made my heart soar. I was eighteen, it was the final year of school and until that point I hadn't had a single girlfriend. I honestly don't know why everything took so long. I was friends with all of them, which basically equated to sleeping with none of them.

I had been directing the school play 'Snow White and the Seven Dwarfs' and Susie had been Snow White. She must have seen something in the way I confidently and calmly brought the play to the stage. Or...she had an overinflated idea of what shagging the director would be like. Either way, I wasn't complaining. Of course, we had the teasing and gossip that comes when two people in the same class start going out. Each day becoming a new episode of the James and Susie show. But none of it mattered. I had a girlfriend.

DANIEL GRANT

A fit girlfriend. I was now within a hare's whisker of finally losing my virginity, the true bane of most male teenagers.

Three months later however, I still hadn't done the mummy daddy dance and I was starting to get annoyed. Now, I'm a patient guy and after waiting eighteen years, you'd think three more months wouldn't be a big deal, right? Well, no. Susie had a bit of a reputation at school and I was getting impatient. I started to wonder why, unlike everyone else who'd dated her, we hadn't progressed much beyond occasional fondling. I figured I needed to up my game, to wine her and dine her with some serious romance.

Susie had always wanted to go to Paris and, being the gentleman I am I thought I'd do something romantic for her birthday. You know, encourage her to put out a little or something. I can't tell you how many extra shifts I had to endure at my part-time job at Pizza Hut but I felt it was going to be worth it.

Having checked off all the things you do, Eiffel Tower, Champs Elysees, Montmartre, tonight was the night. We got dressed up. I wore a grey suit I'd bought for a steal at the local Age Concern which bulged at the seams. She sported a black BHS mini dress with high heels and potent Jean Paul Gautier perfume. I watched with fascination as she applied her makeup having never really studied the ritual in detail.

'What are you looking at?' she asked, glancing up at me, an eyeliner pencil in her hand.

SEX LESSONS

'Nothing. Just watching,' I replied. She rolled her eyes, smiling. She really was very pretty, I could see why so many of my friends wanted to jump into her pants.

'Ready?' she asked, standing up.

'Yep, let's go.'

We walked out of the hotel, arm in arm. The restaurant was a place I'd found in the Lonely Planet called Polinor. From the outside it looked like it had been there since the nineteenth century and the inside wasn't much different. Long tightly packed tables, the smell of cigarettes and cigars lingered in the air. On the walls there were mirrors with French writing, none of which I understood. We were shown to our table and sat down opposite each other. I glanced at the menu which I was dismayed to find was all in French.

'What's the matter?' Susie asked.

'Hmm, nothing,' I replied, a vague attempt at winging it.

'Do you want some help with the menu?'

'No,' I said too quickly. 'Okay yes.'

'Luckily one of us has a GCSE in French,' she said. From that point onwards, anytime we needed service it was Susie that did the honours. First order of the day, vin rouge. The waiter quickly produced the goods and we were off.

'So,' Susie said.

'So,' I replied, covering my nerves.

'I've had a great time James.'

'Me too. Me too.'

'I've never seen you in a suit.'

'I've never had one. The trousers are a bit tight.'

'Makes you look distinguished. Like Patrick Swayze.'

'Thanks. You look nice too.'

'Nice?'

'No I mean, beautiful.'

'Yeah? I love this dress.'

More wine was required and before long, we were soon at the happy stage of drunk.

'Why did it take you such a long time to ask me out?' Susie asked, a twinkle in her eye.

'I just thought we were friends.'

'I fancied you for ages but you just seemed, I dunno, uninterested.'

'Believe me I was interested, I just thought, there's no way someone like you would ever fancy me,' I replied. Susie took my hands in hers across the table.

'You're so sweet.' I looked away, embarrassed at her compliment. 'Did you fancy me?'

'Of course. You're...gorgeous and sexy and I dunno. I just think you're great.' She breathed in, a smile appearing. She leaned forward.

'Come here,' she whispered.

'What?'

'I want to tell you something.'

'Oh, okay,' I replied and duly leant in.

'You are going to get so lucky tonight.' She sat back, flicking her eyebrows. I smiled but I really didn't know what to do with that one. I was excited but at the same time terrified. This was going to be the night.

We'd had a perfect evening. Lots of wine, lots of silliness and flirting. I had allowed Susie to believe I had had a number of past girlfriends. Considering her well documented experience, I thought it best I keep the small detail of my virginity strictly on a need-to-know basis.

In the lift up to the hotel room my confidence seemed to diminish. My mind started an unhelpful conversation with me.

MIND: You're going to have to be amazing, she's slept with quite a few guys. She'll know if you come across as inexperienced.

ME: Yes thank you.

MIND: This is assuming you manage to get it up in the first place.

ME: Yes thank you!

And so on. By the time we reached our room, I had managed to work myself up into a state of unmitigated terror. All I wanted to do was turn the lights off and go to bed.

'You okay?' asked Susie. I looked up, wrenched from my thoughts.

'Hmm? Yeah, great,' I said as convincingly as I could. Susie took a step towards me.

'You look very handsome tonight James,' she said, a smile forming across her face. I swallowed and tried to smile back. Okay, this was it. Jesus. I walked forward with as much confidence as I could muster and kissed her. It may have been more like a head-butt but she seemed to get where I was going. Passion unexpectedly flooded through me. This was good. My hands started running over her body. We guided each other to the bed and lay down. My hands moved over her breasts then under her dress. She started to moan. I gave myself a mental pat on the back. Things were moving in the right direction, I surmised. However, there was still no action in my groin and that concerned me. I carried on. Then...something started happening downstairs. Thank you Lord! When the time came, I was rock hard, it was now or never. She whimpered slightly and I was away, straight out of the blocks and finding my stride. It felt like I'd dived into a warm chocolate swimming pool. Ripples of pleasure deluged me with each stroke. I grabbed her hips and held on for dear life. The feeling soon overwhelmed me. I needed to stop, slow down, but I didn't know how. Mayday, mayday! It was no use, I had no control. I closed my eyes and prepared for a crash landing. I came. My soul rose through the ceiling and out into the dark Parisian night. I did it! For the briefest of moments I felt as though I could do anything. Be anyone. It was as close to Nirvana as I had ever come. The entire session had lasted, I dunno, maybe two minutes but I didn't care.

I was no longer a virgin. I wanted to jump up and do a lap of honour around the room. It was neither pretty nor perfect but I got it in there and did what needed to be done. Good man. Well done.

SEX LESSONS

Susie turned over and was now lying on her back. She wasn't smiling.

'James...' she began. My mind stopped in mid-celebration. I looked at her. 'Is that it?' she said. What? Is that what? I just did it, Susie, what are you talking about? She stared at me, a concerned look on her face. Suddenly my soul was not only back in the room, it had shrivelled down to fun-size. I looked at her. She knew. I could see it.

'I know it was a little quick...'

'A little quick? You said you'd done this before.' Her words peppered my essence to shreds, machine-gunning my soul with ruthless accuracy. I swallowed.

'I know but...'

'Have you? Because that was like fucking a virgin. Well?' I breathed out, lost for the right explanation. I'd saved up every penny I had, taken her to Paris, she was the one. This wasn't how things were supposed to go.

She got off the bed and strode into the toilet leaving me to ponder my failures by myself. I don't know how long I sat there but it felt like hours. I was destroyed, I wanted to justify myself but what could I say? 'Sorry Susie, honestly, I don't have a clue what I'm doing.' It was pitiful. Why didn't she understand? It wasn't deliberate. You are fucking worthless James Kennedy, I told you she'd know. That was a truly shameful display, it's a wonder she doesn't dump you right now.

Eventually I stood and crept over to the door. I knocked.

'Suse?'

'What?' she replied.

'I'm sorry, I should have been honest with you. I didn't want to tell you because you said you didn't want someone inexperienced. I didn't know all this would happen. I was terrified to tell you the truth in case it came to this. But I guess, as we're here now there's no point in pretending anymore.' I waited. Long moments of silence. Then the door clicked and opened. Susie stood there, a frown on her forehead.

'All this time? Why didn't you just tell me?'

'I was scared. You kept saying how you hated virgins and how glad you were I wasn't one,' I replied. She shook her head.

'So you're a virgin?'

'As of five minutes ago, no. But before that, well maybe.'

'That's why it was so quick, it all makes sense.'

'I should have told you up front but...I liked you. I didn't want you to not give me a chance,' she smiled and stepped towards me, putting her arms around me.

'You are so silly James Kennedy.'

'I am.' We kissed and for the first time I felt okay about it all. Everything was on the table, it was as though I'd been carrying around an anvil on my back and suddenly someone had taken it away. I felt light. Honesty had set me free. I kissed her without a worry in the world. She

SEX LESSONS

knew my horrible little secret and she still liked me.

Suddenly we were in this new place. Where I didn't have to pretend to be something I wasn't. I could just be me. And Susie would understand from now on, whenever things didn't go according to plan.

Well sort of. The irony of all this was we split up less than two weeks later. We never did it again. She said it was to do with her parents but a few days later at a Christmas house party she was discovered in bed with Richard Taylor, the captain of the school rugby team. She gave me pretty much every excuse going except the one I believed. That I, James Kennedy, had brought this about by my utter failure as a man.

# FIVE – SATURDAY SLEEP IN

The alarm wakes me at seven thirty. I attempt to hit it, instead I end up whacking the side of the bed table. Pain rushes through my hand. I locate the ear-splitting noise with one eye then batter it until it shuts up. Peace. Silence. Better think about getting up. Suddenly a horrible thought enters my mind. Today is Saturday. Damnit, I forgot to turn the bloody thing off. I lie back and groan. I feel like crap; Mark took me to Jo Jo's last night, this club near Bishopsgate. I can't remember how I got home, there was definitely some walking involved because my feet are sore. I'm still drunk. Was I sick? Don't feel that post-hurl burn in my throat. My eyes are heavy, Going back to sleep. Sorry, too tired.

SEX LESSONS

SIX – INTERROGATION GAME

Slowly consciousness returns. One eye leisurely opens, then the other. I feel better, the room isn't spinning any more. The remnants of a headache thump around my brain but a couple of Alka Seltzers will sort that. The other eye opens and I remember my love of binocular vision. I breathe out slowly, stretching my arms and legs. The covers are half around me, half draping off the bed. I yawn. The inside of my mouth tastes like I've been drinking sand. I glance at the time, the clock reads two thirty. Two-thirty. The numbers roll around my head. Hmm, there was something I needed to do. Two-thirty. OH CRAP! People are coming over at three to watch the football! I haven't even...shit, uhh. Okay. I leap out of bed and throw myself into the shower. It's a quick in and out job, I'm sure a long-term girlfriend would have had me do it again but sod it. I yank on some clothes I find next to the wash basket. Should have done some laundry today

DANIEL GRANT

but there we are. I run into the living room in jeans and my dark grey t-shirt that reads 'If a Man Speaks in a Forest Where No Woman Can Hear, Is He Still Wrong?'

I stare at my fifty inch, high definition plasma TV. The set-top box sits on top of it, unwrapped. Yeah, small matter. I haven't got the HD working yet. I know I should read the manual but I prefer putting cables in sockets until something happens. It's not scientific but it works for me. I start plugging wires in and switch everything on. All I see is the Sony logo and a message saying 'No Input.' I glance at the clock. It's five to three already. This is not going to go well.

The buzzer clangs. Damnit! I leap over leads and packaging and snatch the intercom phone. An LCD screen lights up showing Mark and friends waiting outside.

'Hello?' I say out of breath.

'Hello there big boy,' Mark whispers theatrically into the microphone.

'What's the password?' I say looking at the screen. There are two girls behind Mark giggling.

'Rodriguez sent me.' I smile and buzz them in. I look around at the flat. It's a mess but it's too late to do anything about it. KNOCK, KNOCK, KNOCK!

'Police! Open up!' says Mark's muffled voice. I open the door and in walk two girls, Gina and Karen and two guys, Billy and Mark. I used to go to school with Billy and weirdly he now works at United in computer support.

SEX LESSONS

'What'd you do, fly up?' I say, Mark immediately starts humming the Superman theme tune. Karen works in accounting on the thirty-seventh floor. She's a mumsy type but with a nice pair. Don't misunderstand, she's not my sort at all, I'm just saying, she's not bad looking.

'Why don't you get a cleaner James?' Karen asks, looking around.

'If I wanted to spend money on a woman who comes to my flat and goes through my stuff, I'd get a girlfriend,' I retort. Okay, it wasn't the greatest comeback I've ever had but what the hell. Karen gives me a fake smile and wanders into the living room.

Karen's friend is Gina. She's from Sitges, just outside Barcelona. She's stick thin, with long Pantene-perfect dark hair. I have a theory she's anorexic but I have no evidence to back it up. Maybe because she's Spanish she's always tanned. I mean always. This is like blind date or something, isn't it? 'Gina likes making daisy chains and drinking almost cold hot chocolate. She paints and likes to have her hair in what I like to call a perma-bun.'

'Nice T-shirt Jams,' Gina says smiling; her accent makes my name sound weird. She's a bit difficult to understand sometimes but just go with it. I find nodding helps. 'God, look at that view.' She walks over to the French doors and looks out across London. I wander out to where Gina is looking. From my apartment I have the most amazing view of the River Thames and Canary

Wharf. In summer you can sit out here on the balcony and watch the boats going past. At night, the river sparkles with reflections of Docklands lofty buildings. Pretty funky, huh?

'Mate, what the hell is all this?' I turn to see Mark staring at the newly opened set-top box.

'Uh, yeah slight problem. Haven't managed to plug it all in yet,' I reply, slightly embarrassed.

'All? Looks like you just opened the box and threw cables and plastic around,' says Billy. He still has the same chubby quality from school but he's slightly taller now. He's not the share-your-emotions type. But, what the man excels at is fixing anything technical you throw at him. 'Let me have a look dufus.'

'You'd better hurry, game starts in twenty minutes,' Mark says, folding his arms and turning to me. 'What kind of Muppet invites everyone over to watch the game in HD and doesn't have the HD set up?'

'Yeah, well life's unfair,' I reply, 'beers anyone? Silly question, course you do.' I slap my forehead theatrically, walk into the kitchen and over to the beer fridge. Yes, I have a separate fridge for beer and wine. Some people think it's wanky, I say they're just jealous. It's got a glass door so you can choose what you want without getting cold. Ace! I grab four beers and place them on the kitchen surface. The fridge door slams shut.

'Can I get wine instead of beer please James?' Karen is standing in the doorway.

SEX LESSONS

'Course you can.' I take a bottle of white from the fridge and hold it up to her. 'Pinot?'

'Perfect,' she replies. I can feel something coming. Karen doesn't hang around me unless...'So what happened with Jenny?' I freeze. Small but important point I suppose I should have mentioned before, Karen is good friends with Jenny. They work in the same department...yeah, major OH! Once again, outwitted by the female of the species.

'Uh well, you know...she's nice and everything but, I dunno. We just didn't click.' My heart starts to thump hard as I busy myself getting a wine glass from the cupboard.

'But you said things were going well, I don't understand. Was she screwing someone else? She does do that you know?' If I'd been drinking at this point, most of it would have ended up on my shirt. As it was, I covered the best I could and replied casually

'Really?'

'Yeah, she always seems to have more than one boy on the go.' I give an involuntary snort of disbelief. What-the-hell? Karen quickly continues, 'I wanted to tell you James, but you said you liked her so what was I going to do, tell you she likes to play around?' I can't believe what I'm hearing.

'You could have said *something*. Jesus. So she was seeing someone when she was with me?' I ask, trying to keep my anger in check.

DANIEL GRANT

'You were only with her for two weeks. It's not like you were going to get married.'

'So? Doesn't mean...so, she was sleeping with other men?' Incredulity was starting to make my dialogue repetitive.

'I think there were only two others,' Karen replies, using her fingers to count! I almost burst out laughing.

'Two! Only two! What the fuck!?' It's not just me, right? I'm not overreacting, am I? You're sitting thinking 'what the fuck' as well, aren't you?

'But didn't you end it with her?' Karen now has her concerned look on; the furrow on her forehead's starting to look like the Valley of the Kings. This, apparently, was what Jenny had told her and I wasn't going to change it. Had to salvage what little pride remained. Most of it was now hanging in tatters.

'What, so it's okay for her to have two other guys while being with me as long as I dump her first, that what you're saying?' Karen walks towards me and places a hand on my shoulder.

'You're better off without her James. Jenny's a good friend, but when it comes to guys...she kinda screws them around a bit.' She's rubbing my arm now in a pathetic attempt to comfort me. Two men! The image spins around in my head. Two men at different times or...maybe it was two men at the same time? I want to hurl. I look at Karen and nod slowly. Laughter fills the living room next door. Glad someone's having fun. I

SEX LESSONS

glance at Karen, I don't want her to say anything else. You know the way someone tries to make you feel better but fails with every consecutive sentence they utter? So you just want them to shut the fuck up and stop making things worse.

At that moment, Mark appears at the door.

'Hello, what's going on here then?' he asks. Karen pulls away from me and smiles at him. 'Mate, how long does it take to get a fucking beer? Kitchen's right next door.' He spots the bottles on the kitchen top. 'I'll get them myself.' He marches over to the table and snatches the bottles. They leave circles of condensation on the surface.

'This isn't a hotel,' I reply, opening the wine and pouring Karen a glass.

'Good job, 'cos people would be wanting their money back.'

'Leave him alone, he's having a bad day,' Karen says. I glance at her. All I can think is 'shut the fuck up!' Mark turns to me.

'I don't blame him, if I'd had a bunch of friends come over to watch the big game in HD and then found out the HD wasn't even plugged in, I'd be having a bad day as well.' I try to smile but my wallowing has started to kick in. Two bloody men. Soon there'll be the over-analysis compounded with the inevitable depression. Where do I find these women? By the way, in my twisted mind, the other two guys have porn-star dicks and last forever. 'What's up mate?' Mark is still holding the four beers.

'Nothing. It's fine. How's Billy coming along?' I reply through gritted teeth.

'I think he'll get there. Come on, grab the wine. Alcohol will cheer you up.' We walk back to the lounge.

Billy has the plasma pulled out and is lying on his side, hidden behind it.

'Our host was distracted, here you go,' Mark says, dishing out the beers. I plonk myself down on one of the white leather couches next to Gina who's reading one of my GQ magazines.

'What is G-spot?' Gina asks in Spanglish. Billy's face appears from behind the plasma, I glance at Mark then to Karen, smiles forming on all our faces.

'I think that one's for you, James,' says Billy.

'Oh yeah right, because I'm the expert,' I say with a little more sarcasm than I intended. The thing is, I'd like to be able to tell Gina exactly what the G-spot is and where to find it but if I'm honest, I haven't the foggiest.

'Anyone got an A-Z, I'll point it out?' I ask. Gina frowns. Everyone chuckles. 'Ask Mark, he knows all about hitting G-spots, don't you mate?' Mark's eyes widen.

'Oh?' Karen says. Mark gives me a pretend evil then begins his story about this girl he used to date called Dawn. She was a screamer and while they were getting down to it, he got her so worked up, the neighbours called the police. They were giving statements until two in the morning. I thought I'd save you the build-up and, frankly, disappointing climax. I've heard this story so many times before, it's like his party trick.

I start to zone out. My mind wanders back to Jenny. Two men. Possibly at the same time? I'm The Third Man. There's an aching in the pit of my stomach. I haven't had these feelings for a long time. Neediness is such an unattractive quality.

SEVEN – UNEXPECTED COMPANY

'I think that's it,' Billy says as the HD picture suddenly kicks in. A blue TV guide has appeared and dodgy copyright-free music plays through the speakers. Everyone claps. Billy nods, a cheeky smile on his face. 'Thank you. Now where's my beer?'

'What channel is it?' Mark asks, fiddling with the remote.

'BBC One, I think,' I reply. Mark hits a button and immediately John Motson's voice booms around the room. The sound is deafening.

'Turn it down!' Gina says, her hands on her ears. Mark nudges the volume down slightly. The game looks like it's about to start, they've already sung the national anthems and the teams are finding their respective sides of the pitch.

'Yes. Come on my Greek brothers,' Mark shouts. The buzzer sounds. I glance at Mark who inexplicably smiles. I frown and walk to the intercom picking up the handset. The LCD lights up. Standing in the street outside is the new girl from the office.

'Hello,' I say, as calmly as I can. She leans into the intercom, a narrow strand of blonde hair falling over her face.

'Hi, is this James Kennedy's place?' she asks, tucking the offending hair behind her ear.

'It is. Come up. Flat three.' I hit the buzzer and watch her open the door. What's she doing here?

'Hey,' Mark says, making me jump, 'can I grab another beer?' I turn around.

'Did you invite her here?' I ask.

'It's possible,' he says, walking into the kitchen, hands in the air. I hear the clinking of beer bottles. 'I suspect she'll want wine?' he calls.

'Twenty quid says she'll have a beer,' I call back. I hear a snort which I take as confirmation of the bet.

A knock at the door. I clear my throat and jerk it open. She's wearing a long, dark, expensive coat with a belt around the waist. She also has a black collar around her neck, for walks perhaps?

'Hi, I'm James,' I say, with as natural a smile as I can manage. She smiles back and offers me her hand. I shake it, not too vigorously but enough to make sure I'm not perceived as limp-wristed.

'I'm Lauren, nice to meet you. Sorry to intrude on your party but Mark Pasty said it would be okay? Is he here?' Suspiciously on cue, Mark walks out of the kitchen, a glass of wine in his hand.

DANIEL GRANT

'Lauren, you came.' He ambles over and kisses her on the cheek. I study her face, she wasn't ready for that. Who would be? 'Wine?' he asks, holding out the glass for her. She takes it.

'Thanks,' she says. Mark glances at me, triumphant. I shake my head. 'Actually, I don't suppose you have any beer? I'm not a big wine drinker, sorry.' My face lights up, a smile the size of the Grand Canyon sweeping across it.

'Of course. I'll get you one,' I say. I'm sorry but this is classic. Mark's face has dropped. 'Make yourself at home; the others are in the living room.' She hands the glass of wine back to Mark and, seeing the disappointment on his face says

'Don't worry if you don't have any beer.'

'Don't be silly,' I interject quickly, 'I have plenty of everything. Let me take your coat.' She pulls it off and hands it to me. Underneath she's wearing a black pencil skirt with a white long sleeve top. Her dark ballet-pumps give her an Audrey Hepburn quality.

I hang up her coat, it smells of perfume. Sophisticated. Chanel perhaps? I saunter into the kitchen. I hear Mark introducing Lauren to the others. I grab a beer out of the fridge and an empty glass then wander back in.

Mark is sitting on the sofa next to Lauren with Billy taking up the other spot. I give Lauren her bottle of beer and set the empty glass down on the table in front of her.

'Thanks,' she says, 'nice place.'

SEX LESSONS

'Yeah, it's not bad,' I reply, smiling as I walk over to the other sofa. I sit down between Karen and Gina who is staring at Lauren with a strange look. I'm no expert in these matters but I swear she's looking at her tits. Maybe it's just my perverted little mind. In my defence however, Gina catches me looking at her and turns back to the TV, her cheeks flushed. She was as well. I knew it. Karen puts her arm through mine and tucks her legs under her bum. Karen's always a bit cuddly wuddly, but it feels uncomfortable in front of Lauren. And her hair is tickling my neck which is annoying.

'So you like football?' Mark asks, turning to Lauren.

'Yes, I don't follow it regularly but I like watching England play,' she replies. Her voice sounds posh; maybe she's loaded.

'That's nice,' he replies, 'unfortunately today they are going to lose. Greece has a much stronger defence and Nikos Samaras was the top scorer for Bayern Munich last season.'

'She doesn't care about any of that, Mark,' Karen says. Lauren glances at Karen and smiles.

'Of course she does, she follows England so she needs to know what they're up against,' Mark replies.

'Actually, I don't really care,' Lauren says, deadpan. Everyone laughs. Mark rolls his eyes.

'You will when we score darling,' he replies. I glance at Lauren, her eyebrows rise slightly. She turns to Billy.

DANIEL GRANT

'What about you, Billy, do you care about football?' Billy, who had been silent until this point blushes slightly, then says

'I enjoy watching Greece lose; it shuts Mark up for a few days.' We chuckle as the game starts. I catch Lauren's eyes, my heart surges; I turn back towards the TV pretending everything is cool.

'Oh sure, gang up on me,' Mark says. Everyone laughs again. Mark smiles but he hates being the butt of the joke.

The game carries on, England have far less possession than I would like. Suddenly Greece makes it through the last defender. It's Samaras versus the goalie, he goes one way and shoots. The ball whips through the air and rattles the corner of the English net. The crowd go crazy. Mark goes crazy. He's on his feet, jumping up and down.

'YEEES!! What did I say, Samaras does it again! Brilliant!'

'Give him another beer Jams,' Gina says.

'Anyone else?' I ask. Billy shows his empty bottle and nods, Karen shakes her head. Lauren stands up.

'Can I use your bathroom?' she asks.

'Sure, this way,' I reply. We walk out towards the kitchen, leaving Mark to do his ridiculous Greek dance around the living room.

We get to the hallway and I point to the bathroom door.

'Just over there,' I say. She starts towards it. I can't help it, I glance down at her bum. It moves

SEX LESSONS

flawlessly under her skirt. One cheek, then the next. It's a little hypnotic. Suddenly, without warning, she spins around. My eyes shoot to the ceiling, too slow. Fuck. She caught me. She knows it too.

'Here?' she asks, pointing at the door. My eyes return to her.

'Uh, yeah that one.' She goes in. Bollocks. Sighing to myself I walk to the kitchen, pull out some beers and get them circulated to everyone. I retake my seat as Lauren reappears and sits down opposite me. She's looking at me again, I feel her eyes burning into my temple but I'm not going to give her the satisfaction of returning her gaze. I keep my eyes firmly locked on the TV.

At half-time, England are down two-nil and Mark is becoming obnoxious. He keeps going on about the two hundred I now owe him and it's starting to get boring. There are empty bottles in places I'd rather there weren't and Karen and Gina have gone outside for a smoke. Billy's been in the toilet more than five minutes. Not sure what he's doing, don't want to know. Mark's iPhone rings. He glances at the display and answers it with another winning smile.

'Mate, looking bad for you...the real question is what am I going to spend your money on...?' He walks away, the phone clamped to his ear. I'm left sitting with Lauren.

'So how'd you like your first week?' I say, trying to breathe normally. An eyebrow rises and she nods.

DANIEL GRANT

'Good. Everyone's being really nice. But I'm sure some people think I'm just a dumb blonde.' I'm not sure how to react. 'Which is fine, I love seeing the look on their faces when they realise I'm not.' So what's that mean? Help me out here, because I could take that in a number of different ways. I clear my throat and, desperate to find something to say, I settle on

'So have you got your desk sorted out yet? The best ones are by the window with the views. Pasty's got one and I'm waiting for George to either retire or die...'

'Well, I'm a senior executive, so I think they're giving me the office next to Mike's.' Jesus.

'So you're in charge of...' I start to say.

'All the trading managers, yes. Including you, James.' She smiles.

'Great. That's great,' I reply. I'm not sure whether it is great.

'Don't worry I'm not that scary,' she says, 'unless you fuck up.' I nod. Not sure I agree, she's pretty scary right now. She takes a swig of beer. I watch her, fascinated and at the same time terrified of this girl I'm now subordinate to.

'So do I call you boss or..?'

'Lauren's fine.' I nod, it's getting uncomfortable again. The French doors open abruptly and Karen and Gina come back inside.

'It's fucking freezing out there,' Karen says, 'James, come here and warm me up.' I breathe out a little too sharply.

SEX LESSONS

'Actually I think I need another beer,' I reply, heading for the kitchen, a half-empty bottle still on the table.

EIGHT – BLAST FROM THE PAST

Friday afternoon. I've just returned from Pret with a small bag of goodies for lunch. I normally have a sandwich and an apple but today I got a brownie and a cinnamon strudel as well! I know it's bad but what the hell, my team downstairs is making healthy gains today so I figure I deserve it. I sit down at my desk, prise the sandwich from the ridiculous packaging and take a bite. My phones blink away but I ignore them, enjoying my BLT. I don't like eating lunch here because I find the constant noise of people on the phone distracting. Every so often someone starts shouting at someone else on the other side of the world and, well the whole environment becomes sort of anti-sandwich.

'Hello James.' I look up to see Lauren standing beside me. She's wearing a grey power suit, the blouse undone one button too many.

SEX LESSONS

'Lauren, hey,' I say, flustering with a mouth full of sandwich. I swallow. It hurts as it goes down. 'Did you get home okay on Saturday?'

'Yes thank you. Have you got a minute?' she asks.

'Uh sure.' Just to keep you in the picture, I'm finding the whole blouse thing distracting. Seriously, I can practically see her bra.

'Let's go in my office,' she says. I feel people's eyes on me as I follow her.

The glass office is sparse, she obviously hasn't brought the cactus over from the previous place yet. There's a small, dark wooden table in the centre, with a sofa immediately to my left. I can see Mike Cartwell typing on his computer in the next office. Prick. Probably surfing for porn. The main feature of the office is the dramatic view of the Tower of London. It's sunny but I can see people walking along the banks of the Thames wrapped up to the hilt. Winter's just about bearable when it's like this.

'Have a seat,' Lauren says, sitting down. I find a place on the sofa and plonk myself down. It's deceptively deep and my knees almost hit my chin as I practically fall into it. The leather makes an embarrassing farting-type noise. I check her reaction to see if she thinks it's me. The whole manoeuvre is about as graceful as a giraffe on ice. I sit up, feebly attempting to salvage some dignity but the damage is done. On the plus side, she's trying not to smile. 'You finished?' she asks. I close my eyes, I want the sofa to swallow me whole.

'Yes, I think I'm done now. Sorry,' I reply.

'Have you seen Mark recently?' she asks. Hmm, didn't see that one coming.

'Uh. No. Not since Saturday,' I reply.

'He didn't show up for work yesterday or the day before. Didn't call in sick or anything. I just wondered if you knew where he was?' She crosses her legs, I try not to watch them.

'No I presumed he'd taken leave to celebrate winning the football. I can call him.'

'I've been trying all day. He's got some papers I'm supposed to give to the FSA tomorrow and...I need them.'

'Oh. Let me try him now.' I take out my mobile and scroll down to 'Mark Mob.' It rings out five times then goes to voicemail.

'Hi this is Mark, sorry you missed me. Leave a message after the beep.' I think he sounds weird on the message, like he was trying too hard to sound normal. As it is, he sounds like he's doing a rubbish impersonation of Prince Charles. BEEP!

'Hi mate, it's James, give me a call as soon as you get this. Cheers.' I hang up. Lauren is gazing at me. I frown. 'Weird, he never just doesn't show up.'

'I sent a courier round to his house this morning, no one answered,' Lauren says. 'James, I need those documents or bad things are going to happen. Understand?' I nod, serious-like.

'When do you need them by? How late?' I ask.

SEX LESSONS

'First thing tomorrow. If we don't have them, it will be my fault. Except it won't be my fault, James. It will be Mark's.' Ahh, pin it on the little guy. I get it.

'I'll find him,' I reply, standing up to leave.

'James-,' Lauren stops me at the door, I turn around. Her face has softened, she looks like she's about to say something. Her eyes are almost luminescent, you remember how I said her arse was hypnotic, well that's nothing compared to these babies.

'I wonder...' I see her change her mind and nod, '...as soon as you can, please.' Suddenly I see what's going on. She's scared, the new girl has a big problem in her first week on the job and she's terrified. She's trying to sound confident and bossy but she's crapping her pants.

'I'll get you the documents,' I say, reassuring her as best I can. She nods, a polite smile on her face. I walk out, glancing at her through the glass door as I close it behind me. She's still looking at me. I turn and head for my desk.

When I get there, I snatch my keys, slap my landlines to voicemail and I'm away. I nearly lose a leg when it gets caught in the elevator door. The lift plummets to the underground car park. I scramble out. The Merc bleeps and I get in. Batman, or in my case, the Boy Wonder to the rescue. I rev the engine and speed out of the building.

* * *

DANIEL GRANT

Mark lives in Blackheath, close to Greenwich Park. It takes less than twenty minutes to get there at this time of day. I could get used to leaving work this early and beating the traffic. I park up near his apartment block. It's a modern building which oozes style and exclusivity. Which I think is the height of irony when you know Mark lives there.

I walk/run up to the entrance and press number eight. No response. I take a step back and glance up to his apartment balcony. There are no signs of life. I optimistically yank the handle on the building door. Unsurprisingly, it's locked. Clouds have rolled in and the sky has turned a muddy charcoal colour. It's going to chuck it down.

I try his mobile. Voicemail again. Where the fuck is he? My mind starts pondering the possible bars he might be in. Then, a light clicks on up in his apartment.

'Son of a...' I press the button again, except this time I don't let go. The buzzer moans with a constant drawl. My thumb starts to ache. Then –

'WHAT!' Mark's voice booms from the intercom, nearly knocking me over.

'It's James, open the door.'

'Go away.' His voice sounds shaky.

'Let me in, what's going on?'

'Nothing, fuck off.'

'Hey, let me in!' I repeat more sternly. At that moment, an elderly man opens the door. He's got a cap on his head and wears a tweed jacket which looks itchy. I attempt to walk in behind him, he blocks me.

'Do you live here?' he asks, his voice rickety and throaty.

'No, but my friend does, number eight.' I try to pass again.

'Well he should buzz you in, you could be anyone,' he says, eyeing me suspiciously.

'Look, Mark Pasty. My friend is Mark Pasty and he lives here. I think he's in trouble and I need to get in.' I push past the old man and hurry up the stairs. I can hear him cursing me but I don't care, I'm already on the second floor. Out of breath, I bang on Mark's door. 'Open up.'

'I said fuck off,' Mark's muffled voice replies from the other side of the door.

'You did, but I assumed you didn't mean it.' I peer into the spy hole. The image looks weird and I can't make anything out.

'Well I did.' His voice sounds broken. However, after ten seconds I hear a click and the door opens slowly. Mark stands in a pink dressing gown that is way too small for him, his cheeks are red and there are bags under his eyes. His hair looks like it's been constructed by migrating birds. I take the sight in.

'Jesus. What happened to you?' I ask. He looks like he hasn't slept in a month. Is this the same guy I saw on Saturday? Did I miss a week or something?

'Jess is what fucking happened,' he says, almost spitting the words at me. I frown.

DANIEL GRANT

'Can I come in?' Mark shrugs and wanders back in, his bare feet slapping on the tile floor.

Mark's apartment is enormous, it must be almost the entire floor. And the guy has almost no furniture. Seriously it's like being in a warehouse where only one corner is inhabited. You wouldn't have known his ex-fiancée had ever lived here. Like me, Mark prefers gadgets and stainless steel fridges to angel ornaments and pillows on the bed. Everything is brand new. He just had a new kitchen put in; cost him over thirty grand! For a kitchen! Don't get me started on that, anyway...

We walk past the bar area towards the floor-to-ceiling windows in front of us. He grabs a half-empty bottle of Johnny Walkers and collapses onto the giant chocolate leather sofa. Outside, I can see the Observatory and Greenwich Park. I sit down next to him. He swigs the whiskey.

'I thought it was over,' I say. After what seems like a fortnight he whispers something so quietly I don't hear what he says. 'What?' I ask.

'I saw her,' he repeats.

'Jess?' He nods. 'Where?'

'At Jo Jo's. Why'd she have to go there, she knows that's where I go?' I consider how to proceed.

'Did you talk to her?' I ask. He nods.

'It was fucking awkward,' he says, chuckling at first then back to his serious face.

'I'll bet.'

'She's pregnant.' I can't hide my shock and a thousand questions hit me all at the same time. I rifle through them and settle on

'Yours?'

'His.' Mark shakes his head. 'She was fucking him while she was with me. And all this time I've been feeling guilty for cheating on her! It's a fucking joke.'

'Who is he?'

'Some fucker she works with. Her boss. I mean, talk about clichéd. She always was a predictable skank.'

'Sorry mate.'

'It's a bitch.' He starts nibbling on a fingernail, then pauses to speak. 'She looked so happy as well. Before she saw me, just...fucking happy. How could she do it James? Who does that?'

'Well...you did, sort of, cheat on her,' I reply. Mark stares at me, a confused look in his eyes.

'So I deserve it?'

'No but...come on mate...' Mark suddenly bangs his fist on the table. The boom echoes around the flat. I stop, shocked at his action. He glares at the floor.

'She's having his fucking baby,' he replies.

'Were you faithful to her?' I ask. He blinks slowly. 'What do you think Jess thought about Paula?'

'Jess never even knew about Paula!' Mark snaps.

'Yeah but she knew there was someone, didn't she? That's enough, isn't it?' I reply.

'I guess so. It's all right for you. You have a new girl every bloody week.'

'No I don't. I was with Jenny until she...we didn't work out.'

'Come on James, everyone likes you. The girls go nuts whenever you look at them.'

'No they don't...look, I know this is hard. But the fact is you went off with someone first.'

'Yeah I did! So I deserve it, don't I? I deserve this because I was shagging Paula! Maybe I do,' his voice suddenly softens, 'maybe I do.' He considers this for a moment then says 'this is different, she didn't just cheat. She's having another fucker's baby, I mean...' I stand, walk over and sit down next to him. I can't think of much to say. We both know there are no words of comfort.

'Yeah, it sucks mate. I'm sorry.' I say. Mark shrugs. 'But look, she's not the one for you. Simple as that. You were fucking Paula for a reason. You didn't want to be with Jess. And that's okay. It's a hard way to find out but you'll meet someone new and think 'thank God I didn't marry Jess.' He nods at my words, taking them in. 'What is with this dressing gown?' Mark slowly looks down at it. 'I mean I know you're upset and everything, but mate, it's fucking pink!' I see an unwelcome smile creep across his face.

'It's Jess's. About the only thing she didn't take.' He replies, chuckling.

'I can see why. You look like you're auditioning for a part in Priscilla, Queen of the Desert.' He starts to laugh. I chuckle with him. 'By the way, I thought not turning up for work was a nice touch.'

'Yeah?'

'Yeah, very dramatic. You got Lauren shitting her pants.'

'Lauren?'

'Apparently you've got some FSA documents she needs and she's not best pleased you went AWOL with them.'

'Shit. I have as well.' Mark stands and goes over to his desk. He opens a drawer and pulls out a pile of papers. 'I think they need them for tomorrow,' he says.

'I know, give 'em to me, I'll get them back to her. I'll tell her you had to go in to hospital or something.' Mark considers this then nods.

'Yeah, like an operation or something.'

'I'll come up with something. Like you dropped a piano on your balls.' He chuckles.

'Yeah. Thanks mate,' Mark says, an appreciative smile on his face. I slap him on the back. 'Hey, you know what we should do?

'What?' I reply.

'We should go to Heaven.' I sigh, already aware there will be no arguing on this one.

DANIEL GRANT

NINE – HEAVEN CAN'T WAIT

I stare at the italicized letters on the dark glass door. 'Heaven.' I turn to Mark who's now got a stupid grin on his face.

'Why have we stopped?' he asks, pushing past me and opening the door. He's sure perked up. I roll my eyes and follow him inside.

We walk down a dimly lit hallway with scarlet carpet and are greeted by a man sitting behind a thick wooden desk. He has a dodgy moustache, wears a cheap suit and wire-thin glasses. Standing next to him is a large bald guy in seemingly the same suit. Maybe they go shopping together. Bald man glares at us. Further ahead I can hear thumping music coming from behind a closed purple curtain.

'Evening gentlemen,' says dodgy-moustache.

'Evening,' I reply.

'Hi,' Mark says, a little too enthusiastically. Dodgy-moustache writes something down on his clipboard.

SEX LESSONS

'Twenty pounds please,' he says. I glance at Mark who's already got the twenty in his hand. He gives it over.

'Thank you. Enjoy the evening.' The bald guy hasn't said anything but I think we know what he's about.

'Oh we will,' Mark replies. I shake my head, pull the curtain to one side and walk through.

Before us is a substantial mirrored room. Men with no ties sit at low-seated tables dotted about the place. To the right is a raised platform with a pole stretching from the floor to the ceiling. Sitting next to the pole are seven girls in nothing but their underwear. They chat amongst themselves as house music thumps from hidden speakers. A redhead is dancing on one of the tables for a fat guy with a beard.

'This is what I'm talking about,' Mark shouts above the music. A blonde with fake eye lashes strides up to us. She wears very little and carries a tray in one hand. Mark smiles at her as she approaches.

'Hi,' Blondie says, 'what can I get you?' She has an eastern European accent.

'Two beers, please. And a menu,' Mark replies.

'No problem,' she says and walks away. One of the seven girls stands up and saunters to the pole. She grabs onto it, swinging herself round and round. I feel dizzy just watching her. Then she pulls herself up and grips the pole with nothing but her legs. Slowly she lets herself hang down, her more-than-enough breasts almost touch her chin. Mark leans into my ear.

'Impressive.'

'Very,' I reply. I scan the other girls. They all have toned, well-proportioned bodies. One stands out. She's got long brown hair, pert breasts and an alluring smile. She's chatting to the girl next to her but suddenly turns to me and grins. I feel strangely embarrassed so I look away. The girl on the pole is now dancing and moving around the room.

'Fuck, look at these chicks dude,' Mark says. The near-naked waitress arrives with our drinks. I pick up my glass and start chugging.

'Yeah,' I reply. I glance back to the brown-haired girl, she's already staring at me. As soon as I look over to her, she stands and starts walking towards us. Fuck. I pretend to be watching the girl gyrating on the fat man's lap.

'Hi,' the girl says, 'I'm Bunny.'

'Bunny, that's an unusual name,' Mark replies, grinning.

'My parents were comedians,' Bunny says, smiling back. I snigger. She places a menu in front of me. It reads:

DANCE AT TABLE: 40
TWO GIRLS DANCE AT TABLE: 70
PRIVATE DANCE: 100
TWO GIRLS PRIVATE DANCE: 150
FULL WORKUP: 400

I stare at the menu and I have only one question. What the hell is a 'full workup?' I mean,

SEX LESSONS

I can imagine what it is but how full does it go? Is it even legal? Mark snatches the menu from under me and peers at it.

'Let's see,' he turns to Bunny, scanning the menu, 'any wiggle room on the full workup?' Bunny shakes her head. 'Okay, what do you get for the four hundred?'

'You get to have your dreams come true,' Bunny replies in a sexy voice. Mark smiles.

'What if my dream involves winning the lottery?' I ask.

'I'll help you spend the money,' she says, smirking.

'I like it,' Mark says, pulling out his wallet. She puts her hand out.

'Not here. Let's go.' I watch all this with fascination.

'Oh no, it's not for me. It's for this dude here.' I glance at Mark.

'Me? I don't want it.'

'Yeah you do.'

'No I don't.'

'You're going.'

'I'm staying right here.'

'Bunny, help me out here.' Bunny takes my arm in hers and stands up.

'Come on, your friend wants to treat you.'

'Thanks, I'm good.' Bunny tugs at my arm.

'What's your name?' she asks.

'It's James. James Kennedy,' Mark blurts. I glare at him. Why not just tell her where I live, give her my bank details.

'James, come with me please,' Bunny says. Fuck. I stand up reluctantly.

'You're dead,' I say to Mark.

'I know,' he replies, smiling. I glance back as I follow Bunny through another curtain and out into a hallway. It's softly lit with deep red walls that make me feel like I'm in an old-style mansion. Now I'm nervous. I glance down to her arse, she's wearing a thong and not much else. Stunning butt though. We get to a door with carvings of naked women on it. She opens it and goes inside. I follow her.

The room is large, most of it covered by what looks like an enormous futon with different coloured pillows. It's lit only by a few candles and dimmed spotlights in the ceiling. The smell of burning incense fills the room.

Bunny lies down on the futon and pats it next to her.

'Look, I know what my friend said but really...'

'Sit down,' she commands. I sigh quietly and park myself down deliberately a little way from her. She stares at me, one eyebrow raised. I feign ignorance. What? 'Okay, I'll come to you,' she says and starts to crawl towards me on all fours, her sultry eyes taking me in. I swallow.

'So, how often do you do this?' I ask, a pathetic attempt at small talk.

'Every hour or so,' Bunny replies as she moves her face next to mine. She smells of vanilla. Her cheek slowly strokes along mine. Then she moves her leg over my head so she's now facing away from me and stretches so her butt flattens. I breathe out fast.

'Are you nervous?'

'No,' I reply, quickly.

'What do you do for a living?' she asks, slowly bending upwards, as if doing a press up.

'Banker,' I reply.

'Ah. The baddies. I think you got a bad rap.'

'Yeah. We're not all money-grabbing, coke-snorting, stripper-paying arseholes,' I reply. She laughs. 'Although some of us are, I guess.'

'You don't look like an arsehole to me James.'

'Yeah well, don't rush to judge, we've only just met.' Her legs are either side of me, her butt moving into my face. I hope she doesn't have wind.

'I can tell things about people. I think you're a nice guy.'

'Look, I appreciate everything you're doing here but I'm not sure I can do this.'

'Married?'

'No, just...it's complicated.' Bunny turns around and stares at me.

'I think you need to relax James. Just go with the flow a little.' She smiles, touching my arm softly. I shake my head and stand up.

'Sorry. It's not you, I just...can't.' She studies me for a second then nods.

'We can go slow. You want to talk?' she asks.

'Not really,' I reply.

'Your friend paid for the hour, be a shame to waste it,' she says. I move towards the exit.

DANIEL GRANT

'Keep it,' I reply and go to open the door.

'James?' she calls. I stop and turn around slowly. She stares at me, her gaze intense as if trying to read my mind.

'Whatever it is. It can be fixed. I'm a good listener, you know?' she says, smiling with sincerity. I frown, staring at her.

'Thanks. I...thanks,' I reply and leave. What the fuck was that?

I find myself outside in the cold, waiting. If I smoked this would be a perfect time to light up. What's wrong with me? Now I'm scared to even get it on with a stripper? Someone I will never see in my life again. What's that about?

I jump up and down and walk around in circles trying to keep warm. Eventually my mobile beeps. It's Mark. 'Hey, where are you?' I reply, telling him I'm outside. Two minutes later he emerges.

'Mate I know you're out of practice but seriously, that was less than ten minutes.'

'Ha ha. She just wasn't...'

'Wasn't...what, your type? What are you, blind? Jesus.'

'No, I...it's not my thing.'

'A beautiful girl with her tits out is not your thing?'

'No, you know...I just felt a bit uncomfortable.'

'Get over it, you big pussy. That was four hundred quid!'

'I know, I'll pay you back,' I say. Mark shakes his head.

SEX LESSONS

'I don't want the money, prick.' I stay silent. Mark shakes his head. 'Unbelievable.'

'You want to get a drink?' I offer.

'Damn right I do and you're buying.'

TEN - THE COURIER

I'm sitting in my car, Johnny Vaughan and Lisa Snowdon in my ear and I'm stuck in the most horrendous traffic jam I've ever been in. It's eight-thirty, I left home over an hour ago and I have an über-headache. I should have just gone straight home from the strip club, what was I thinking? We ended up going on a bar crawl till three in the morning. Clever James.

The radio starts playing 'Cheater', a track by this band I've got into recently called the Time Travellers. Johnny Dougan, the lead singer, was on the front of Rolling Stone this month and... oh here's the chorus, I start to sing along momentarily forgetting where I am. *'My heart crushed, drip-fed the scraps from your table... cheater...cheater.'* Brilliant.

This journey normally takes no more than forty-five minutes in rush hour. I would call into work and tell Lauren I've got the papers and everything is going to be okay. However the other kicker to this story is I am currently underneath the Blackwall Tunnel and the car in front hasn't moved in twenty minutes. It's frustrating the tits off me. I'm trying to keep a lid on it but panic has already started to work its evil trickery. If I don't get the papers to Lauren by nine, at the latest, Mark will be out of a job. Which means he will not only hate me, he'll also become the biggest moaner the world has ever known. That is not an option.

The carrot-top behind suddenly beeps. This makes me supremely angry. I glare at the rear-view mirror, shooting him evils. What the hell am I supposed to do, bash the guy in front of me? WAKE UP MAN! I notice he's driving a BMW. Shocker, eh? London's full of guys like this. Two-to-one he sells insurance.

It's eight thirty-five. I'm about ready to go on a violent, gruesome rampage when, suddenly, the guy in front creeps forward. Hope shoots through me like a heroin jab. I slap the car into drive and move forward...three feet, then come to rest again. I shake my head and grip the steering wheel till my knuckles turn white. The clock is fast approaching eight forty. I close my eyes. Please GOD! I should have just taken the tube. What am I talking about? I never get the tube, stand in one of those cattle trains? I'd rather staple-gun my balls to a sofa.

'Ninety-five point eight, Capital...' I switch Johnny off. Sorry, I can't be dealing with all his happiness when life is about to take a dramatic, Eastenders-style turn for the worse. Suddenly we're moving again, thank fuck. I can see the end of the tunnel. It's slow going but we're moving. The opening gets lighter and lighter. Come on. I glance at my mobile, still no signal. Be just my luck if the guy at Vodafone had decided this spot didn't require a transmitter. I'm almost there, I can see blue flashing lights, come on baby! I'm out, the sense of euphoria is almost overwhelming. In fact, I feel strangely emotional. My Blackberry has two bars. I whack it onto speaker, dial the office and get one of the anonymous switchboard operators.

'United, good morning,' she says cheerfully.

'Lauren Bates, please,' I say, swerving to avoid hitting a police motorcycle that cuts me up in the outside lane. I resist the urge to fire a round of obscenities at him and drive on.

'Who shall I say is calling?' the operator replies.

'James Kennedy, it's urgent.'

'Hold the line, please.' I get a copyright-free, panpipe rendition of Titanic echoing around my car. It's so bad I consider hanging up.

'Hello?' Lauren's beautiful voice interrupts the climax of the 'musac.'

'Lauren, it's James,' I say. Her voice becomes harsh and whispery.

'Where are you? Have you got the papers?' she asks, unrestrained panic in her voice.

'Yes, I've got them. I'll be there in ten minutes.'

'Thank God.'

'I told you I'd get them.'

SEX LESSONS

'You didn't say you'd give me a coronary in the process. The FSA guy is in Mike's (wanker) office. I'll stall him until you get here. Thanks James.' Now, maybe it's because I'm on a natural adrenaline high or maybe I was getting more out of the panpipes than perhaps I originally thought but something in me triggers and I suddenly feel no fear. So in a classic Kennedy moment, here's what I say

'Maybe you can return the favour sometime. I think dinner would be a nice start.' A long silence. I start to consider the ramifications of what I've just allowed to spill from my mouth. Oh God. Say something. Please.

'Just get the documents to me. Okay?' I close my eyes (only briefly, remember I'm driving a thirty thousand pound automobile fifteen miles per hour over the limit.)

'I'll be there as soon as I can,' I reply. She hangs up. I continue my self-flagellation all the way to the office.

I throw the car into my spot and run to the elevator. It takes a butt-clenching amount of time to get to me but I jump in and hit twenty-seven. The elevator accelerates and before I know it I'm running into the office, papers clutched to my heart. I slow down to a fast walk as Lauren steps out of her office with Mike and some tall, bald guy in an expensive suit. I catch Lauren's eye and hand her the papers in a transfer so seamless that if you'd seen it, you'd have thought we'd been practising all week. I stand back and watch them walk over to the videoconferencing suite. The door closes behind them. I want to jump in the air and shout 'YES!' But, of course, that would draw unnecessary attention and cause a scene.

It's a little strange then, as I turn around, the whole office has gone painfully quiet and almost everyone is staring at me. For about a second I genuinely don't know what they're all gaping at. However, my mind, being the efficient keeper of memories that it is, immediately replays it for my (and arguably your) viewing pleasure. It seems that although I'd thought I hadn't jumped in the air and shouted 'YES!' The reality was, I had. What's worse, afterwards I had also done a small moonwalk followed by a Doctor Benton, E.R. style air-punch. Now, I don't want any of this to be true. But there we are. The looks on people's faces and my memories of the incident are compelling evidence. My cheeks turn scarlet and I excuse myself to the gents as fast as possible.

When I eventually come out, I go straight to my desk and sit down quickly. I log on to the computer and set about doing some work. I glance up every few minutes to check the door of the conference room. Nothing so far.

An hour goes past. Still nothing. My mobile rings. It's Mark.

'You still have a job,' I say.

'Thank God,' he says, 'was she angry?'

'Angry isn't the word I'd pick, something more akin to terror.' Mark chuckles. I'm unconvinced it's a laughing matter. At that moment the conference door opens and the three of them walk out. The bald guy shakes both their hands and leaves. Lauren smiles at Mike who nods with a congratulatory look on his face (arsemuncher). He turns and walks into his office. Lauren goes back to her office and closes the door. I breathe out. I don't know why, but somehow it feels like I'm the one in trouble.

The rest of the week goes slowly. Mark returns to work on Friday and makes up this rubbish story about having heart palpitations. Everyone buys it. I swear, I'd believe him if I didn't know the truth. He's such a good liar, no wonder Jess never found out about Paula. Lauren calls him into her office, they have a ten minute chat then he's out. He tells me she gave him a slap on the wrist and he's now sure Lauren's in love with him. I roll my eyes but something stings when he says it.

Evening arrives and Karen wants to go out for drinks after work at Park Magoo's which is this power bar near Liverpool Street. To be honest all I want to do is go home and get some sleep. Karen being the persistent girl she is bullies me into going. Mark and I finish around five thirty and are in the bar by six which I thought was good going. It's only when we get there that we realise we've been beaten not only by Karen and Gina but also Darren Hargreaves. Remember him? The bloke whose head I bit off at the beginning of the story. Don't worry I'm shit with names as well. Also Marcus from HR has decided he's invited as well. He has a silly bowl cut and wears this strange collarless shirt. Guess he thinks it's fashionable or something. It's weird, I've known Marcus for the entire time I've been at United but I can never remember his surname. It's something stupid like Marshmallow. Like I said, I'm crap with names. Leave it with me, I'll let you know if it comes.

Park Magoo's looks like nothing on the outside, just a black door off Middlesex Street but go inside and a whole world opens up. High-backed tables and chairs surround the bar and there's a large area for standing. The whole place is low-lit with leather red couches dotted around the edges. Since it's early, Karen has already nabbed one of the couch areas. It looks like everyone's settling in for a long evening.

'What do you want?' I say to Mark.

'Mate, I'm buying. I think I owe you that much. In fact, let's just say all drinks are on me,' he replies, slapping a hand over my back.

'That's very generous of you.'

'It doesn't mean you're suddenly not a tosser. And it doesn't mean you don't still owe me for the football. Just that I appreciate your efforts,' Mark says. I nod.

'Where's your girlfriend?' I ask. Mark frowns slightly, his brain scanning through all the prospective candidates. After a few seconds I complete the question. 'Lauren?'

'Ah. No idea, I asked her to come, said she had some crap to do at home. I tried. Why, you missing her?'

'Mine's a Grolsch,' I reply, patting him on the back. He shoots me a sarcastic smile and walks over to the bar. I settle in next to Karen and try as best I can to integrate myself into a conversation I've not been part of. What's it about? Who cares? I just sit and listen. After what feels like a decade, Mark returns with my bottle of beer.

'Were you growing the hops or something?' I ask.

'There was a queue,' he replies.

'More bar presence in an Ewok,' I say.

It gets to nine-thirty and I'm starting to feel tired. I'm pondering which excuse I should use to ditch my buddies and get a cab home when I look over to the door and see Lauren walk in. I'm pleased, but I pretend not to have noticed her until she's standing next to me.

'Hi Lauren,' Karen says, smiling. I glance up at Lauren, surprise on my face.

'Oh hi,' I say. Keep a lid on that enthusiasm, James.

'Hi,' Lauren replies smiling, looking for somewhere to sit. Mark's already moving down, trying to form a space next to him but he's boxed between Darren and Gina. So I say

'Have a seat,' signalling a place next to me, 'Mark's buying tonight.' Mark glares at me but before he can speak, Lauren says

'I should think so too after all the hassle you caused me, it's the least you can do.' Mark huffs when he gets up.

'Mine's a beer, please.' Mark forces a smile and wanders back to the bar. He'll be there till Christmas. Lauren apologises for being late, gives some crappy excuse as to why. I don't buy it but whatever, she's here now. I'm suddenly not so tired. The others start to carry on their conversation. I figure this is my moment.

'So everything went okay with the FSA?' I ask.

'Yes, thank you. He was pleased we had all our documentation in order,' she replies.

'You should keep back-ups of that sort of stuff, if it's that important. Certainly don't trust it to someone like Mark.'

'Really? You think?' Her tone is playfully sarcastic but somehow it still feels like a slap. Her face softens.

'It's been a long week. I did have back-ups but I...couldn't access them.' I feel the hesitation in her voice and pounce.

'Couldn't access them?' She's annoyed at the question, I can tell, but I watch as she considers her answer. This girl is so beautiful, my heart aches every time my eyes meet hers.

'Okay, I forgot the password,' she admits finally. I say nothing at this, just smile. Then the

SEX LESSONS

smile turns to a spluttered chuckle. 'Laugh it up. It wasn't funny on Wednesday.'

'No I'm sure,' I say. She glances my way then slowly, the slightest of smiles forms on her lips. We stare at each other a second longer than necessary. I look away first, I need to work on holding people's stares. Mark appears at the table and sets Lauren's drink down.

'Thank you,' she says, her eyes returning to me.

'No problem,' he mutters and takes his seat next to Darren.

'So, is asking the boss out on a date a normal thing for you?' Ouch! That felt like a punch in the stomach. Must say something cool.

'You're the first,' I reply. Not bad. Not great, but not a dog's dinner either.

'Should I be flattered or place an inappropriate behaviour warning on your record?' she asks, her face suddenly serious. My heart is racing faster than an athlete on steroids. I laugh but it comes out hollow. Her eyes are suddenly playful, I can't tell if she's joking or not.

'Flattered?' I ask, unsure if this is the correct answer. She turns to collect her drink from the table. Her lips enclose over the rim as the sparkling liquor moves down her throat.

'Well, the proper course of action would be a meeting with Mr. Buchanan in my office first thing Monday.' She nods towards Marcus. Buchanan! That's Marcus' second name! Thank God, that was going to annoy me all night.

DANIEL GRANT

'You wouldn't want to do that. Think of all the paperwork and hassle. And those suspension meetings with HR are always such a drag,' I say, as playfully as I can muster. She looks at me, I smile weakly.

'I am curious to see what kind of person you are on a date.' What did she say? A date? I wait patiently for her to say something else. It's at this point Karen butts her big butt in.

'...exactly, *some* women like to talk about their problems, I'm just saying not all. Lauren, I bet you don't tell *all* your problems to your friends, do you?' Everyone at the table is now staring at Lauren. She considers her answer then says

'I have a few good friends but generally, if I have a problem, I'll deal with it myself.'

'See. It's not *all* women,' Karen says. Mark tries to backtrack.

'I wasn't saying *all* women, I was saying *most* women. Come on James, help me out here.' I hold up my hands, I'm not getting involved in this one.

The night carries on and I don't get to talk to Lauren properly again. Which kills me because I feel like I'm on a rope bridge with no handrail. Before long it's midnight and the others want to head off to Jo Jo's. Lauren says her goodbyes to everyone. She gives me a peck on the cheek, saying nothing further. Not even a suggestive look. Then she moves on to Darren as if our conversation had never happened. Was I dreaming it? She said 'I'm curious what you'd be like on a date.' Right? You were there, I'm not going crazy.

She starts to walk away. I want to go after her, finish our chat but with everyone milling around like this, I don't have the conviction to do so. I glance at Mark who's also watching her. He, on the other hand, has no such hesitations. Suddenly he breaks into a run and goes after her. I watch him disappear into the night and sigh to myself, regret playing me like a cheap fiddle.

DANIEL GRANT

ELEVEN - DATE

After what Lauren said in the club, I spend the next week fully expecting her to ask me out on this date she'd mentioned. So I make myself available whenever I catch sight of her.

Carefully and deliberately I craft all kinds of excuses to talk to her. I try to catch her eye when she goes for lunch. Nothing. She seems busy and preoccupied. There's no friendliness when I ask her to go over my figures for the week. She just tells me to e-mail her a copy and resumes typing. It's really frustrating. Maybe she was drunk or something? I dunno.

The real kick in the nads comes on Thursday lunchtime. I pop out to grab a sandwich. Pret's opposite my building and I run across the road, trying to avoid being killed by the mad taxi-driver haring along the bus lane. As I get to the window I glance in and am shocked by what I see. Mark and Lauren are sitting on the stainless steel chairs, munching sandwiches together. I stare at them, disbelief throwing up all over me. My hunger evaporates. They are giggling with one another, she can barely hold onto her sandwich she's laughing so much. My eyes glare at them, my feet frozen to the ground. Suddenly, Lauren looks up and spots me at the window. My heart skips a beat. I turn quickly and run back across the street. What the hell is going on? So she's just a cock-tease, that it?

I'm not even sure why I care so much. She's more of a fantasy anyway. Maybe I read more into the date comment than I should have. Damn you Pasty. I feel betrayed somehow. Not his fault, he's just doing what he always does. A strangely familiar sensation starts creeping through my abdomen, like a fat man sitting on me. I drift back to work, lost in thought, and find my way to the office kitchen. I need a cup of tea.

I don't know how long I'd been staring at the wall when I'm interrupted by Gina.

'Hi Jams, what's up?' she asks, I come out of my mini daydream and smile softly at her. There's something different about her and I can't put my finger on it. She busies herself getting a mug from the cupboard whilst searching for tea bags.

'Mmm? Nothing, just, you know...getting some tea.' I say, dejection clear in my voice. She turns. I know she'll pick up on it. Gina is annoyingly good at reading people. One reason we became such good friends when she first arrived at United. I was the one assigned to 'train' her up. Most of the time we just ended up going out on the piss and telling each other things we

DANIEL GRANT

shouldn't. Never found her attractive though. Not saying she isn't, just...not my type I guess.

'You okay?' she asks. I consider telling her that I'm not okay. That my best friend and the girl I'm in love with (okay infatuated with) are sitting across the road practically having oral sex. I think about telling her how I thought I was in with a chance and how crap I feel now. And I still feel pissed off about the whole Jenny thing too. Instead I smile politely.

'Yeah. Thanks,' I reply, 'how are you?' My heart's not in this.

'I'm okay. Can I tell you something?'

'Sure.'

'You can't tell anybody.'

'I promise.' Gina considers her next words before saying

'I think I love somebuddy I can't have. You ever have that?' I turn to face her, suddenly interested. She pours hot water from the boiler into the mug.

'Yeah,' I reply.

'Sucks,' she says. I nod.

'Yeah,' I agree, 'what can you do?'

'Someone said that love is a decision. You choose the person you love. You think that's true?' I consider her words.

'I don't know. It's possible, I guess.'

'Maybe I need to choose someone else,' she says, turning to me as she throws her tea bag into the bin. She sips the tea. 'Too hot,' she says, blowing into the cup.

SEX LESSONS

'So who are you in love with Gina?' I ask. She sighs.

'Lauren. You know, the boss? Since that day at your place, I not stop thinking about her.' I'm surprised, I had no idea Gina was gay. She never mentioned anything before. I've never seen her with a boyfriend but I just assumed she had someone in Spain or something. For reasons unknown to me, I start to smile. I can't help it. Gina gives me a look that says 'it's not funny.' I try to stifle the smile but that doesn't work because the smile has swerved out of control and become a chuckle.

'What? You think is funny?' she says, a frown appearing on her forehead. I shake my head, the chuckle now becoming a full-blown laugh.

'No, it's not funny.' I want to stop, it's not cool. Horrified, Gina slams her mug down. I try to stop her from leaving but I'm nearly on the floor. Why am I laughing? No idea. Maybe it's just the absurdity of it all. The four of us in some fucked up love...square. I make a mental note to apologise to Gina when I see her again. Poor girl. She was trying to tell me something and I...oh God, I'm laughing again.

The clock ticks over to six and I gather my gear together. I wander over to Gina's desk, she's already gone for the night. I consider leaving a note saying sorry but I figure I'll see her tomorrow. I glance over to Lauren's office. The light is off, she's also called it a night. Weird, I normally see her go. I do feel better about her. At least now I know the score.

I walk inside the elevator and hit the car park button. I'm starting to feel guilty about Gina now. I whip out my phone and write her a text saying sorry. I hit send but the signal has gone. Damn. She'll be fine once I explain everything to her. The elevator doors open and I walk over to my car.

'Hi.' I spin around to find Lauren standing next to me.

'Hi. What are you...?' I start to say.

'Look, I just wanted to apologise,' she says, looking straight at me. I frown, faking ignorance.

'For what?' I reply. She doesn't respond immediately. Finally after some thought she says

'I'm trying to be professional about all this. I'm new here and I need to make sure I don't mess it up.' She shakes her head, not quite how she wanted that to come out. 'I can't make any stupid mistakes, you understand?' Suddenly my heart is galloping with a full wind behind it.

'Yeah, I understand. Of course there is the possibility I may not be a mistake,' I say. She sighs and stares back at me.

'You're pretty sure of yourself,' she replies. I control the urge to burst out laughing. Maybe the fact that she's even thinking about any of this spurs me to say

'It's one date. You don't like it, we stop.'

SEX LESSONS

'How do you know I don't already have a boyfriend?' she asks. Good point.

'Do you?'

'No,' she replies, leaning up against my Merc. I try not to notice. I'm hoping there's no zipper on the back of her skirt because that could cut up my paint job something awful. Although saying that, her arse on my car is no bad thing, I guess. She taps her high heel on the concrete pondering her next move.

'Alright. One date. There's an Italian near where I live called Carpaccio's. Saturday, eight o'clock?' she says. Oh my God.

'Where?' I ask, out of breath suddenly.

'Moreton Street in Pimlico.' I nod excitedly, I can't believe- 'James, you tell one person about this. Anyone. Including Mark or any other person living or dead, the date's off, understand?'

'Absolutely. I will tell no one. Not even myself.' She looks unimpressed by my attempt at humour. 'No one will know,' I say trying to reassure her. She stares at me, then nods and walks towards her car. Her heels clip-clop on the ground. I watch her go, there's that bum again.

'Stop looking at my arse,' she says, not turning around. I laugh.

She gets into her car, a white Porsche. Nice. She revs the engine hard, the noise echoing around the car park then shoves it into first and races out the exit without looking back.

* * *

DANIEL GRANT

I open the front door and throw the keys onto the table. I can't believe this. I grab a beer from the fridge and park myself on the sofa, flicking the plasma on. My mind is conjuring all sorts of images for me. Me and Lauren at the meal, me and Lauren kissing, me and Lauren baking a cake (the mind does what it wants.) I'm so excited I can't focus on anything. I want to tell someone, call a friend, anyone. I try to watch TV. As usual there's nothing on. With Sky, I have over a thousand channels to choose from. Can I find one thing worth my time? Eventually I settle on a re-run of Planet Earth. Lauren and I are going on a date. Lauren! My fantasy girl. How did I do that? You are one smooth talker James. I am. I must be.

Maybe it's the HD pictures of lions mating. Or maybe it's just the fact I'm hungry and keep replaying the picture of Lauren's arse on my car. Whatever it is, a tiny thought shimmers into my mind. Here's what it forms as: 'You realise that if things go well with Lauren, you may end up having sex with her.'

I consider this detail brought forward by my subconscious. I no longer have my blue pill safety net. This starts an unfortunate chain reaction in my mind. What begins with the smallest of ideas soon swells and starts stomping over the fertile feeding ground of my subconscious, devouring everything around it. What does happen if I get Lauren into bed? She's the sort of girl that needs proper satisfaction. She won't put up with any nonsense. Christ, how could I have got myself into this situation without considering the implications? I start to panic. I need to, no, I have to find another source of pills. Someone could maybe get them for me. Who? I don't trust anyone that much. I don't even tell God about my problems any more.

I sit on the sofa while my mind replays a 'Greatest Hits' of the worst moments of my short sexual history. Erectile dysfunction, premature ejaculation, various disappointed female faces flash before me. Then a vision of 'Bunny' the stripper I 'ran' away from. All this imagery is about as useful as a one-legged man at an arse-kicking competition. I need a solution and quickly.

TWELVE - SEARCHING FOR SOLUTIONS

I've been sitting on my sofa for about half an hour going through things in my head. I stand up and walk over to the French doors. My hazy reflection moves closer as I reach for the handle. I pull open the door and step outside. It's chilly but I figure my brain needs the wakeup call. I peer towards the twinkling lights of Canary Wharf and ponder a solution to the developing storm before me. I have to source the blue pills from somewhere else, there *is* no other alternative. My mind flashes to Doctor Moore's so-called advice, 'You have a problem and I don't think it's necessarily a physical one. You need to see a psychologist...'

A psychologist? That's not going to get this sorted quickly, is it? There'll be going back over my past and childhood, the whole thing will take months. I do agree with Moore that I have to get this sorted out, not keep relying on the boys from

SEX LESSONS

Pfizer. You know what I really need? Someone to show me what I'm doing wrong. To guide me through the various stages and give me advice on what not to do. Who would do that though? All the girls I've been with recently ended so badly, most of them are either not talking to me or hate my guts. Who could I ask? An idea faintly enters my mind. I try to think it through. Before I know it I'm back inside the apartment. I lock the French doors and grab my jacket and keys. Fuck it, you only live once.

Okay, so you know how sometimes an idea can seem more appealing in your mind. Well I think this idea may have slotted itself nicely into that category. I'm standing outside 'Heaven' once more. I've been here for maybe ten minutes debating with myself on how to proceed. I take a step towards the door, then stop. A bunch of guys arrive behind me. Fuck, no choice now, I have to go in. I pull open the door and walk inside. A quick prayer and a deep breath later, I'm paying the entrance fee and I'm in. Everything feels the same, the music, the decor, even the smell. I glance at the girls waiting for their turn on the pole. I can't see Bunny. I find a table and take a seat. There's that fat guy again who was in here last time. Jesus, does he live here or something? A waitress appears at my table. She's different to the last girl that served me but wears a similar

DANIEL GRANT

wardrobe (not a lot.) Shorter hair, smaller breasts, more defined eyebrows.

'Hi there, how are you?' she asks, her Geordie accent barely audible over the music.

'Good. Listen, is Bunny working tonight?' I ask.

'Yeah, I think she's with a client.'

'Oh okay.'

'You want me to send her over when she's back?'

'Yeah, thanks.'

'No problem, can I get you a drink?'

'Just a beer please.' She potters off. I watch one of the girls fly around the pole. How do they do that? I guess if things don't work out here, they could always make it at the circus. The waitress brings my beer and I watch the girls around me. A short, pretty black girl wearing thigh-high boots sits down next to me, placing the menu in front of me.

'Hello. Can I get you a private dance?'

'Uh, I'm actually waiting for Bunny?'

'I think she's with someone at the moment, I'm...'

'Thanks, but I'll wait.' I don't mean to cut her off quite so abruptly but it's too late now.

'O...kay.' She swipes the menu and strolls back to sit with the other girls. She whispers something to them, they giggle and point at me. Great.

SEX LESSONS

'Is it...James?' I look up to see Bunny standing over me. She's got a dress with poppers down the front and knee-high boots.

'Yeah. Hi. Good memory.' I go to stand up, my hand extended.

'I'm a MENSA girl, what can I say. You want a private dance?'

'Uh, yeah. A private dance, yeah.' She smiles and reaches out her hand. I take it and stand, grabbing my beer. I follow her to a different room to last time. The theme is ancient Greece. A couple of statues with arms cut off. The futon is the same though, with yellows instead of purples. Bunny closes the door.

'Lie down.' I do as I'm told.

'Listen, Bunny...' I start. She looks over to me. Okay, how do I phrase this? 'Uh...'

'It's one hundred.'

'Huh? Oh, right.' I fumble and give her the cash. She takes it and places it on a table next to the door. Then she turns and stares straight at me. She takes a step forward then suddenly spins round and bends over. Her arse comes within centimetres of my groin.

'Look, I need your advice on something,' I say.

'What's that?' she replies, revolving her hips to the music.

'Well, I have this problem. And I thought, maybe you could help,'

'I'm sure we can do something? But the full workup is four hundred,' Bunny says on autopilot.

'No.' I slide out from underneath her and stand. She stops dancing and looks at me, her hands moving to her hips.

'Look, I like this girl at work and we've started to go on dates. The problem...my problem is, I can't...' Please don't make me say it. She waits. Fine. 'Get an erection and keep it up.' I want to die of shame.

'Lots of guys have the same problem. You tried pills?'

'Yes. That's what I've been using. But I want to do it properly, not rely on pills every time.' She listens and waits for me to continue. Man, she's not making this easy. 'Look, I don't know if it's something you'd be interested in but what I really need is someone to show me what I'm doing wrong.' I pause, looking for a reaction. She nods slowly, suddenly understanding, 'I'd pay you of course, for your time. I'm sorry if this isn't your gig or I'm completely off-base here...'

'So, what you're asking is whether I'll sleep with you then tell you what you're doing wrong? Am I warm?'

'Yes, I've got money...'

'I don't do house calls.'

'It doesn't have to be at my house, we could go to a hotel...?'

'Look at me James.' I do as I'm told. 'You think I'm stupid?'

'No I...'

'I'm a stripper, not a whore. You think, because I work in a strip club and get my tits out that somehow I'm lacking in brains?' Jeez, feels like a telling off.

'No,' I say. Silence. Then

'Maybe you should go,' Bunny says. I nod slowly.

'I'm sorry if I offended you...'

'You didn't, I just think you should leave.' I sigh and nod slowly. I walk past her towards the door, then stop and turn around.

'I've had this problem my entire life. I want to get it sorted out without relying on pills. I'm sorry for asking you, I obviously got it wrong. I just wanted help finding a solution. Here's my card, my address is on the back. Here's two hundred. For your trouble.' I lay my business card and the money on the table. I glance at Bunny, she watches me suspiciously. I open the door and leave. As I walk back towards the club, feelings of hopelessness course through me. I stride faster, out through the main bar making eye contact with the short stripper before pushing through the curtain and out.

The cold air hits me. I cough, taking stock of what I've just done. Let's see, I offered a stripper money to come back to mine and give me sex lessons. Good one James.

Well, what the hell else was I supposed to do? I don't know how to solve this fucking thing. If I do ever end up with Lauren, I can't do nothing or it will be over before I've even got her bra off. I know it's pathetic having to pay for this and it's not something I'm going to stick in an e-mail and group message to people. Nightmare. All of it. I guess I need to fall back on Plan B and source more pills. Just not sure how exactly. Then suddenly, an inspired idea. Order them online, dipshit! Could it be that simple? I just need to find a reputable site and bulk-order the fuckers. Why didn't I think of this before? Just get them delivered, brilliant. You probably thought of this ages ago. James Kennedy, sometimes you can be so fucking dumb.

SEX LESSONS

THIRTEEN - QUESTIONS

I arrive at Carpaccio's ten minutes early. I peer inside, it's already rammed. I debate with myself whether I should go in or wait here. In the end, I opt for going in. At least I can get some alcohol into my system before she arrives. I'm expecting Lauren to be late, not sure why. Maybe she just gives off that 'late girl' air.

Carpaccio's is a small old-style Italian. The smell of pizza dough and herbs fills the air. There's a long bench running along one side of the restaurant with tables packed tightly together. Above the bar is a blackboard with the specials written in chalk. The waiters all look like they flew over from Naples especially. Everything is low lit with small candles competing with one another for brightness. It's rowdy, the sounds of cutlery hitting plates and diners chatting seemingly having nowhere to go. I find the only spare table and sit down. A waiter wearing a white apron walks over.

'Good evening sir, table for one?' He asks in a thick Italian accent, laying a menu down next to me and turning the wineglass up the right way.

'Two, I'm expecting a guest,' I reply.

'Very good sir, something to drink?'

'Just a beer, please.' The waiter nods and leaves. I think I got lucky with the table, it's right next to the window. I peer out to the street and watch people wandering by. I discreetly check my breath with my hand. Seems okay. I glance at my watch. 20:02. I hear one table talking about the war in Afghanistan. Another couple are having a quiet argument, he's obviously done something wrong and is trying to make up for it. Poor bastard. The barman is a pro, he's shifting drinks out as fast as anyone I've seen.

The waiter brings over my beer. I take a large gulp and swallow. Feels good. I look out the window again, scratching my eyebrow. Okay, where is she? The possibility of being stood up occurs to me for the first time. She wouldn't do that. I mean, it would be awkward for the both of us at work.

'This seat taken?' I turn. Lauren stands next to the chair. She looks incredible. She's wearing a tight-fitting black dress with a shawl over her shoulders.

'It's all yours,' I reply, standing. She takes her seat. 'You look great.' She smiles.

'Thank you,' she replies, 'what are you drinking?' I show her my bottle of Peroni.

SEX LESSONS

'Want one?' I ask. She nods. I try to catch my waiter's attention but he's jabbering with the manager. Eventually I catch his eye and show him my bottle of beer and two fingers mouthing the words 'two more.' He nods.

'So you found the place okay then?' Lauren asks. I resist the urge for a sarcastic comeback.

'Yeah. Nice.'

'I used to come here a lot but, it's been a while.' It's uncomfortable, I feel like I'm broadcasting nerves on all frequencies. Quickly, I take another swig of beer. She watches me. I place the bottle back on the table, swallow and smile.

'You okay?' she asks. I nod and widen my eyes.

'Mmm, yeah. Just, you know...'

'No.'

'I dunno, just...first date stuff.'

'Is that what this is?' She's staring at me intently.

'Well yeah...isn't it?' The edges of her mouth rise into a smile. The waiter puts down two Peroni's in front of us and, stealing a lingering look at Lauren, walks slowly back to the bar. I see him pointing over towards our table, smiling with the other waiters. I ignore him.

'Yes James. Don't be so nervous.'

'I'm not.' I take another sip

'So what happened with Jenny?' I almost choke on my beer.

'How do you know about that?'

'I ask around.' If this is her attempt at making my nerves go away, she's rubbish.

'We weren't right for each other,' I reply.

'She's a pretty girl.'

'Yeah.'

'Okay sorry, I know it's quite a personal question but what's the point of small talk. Much more interesting to get down to the nitty-gritty, don't you think?' Uh, not really.

'I...don't know.'

'Okay, how about this, we'll order our food then you can ask me any question you like and I promise to tell you the truth.'

'Okay,' I reply. We stare at our menus but my mind is now racing with all the possible questions. Where do I start? I need something that will test her. When the waiter comes over I still haven't decided so I just pick the first thing I see on the menu. We fold our menus and hand them back to him. I swear he just glanced at Lauren's tits. Italians, unbelievable.

'So? Have you thought of a question?'

'I have actually,' I reply, 'what's your magic number?'

'What?' The smile disappears from her face.

'How many men have you had sex with?' Her eyes widen. I got her. Women hate that one. She breathes out heavily.

'Damn you,' she says, flashing a quick smile. I raise my eyebrows playfully.

'You said any question.'

SEX LESSONS

'Yeah I know. Are you sure you want the answer?'

'Uh-huh. Don't try and squirm out of it.'

'Okay James. If I answer this, you have to answer one of my questions.'

'That wasn't part of the deal.'

'Are you afraid?'

'A little.'

'Come on, fairs fair.' I love this, it was her that came up with this hare-brained scheme and now I've got her in a corner she wants to change the rules. 'Okay, the honest answer is I don't know.'

'What? You can't get away with that.'

'It's true, I honestly don't keep count.'

'So it's a lot then?'

'More than my grandma, less than a hooker.'

'Come on. Are we talking, what, twenties?' She looks up to the ceiling. 'More?' I ask. 'Forties? Over a hundred?' I was joking with the last part.

'No! Definitely not more than a hundred. And that's all you'll get from me Mr. Kennedy.' Jesus, she's fucked a hundred men.

'Now my turn,' she says, grinning.

'Okay,' I mutter.

'What happened with Jenny?'

'That's your question?'

'Yes. Honesty please.' Fuck.

'We weren't right for each other.'

'Weren't right how?'

'She broke my coffee pot.' Lauren stares at me then laughs.

'It's not funny, I need coffee in the mornings. She had to go.'

'Okay smart-arse, what really happened?' I sigh and consider my response.

'She was nice but we just didn't click, I don't know.'

'Was she rubbish in bed?'

'No, you know...hang on you've had your question.'

'Yes and you haven't given a complete answer.'

'She was great and she's a lovely girl we just didn't...'

'...click, yes.' Lauren finishes the answer for me. Then a new idea comes to her. 'Okay, how about this one. Do you think pretty girls are better in bed?'

'Not always,' I say, taking another sip of my beer. 'You've got nothing to worry about.' Lauren suddenly bursts out laughing.

'I'm not talking about me. Why would I sleep with you anyway?'

'Easy, my ego can only handle a certain number of compliments in a day.'

'It's one date James.' Is it me or is this girl sending out mixed messages? I can't for the life of me figure out what she's trying to say.

Our food comes and frankly I'm grateful for the interruption. Feels like I've gone three rounds with Mike Tyson. My stomach is a big, hard ball of tension. I'm not even hungry. We eat silently, then she says

SEX LESSONS

'Sorry for all the questions. It's just what I do when I'm...in new situations.'

'If you've had a hundred men, this can't be a new situation.' Her mouth opens with surprise and shock.

'I have *not* had a hundred men!'

'I mean that you must have been on a few dates before.'

'So now you think I'm a slut?' She has stopped eating. My stomach is now doing Fosbury flops, need to get this under control and fast.

'No, of course not. Look, I don't think anything. You're obviously pretty driven and maybe the result of that is you don't have much time for relationships. I don't know.'

'You try working sixty hours a week plus all the crap I have to take home with me, half of which isn't even my job. United is slightly better than the place I was at before but it's still bloody hard work. And I don't care what people say about smashing through the glass ceiling, in our business it's still a man's world.' I nod in understanding. 'You know how hard it is for someone like me to make it where I am without either sleeping with every boss I have or using my looks to get where I want.' She really has a thing about her looks, doesn't she?

'I understand.'

'You don't understand James.' She's calming down, which is a relief. 'People look at me and think, oh look at her, she's got blonde hair, big tits and a nice face what could she possibly know about managing traders? I see it every day. From everyone. Mark thinks it. I play along because I need people to be on my side but don't think I don't know what's going on.' I'm lost now.

'What *is* going on?' I ask.

'You seem like a nice guy James. I just don't want to get into any sort of heavy stuff, I can't deal with it at the moment.'

'As you said, it's one date, I'm not asking you to marry me.' I reply. She glances up at me and a smile creeps across her face. She is beautiful. She giggles a little then breathes in hard, sighing loudly.

'Okay, sorry. I don't know what's wrong with me. I'm never like this, I'm always...'

'...in control?' I finish for her. She nods, staring at me. 'Maybe you just need to take your foot off the accelerator a little. It's okay to have some fun. Even if you are working yourself into an early grave.' She nods and takes a swig of her beer.

'You're a smart man James.'

'Thanks.' We stare at each other, then carry on eating.

Once we finish dinner a small 'discussion' takes place about who should pay the bill. In the end I go up to the bar and give the waiter my card. She huffs but I think she appreciates it. Maybe.

The streets outside are raucous with drunk teenagers walking to clubs. Buses and cars rush

SEX LESSONS

past, the streets bustling with Saturday night traffic. We face each other.

'Do you want to get a cab?' James, the sex thing, remember? What are you doing? Fuck, yeah. Don't go for the cab idea Lauren.

'I'm not sleeping with you James.'

'I never assumed...'

'Yes you did.' I know I probably couldn't have done it anyway but a part of me is still disappointed. Did she wait with all those other guys or jump straight in to bed with them? I turn and scan for a free cab.

'Well, let me see if we can get you home.' There's one, I go to hail it. Lauren suddenly grabs my shirt and pulls me in. Our lips connect. POW! Electricity shoots through me. It's unlike any kiss I've ever experienced. Our tongues find each other. Her smell fills my nose and courses through my lungs. I run my hand through her fine hair and push her head harder into mine. So soft, so fiery. I can barely control my breathing as our lips break contact and I slowly pull away. My eyes flick open, yanking me back to reality. I watch as she opens her eyes, her mouth is still slightly open from the kiss. She's bowled over, it's written all over her face. She swallows and stares at me. We stand in the freezing cold, just staring at each other for what feels like years. Inevitably, speech breaks the spell.

'Well, I guess I'll see you in the office,' she says. I nod, not breaking eye contact.

DANIEL GRANT

'Yeah.' I blink a few times then turn and look for a cab. One's coming with his light on.

'TAXI!' I shout, he pulls over. I open the door and Lauren walks over. She touches my hand as she climbs inside. I close the door and watch her drive away, wondering what just happened.

SEX LESSONS

FOURTEEN - A LESSON LEARNED

The following day at home, I manage to find a web site called www.onlinepharmacy.org and order a box of fifty Viagra. When I click the order button, there's a small part of me that feels like I'm heading backwards. What the hell, I need these pills, at least until I can work out a more permanent solution.

It gets to one o'clock and I am just sitting down to start on my microwaved lasagne when the phone rings. Cursing and swearing I stand up and yank the cordless off the base station which promptly crashes to the floor. Fuck!

'Hello?' I say, flustered.

'Where were you last night?' It's Mark, I can't be bothered.

'Out, what do you want?'

'Touchy, what's up?'

'I'm trying to eat my lunch.'

'So? Just heat it up again. Come on then, who was she? I thought you were coming out with us.' Bollocks, I do vaguely remember saying I'd pop down for a few drinks. But that was last week, a lot has happened since then.

'Yeah, I wasn't feeling that great to be honest,' I say, uncomfortable with the lie.

'Oh...yeah? Going blind 'cos of all that porn.'

'Something like that. Where'd you go?'

'Karen dragged us to Arthur's on King Street, have you been there?'

'Nope.'

'It's such a meat market, I know she's desperate for a bloke but this place was offensive, even to me.' I chuckle but only slightly. Mark detects my tone. 'Well anyway, what you up to today?'

'I was going to finish my lunch and probably go back to bed.'

'Okay fair enough. If you're feeling up for it, maybe go down the Archers for the quiz?'

'Maybe,' I reply.

'Cool, laters dude.'

'Bye.' I hang up. I know I should make more of an effort but my lasagne is getting cold. I walk back to the table and suddenly my Blackberry rings. I mouth the 'f' word and look to the ceiling.

'Hello?'

'Is this James?'

'Who's this?'

'It's Bunny.' My mind does a search and comes up with a big flashing light. Holy shit. 'I've...been thinking about what you said and...I just thought I'd call.'

'Oh right, yeah. How're you doing?'

SEX LESSONS

'Fine. Were you serious, before?'

Fuck, now what? Not sure I want to pursue this. What's the moral thing to do here? I'm sure Lauren wouldn't be amused at me even thinking about this but then if I have to get into that shitty 'no wood' situation one more time. Maybe just once. We wouldn't even need to have sex, just talk maybe?

'Yeah. Are you interested?' I reply. There's a long pause on the phone.

'How much are we talking?'

'Uh...' I have no idea, what's the going rate for whoring nowadays?

'Two hundred a session?' I try.

'I make more than that at the club.'

'Five hundred?' Jesus James, sounds like you're haggling over a sofa.

'Five hundred, how long is a session?' she asks. I have no idea.

'Two hours?' I venture. The phone goes quiet again.

'Okay, it's a deal. You got the money now?' Fuck no. Maybe in a sock drawer somewhere.

'Yes.'

'Then let me in, I'm outside.' What the...I walk over to the intercom and pick up the handset. The LCD flicks on and sure enough, there's Bunny. I buzz her in. Shit. Am I supposed to clean up? Fuck that, I'm paying her. I don't want her to think I'm a slob though. I move the barely touched lasagne into the fridge and throw the knife and fork into the dishwasher. A knock at the door prevents me from doing any more. I walk over and open it.

Bunny looks different somehow, shorter than in the club. She's got a silver puffer jacket on and her high heels make a loud echo on the wooden floor as she walks. She wears less makeup than before. She's cute but not amazing, not like Lauren but she's got something. Sexiness. More than that though, supreme confidence perhaps. A black handbag hangs over her shoulder.

'Hi, come in,' I say. She walks in, glancing around. I watch her reaction to the apartment.

'Nice place,' she says. Ha! Brilliant. Everyone loves this place. Maybe now she's convinced I'm not going to hack her to pieces with a saw. Stop thinking those things James, you're scaring everyone.

'Thanks,' I reply. She wanders into the living room and takes in the French windows.

'Jesus, that's some view.'

'Yeah. Glad you like it. So...were you christened Bunny?' I ask. She turns around.

'No,' she smiles, considering her next words. 'But let's stick with Bunny for now.' I don't know why but she has a different vibe to when I met her at the club. Feels more relaxed.

'Do you want something to drink?' I ask.

'Just a glass of water, thanks.'

'Make yourself at home.' I walk into the kitchen and pour a glass. I hear her clopping around the living room, hope she's not stealing the TV. Although let's face it, that would have a certain comic element to it. This small girl trying to lift the fifty inch plasma. When I saunter back in she's staring out at Canary Wharf. I hand her the glass.

'Thanks. So you're a banker.'

'Yeah. As I said before, we're not all arseholes.' She shrugs.

'I know some very nice bankers.' She looks down at my GQ magazine. 'This girl you're seeing doesn't come over too often, does she?' I eye her suspiciously. 'I spotted the dirty plates. There's no girl stuff in here either.'

'Clever.'

'Yeah, well I'm doing a psychology masters so I guess I should be.' Is she serious? She's not smiling. Fuck. An intelligent stripper. She must see my thought because she says 'Surprised?'

'No. It's great. The two things just seem...different.' She laughs.

'Different yes, but not incompatible. I know, I'm a walking cliché. Student by day, stripper by night.' I don't know what to say to this so I keep quiet. 'So what's the problem James, you seem like a nice guy, everything not quite working under the hood?' I breathe in and let it out slowly. Go on then, tell her.

'Uh, have a seat.' I point towards the sofa. We sit down next to each other. She places her handbag on the table and removes her puffer jacket. She's wearing a low-cut top and a Tiffany's heart around her neck. 'Okay, so the thing is...well it's two things really...' Jesus, I'm nervous now. Deep breaths, James. Okay. 'I can't keep my...thing up and uh...sometimes I can't even get it to go up in the first place.' A deep sense of shame fills my being as I utter the words. I study her reaction, she gives nothing away. I elect to carry on. 'I mean, not all the time, just mostly. I've been taking, Viagra but...I dunno, I want to get it sorted out properly. My doctor, Nazi that he is, says I should see a psychologist. Although with you being a psychology student, I guess I'm getting a two for one deal.' I chuckle nervously at my own joke. Bunny smiles politely.

'Okay.' She stops and stares at me. Then she nods as if making her mind up. 'I think I can help you, James. There are a few things we can try. First I want to chat about everything that's happened to you sexually up till now. It might take a couple of hours but it's worth doing. Are you up for that?'

'Sure, I guess. The only thing is, I don't know whether I have the five hundred here. I wasn't expecting you to call so...'

'You said you had it on the phone.'

'I know. I might have, I haven't counted it for a while.' Bunny stares straight at me, her smile is gone. I want to look away but her gaze is intense. Finally she says

'This breaches every rule I have...but you look like you're good for it. Give me what you can, you can pay the rest on my next visit. You screw me James, remember I know where you live.'

SEX LESSONS

'Yes. Right. Of course.' I fumble, deciding to exit stage right before I say anything else that might confirm her suspicion I'm a fuckwit. I walk into my bedroom and grab the sock drawer money. I count it out plus what I have in my wallet. I have exactly three hundred and thirty-five pounds. I wander back to Bunny and hand all of it over to her. Feels strange giving this girl money. Doesn't feel wrong exactly, just...I dunno. Am I really this sad? That I have to pay a stripper to...fuck it, I don't know. She places the money in her handbag and turns back to face me.

'We might go over our allotted two hours but don't worry I won't bill you more.'

'Cheers.'

'Yeah, just the kinda girl I am. Okay, so tell me about the first time you ever had feelings for a girl.'

'Really? So we're starting now?'

'Yeah. This is what you wanted, isn't it?'

'I don't...know. I just kind of assumed, you'd...show me.'

'We'll get to that. It doesn't sound physical with you, your Nazi doctor is right. I want to understand what led you to where you are now. Trust me, it will pay for itself a thousand times over. Don't worry, we'll get to the practical side later.'

'What about you? I don't know anything about you?'

'I'm not here to talk about me James.'

DANIEL GRANT

'What's your real name?' She sits back.

'Come on. I want to open up but the name Bunny...it's not you.'

'You don't know anything about me James.'

'Exactly, that's why I'm asking.' She puts her thumbnail between her teeth as she thinks.

'It's Sarah.'

'Sarah, I'm James. That wasn't so bad was it?' By her look, I can tell she's not sure if she did the right thing there, but it's done now.

'Tell me about your past girlfriends.'

So we sit and we talk. Rather, I sit and tell her everything I can remember about my past. Susie, of course, plays a big part in the story. There are others, of course, girls that were just screws, others that were friends that became screws then subsequently became strangers. I tell her everything, and you know what? It feels strangely freeing. She listens, sometimes she interrupts me for clarification on something or asks how a certain person or event makes me feel. It's like being in therapy, I guess. I try to be as honest as I can. Some of it is harder than I expect. As I speak, I feel like I'm suddenly right back in that place. Sandra Cummings screaming at me to 'sort it out' because I couldn't get hard for the third time in a row. Asking Jane Weller out in front of my entire school year, and her smirking as she said no. All the shame, dejection, rejection, humiliation. Every event in my life that had ever turned sour and caused me no end of pain and over-analysis. We talk about my relationship with

SEX LESSONS

my father which is pretty good. He lives in Norwich now which is too far to see him on any regular basis. My relationship with my mother, which is non-existent. I can't remember the last time I spoke to her. I speculate on whether she's still with that George bloke she left my father for. Or whether she's got some other faceless man in her life. There's always someone as I recall. I pretend not to care when I talk about these things but Sarah calls me on it every time.

I ask her questions as well. I find out her lifelong dream is to go to Argentina. She loves to tango and goes to lessons. She explains how ethics don't get in the way of what she's trying to do. She says the human body is the most natural, beautiful thing in the world and getting paid to take her clothes off is easy money. Whatever works for her I guess, I'm not complaining. She's still got her shields up, but I think I'm getting in there.

The neighbour's cuckoo clock sounds five o'clock and day has quickly become night.

'Well, I think that will do for now,' Sarah says, standing. 'I have to say, you're remarkably honest James.'

'Yeah?' I reply, my insides feel like they've been on a high spin most of the afternoon. She nods.

'I don't know many guys who would tell a complete stranger so much about their private life with so little...defensiveness.'

'What are you going to do, tell the papers?' I'm joking, of course, but I study her face just in case.

'I reckon we can get this thing sorted out without pills.' I nod.

'Hope so,' I say. She grabs her puffer jacket and I follow her to the door. She opens it and turns to me, handing me a card.

'Here's my mobile number. Text only. Weekend nights are busy for me and I study most of the week but text me and we'll work out a time that suits.'

'Thanks. I'll do that.'

She nods and walks out, her heels echoing down the stairs. I close the door, feeling like Sarah somehow just took part of my soul with her. I hope she keeps it in a safe place.

SEX LESSONS

FIFTEEN - COMPLICATIONS

Monday at work is, frankly, a pisser. I'm way behind in my correspondence with some of the other banks we deal with and I had promised to have it all wrapped up by today. So here I sit, tapping away.

By midmorning I want to throw myself off the atrium. I watch Lauren in her office. She takes meetings with Mike (bell-end) and other senior executives, she looks so damn hot I want to just go in there and take her now. Of course, knowing my lower body the way I do, I probably couldn't if I tried. So here I sit and wait and watch. She's started wearing reading glasses when she looks at her computer too and frankly it's enough to give me a small coronary.

I ponder on how long it could take Sarah to sort my issues out. I'm also wondering what she has in mind by way of a solution. I'm sure it won't all be talking. I feel strange about the whole thing, not sure why. Am I being deceitful to Lauren? We're not technically anything at the moment, we had one date and we kissed. Not like we promised to honour and obey. And yet, something in me still doesn't feel comfortable. Plus if it ever got out that I was paying for this, I don't know...Christ let's not go there. I decide all this is probably just a bad bowl of Frosties this morning and nothing more.

Lunchtime arrives. I watch and wait for Lauren to leave her office. She's sitting at her desk typing, her hair tied back in a ponytail. She's concentrating hard on something. She stops, leans back and takes off her glasses, rubbing her eyes slowly. She places the glasses in their box, turns off the computer and stands to leave. I'm up quickly and heading towards her. She walks towards the toilets, don't think I'm going to get to her before...damnit, she's inside. I wait. I'm not sure if this is a good move or not but I'm committed now so I can't walk away. I lean against the wall, a spotlight in the ceiling shining down on my face.

The door opens and Gina walks out pausing as she sees me. Fuck.

'Hi,' I say. She's got her 'I'm pissed off with you look' on.

'Jams,' she replies and goes to walk away. I move to block her.

'Listen, I'm sorry for laughing before. I do understand your predicament, can't be easy for you.' Her face softens faintly.

'Whatever Jams. It's fine.'

SEX LESSONS

'No it's not fine, I was a prick. I'm sorry. Forgive me?' I blink my eyelids fast, giving her the best puppy dog look I can muster. She raises her eyebrows, unimpressed. I carry on regardless. Slowly a smile creeps across her face.

'Alright, I forgive you. Stop doing that with your eyes, it's weird. You want lunch?' Yes but with Lauren...

'Uh, okay yeah sure,' I reply glancing at the door.

'I get my bag and meet you outside,' Gina says. I nod.

'Sure.' I want to wait but now I have to move away. I keep glancing back to see if Lauren comes out, she doesn't. Maybe it's a number two.

Gina takes her handbag from her desk and we walk out. We head over to Johnny's Sandwich Bar on Queen Street. It's a little way to get there but the sun is out and we both fancy a walk along the Thames.

'So, you still in love with Lauren?' I ask. Gina looks up to me, a little surprised then considers her response.

'Yes. But is not going to happen. What about you?'

'Me? No, why would you think that?'

'You are a man, she is very attractive no?'

'I guess.'

'Come on Jams. She is beautiful. Are you gay?'

'What? No, I just don't think she's as amazing as you say she is.'

'Liar.'

DANIEL GRANT

'What?' I smile, I can't help it.

'You are such a liar, look at you.'

'Look at me what?'

She shakes her head, beaming. We walk on further, not saying anything. It's frosty but there's not a cloud in the sky. London is the greatest city in the world on days like this, especially by the river. A tourist boat motors past; I get faint clips of commentary murmuring in my ear.

'So you didn't like Jenny?'

'Why does everyone keep asking me that?' I reply.

'I heard she's a bitch,' Gina says.

'She wasn't a bitch, just not right for me...look, she had implants, what else is there to say?'

'What is implant?' I make an exaggerated shape of breasts using my hands. She gets it. 'Oh. Fake boobies.'

'Yeah,' I reply, chuckling.

'I think you can get someone better than her Jams.'

'Thank you for saying so Gina.'

'You think Mark likes Lauren?' I frown and glance at Gina.

'I...don't know. Why?'

'I think he look at her strange.'

'Really?'

'Yeah. You don't think?'

'I've not noticed,' I lie, 'but now you've brought it up I'll keep an eye out.' Gina smiles and nods.

'Good,' she says.

* * *

SEX LESSONS

I get back to my desk a little late, almost two o'clock. I glance around nervously, don't think anyone noticed. I carry on typing up those endless e-mails. I ponder on how much further up the company I need to travel to get myself a secretary or a PA or something.

'Hey!' I nearly fall out of my chair. Mark stands next to my desk. 'Long lunch?'

'Something like that. What's up?'

'Nothing I just thought you sounded a bit off on Saturday, everything okay?'

'Yeah. Just wasn't feeling great.' He can't tell when I'm lying, but I don't make eye contact anyway, just in case.

'Listen,' his voice becomes almost a whisper, 'I'm thinking about asking Lauren out. What do you reckon?' I think you should get back to your desk and never mention her name again you sick son of a bitch.

'Uh, really?' My voice sounds surprised and comically high-pitched.

'Yeah really. We've been getting on really well and I dunno, I think she digs me.' I involuntarily breathe out hard. 'You sure you're okay?'

'Yeah, you know, still not feeling a hundred per cent.' Actually I feel like an elephant just shat on me.

'Mate, should you even be in?'

'Yeah, no, I'm fine.'

'Sure?'

'Yeah. Thanks,' I reply. He pats me on my back.

DANIEL GRANT

'So, what do you reckon?' I play dumb.

'About what?'

'Duh...Lauren?'

'I don't know man, I mean...' I'm floundering here, 'you really think she likes you?' Mark smiles.

'Yeah, why...you don't think so?'

'No, I just...I dunno. She's still getting her feet under the table.'

'So what? That's the time to do it, when they're disorientated.'

'Can't quite see her as the confused, vulnerable type.'

'So you think I should hold off?'

'Yeah maybe.' Mark considers this, glances at me and nods.

'Okay, maybe you're right.' What are you doing James, this is going to start getting nasty.

'Actually, fuck it. If you want to try something, go for it,' I say. My mind kicks in. What's that now? You're opting for him to ask her out with your blessing? Either you're a genius or fucking stupid. I know which one I want to be.

'Okay, thanks man. I'll do it now. Wish me luck.'

'Now? You're going to ask her out right now?'

'Yeah? Why not?' I can think of a million reasons, none of them seem appropriate at this point.

'Good luck.' I actually feel pain as I say the words.

SEX LESSONS

'Cheers,' Mark replies and wanders over to Lauren's office. I watch him go, my heart a shrivelled prune on the floor. I'm so nervous I start sharpening pencils. He closes the door behind him and starts talking to her. She looks up from her computer and listens to him. I check my watch, 14:05. He says something then laughs, she smiles. Suddenly she glances over to me, I hit the deck immediately. My chin smacks the desk, the resulting bang stops everyone temporarily in their tracks. Poppy, the loudmouth on the desk in front stands up and peers over.

'You okay?' she asks.

'Yeah, just hit my chin on my desk,' I reply, as if that's the most normal thing in the world.

'Oh, okay,' she says and sits back down. I rub my bruised chin, it fucking hurts but nothing like what's going on inside my gut which feels tighter than my old school Speedos. I glance over to Lauren's office. The door is open, Mark has already left. Shit. I look around, trying to find him.

'Who said I'd lost it?' Mark says, making me jump again.

'Jesus, stop doing that!' I reply, turning around. He has one of those classic Pasty smiles on his face. 'Well?' I ask, but I already know the answer.

'We're going out on Thursday, just drinks she said but I think I may well be...how do you say...in there!' He's almost dancing with glee. My heart feels like it's had a twelve gauge fired into it.

DANIEL GRANT

'That's...great. Well done mate.' He bows slightly.

'Thank you, thank you. Drinks tonight? I'm going to need some serious advice on the best approach.'

'I don't think I can...' I start to say.

'Course you can. We don't have to get drunk.' I'm unimpressed. 'Okay we probably will, but come on. I need you buddy. This is the perfect antidote to Jess. I've never had someone like Lauren.' Interesting, the way he said 'had' just then. In the past tense. Like it's already happened.

'Fine, one drink,' I say. I just want him to go away.

'Great, I'll find you at six.' I nod and watch him walk away, almost skipping as he does so. Anger is bubbling inside me. What the hell is going on? I need to keep a lid on this, not have a scene. I stand up, my stomach groans at me. I walk over to Lauren's office and knock on the door. She looks up from her computer and when she sees it's me, gestures for me to come in. I open the door and go inside, carefully closing it behind me.

'Hi,' I say.

'Hello James. This isn't what I would call subtle, but it's good to see you.' An admirable attempt at redirection but I'm focused.

'Is there some reason you're going on a date with Mark on Thursday?' She lets out a sigh, leans back on her chair and examines me.

'Sit down.'

SEX LESSONS

'I don't want to sit down, I just want an answer.' My voice is getting loud. She frowns.

'Shh. It's not a date, it's drinks. I don't want anyone knowing about us James and...'

'So instead you agree to go out with Mark, that makes sense.' My anger is spilling over now, I don't want it to but emotion is starting to get the better of me.

'James, sit down,' she commands. I do but I make sure I shoot her a look that says you're not the boss of me. Although I'm aware, of course, that she is.

I slouch on the sofa, knees together feeling about as comfortable as tweed pants. On her swivel chair she is higher than I am. I can see why she wanted me to sit down. She leans forward.

'It's not a date. Karen and the others are coming as well.'

'What?'

'It's the two of us to start with, then Karen and Gina and probably Darren will come down after us. That was my compromise.' I don't know what to make of this.

'Why go out with just him at all?'

'It's sweet you're jealous but we've been on one date. Okay. You're not going to start being weird, are you?' I consider my response. I know what she's doing here, she's trying to make me feel like a freak. Damnit I think I have a right to feel a bit jealous. Maybe I do need to calm myself a little but what the fuck?

DANIEL GRANT

'No. You're right, I don't have any right to be jealous...I just wanted to get the facts straight, that's all.' Lauren tilts her head to the side.

'I don't want Mark or anyone else knowing about what happened on Saturday, James. If this shuts him up for a bit then all the better.'

'It won't shut him up, he'll keep hassling you until he gets what he wants.'

'I'm perfectly capable of dealing with men like Mark thank you. I think you should go now.'

I stand up and head for the door, shaking my head like a sulky teenager.

'James..?' she says. I turn, my fingers on the handle. 'I had a great time on Saturday. I hope we can do it again soon.' She stares at me with sincerity. I swallow and nod, then open the door and walk out.

I find my desk, all kinds of emotions zipping around inside in my head. Am I being taken for a ride? Sure feels like it. But then that last comment. She wants to go out again? So I just have to stand by and wait for her and Mark to go out then I get my turn? Well you know what I think? Fuck. That.

SEX LESSONS

SIXTEEN - KEEP IT IN THE CLOSET

I get back to my desk and whip out my Blackberry. I write a text. It reads: 'Hi Sarah, its James would luv 2 c u again Im free most nights this week. Let me know whats good 4 u.'

I hit send and drop it on the desk running my hands through my hair. This feels horrible. Is Lauren just fucking with my head? Wanting her pie and eating it? Am I supposed to compete with my best friend for this girl? Sure looks that way.

I spend most of the afternoon pinging ideas back and forth in my head like a rally at Wimbledon. Most of them aren't helpful. I look down and notice I've drunk two cups of coffee and a Red Bull. Jesus, how did that happen? My colon's going to be one unhappy clapper tonight. Speaking of which, I stand and head down towards the Gent's, my mind still whizzing with all kinds of weird and wonderful notions. I get to the urinal and unleash. Feels good, I hadn't realised how badly I needed to go but now that I'm here, I'm glad I didn't wait any longer. I get to the basin and throw some water on my face. It's warm, feels good. I look up, see myself staring back. What a mess. I grab a paper towel and dry off, chucking it towards the metal bin and missing by a mile. I walk out. I get to the narrow corridor and start heading towards the trading room.

'Psst.' I turn at the noise. The cleaner's closet door is slightly ajar. I walk over to it.

'Hello?' I whisper. I'm not sure why I'm whispering but it feels right.

Suddenly, a hand grabs my shirt and hauls me into the dark closet. The shaft of light from the corridor only barely illuminates the room. Lauren stands in front of me, her hands grab my neck and she kisses me full-on. I unintentionally take a step back, banging into a metal mop bucket. It makes a hell of a noise.

'Shh,' Lauren says, frowning.

'Sorry,' I whisper. We kiss again, I feel her hand move around my back and down to my arse. She grabs both cheeks hard. Then a feeling. And it's not a feeling I want right now. No, not that. You won't believe this but I suddenly have an urgent need to fart. Like badly. Don't ask me why I didn't do it in the toilet, I have no idea. I move my hands over her breasts and down to her skirt. I clench myself as tightly as I can, there is no way I can let this one go. She leans her head back exposing her neck. I feel like my lower body is going to explode. I breathe in, trying to suck back the force. Suddenly, muffled voices outside. We stop in mid...whatever you call this. Oh God, hold on.

'...exactly but Jerry over at Morgan Stanley said it was a sure thing,' says the first voice, a man that sounds like he could be doing voice-overs for movie trailers.

'Really? I might buy in to some of that,' the second voice replies, almost a man but weedier. We look at each other trying not to laugh, or rather she tries not to laugh, I smile uncomfortably. I can't hold this in much longer. Lauren starts giggling and holds up her hand to cover her mouth. I'm smiling but she needs to be quiet. The voices get softer as they move away. I glance down to Lauren's untucked blouse then up to her now messy hair.

'I think we'd better go,' I say. She nods, tucking her blouse back in. She pulls her hair back and ties it with a band. She leans in and kisses me gently, one hand on my shoulder. Please go!

'I like you James, okay?' she says. I nod, blinking fast. 'I just can't show you I like you. Not around here.' I nod again but she needs to leave, right now.

Suddenly my phone beeps. Loudly. It makes me jump. Shit! Something escapes, I tighten up. We stare at each other, listening. Please go before...

Lauren kisses me on the cheek then walks out. Something awful enters my nostrils. Like the inside of a dumpster or rotting baby poo. Jesus

DANIEL GRANT

H...thank the Lord she left when she did. It's fucking horrible. So bad, in fact, my eyes start to water. I take out the Blackberry and, wiping my eyes, look at the message. It's from Sarah. I click open. It reads: 'Free Thursday night and Saturday daytime. Let me know. Sarah'

I put the Blackberry away and walk tentatively towards the doorway. I peek through and listen. Nothing. I walk out and let the rest of the fart go as I stroll slowly along the corridor. It feels like I've passed a gallstone, I actually feel lighter. My cheeks are hot. Mark is at my desk, waiting. He throws out his arms in despair.

'Dude, what happened?'

'What'd you mean?' I say, as composed as possible.

'I've been here for like ten minutes.' I glance at the clock, it's 18:14.

'Sorry mate, I...had a slight problem.'

'Thought you'd gone without me, then I saw your jacket.'

'Well I'm here now,' I reply. A door bangs shut, we both look over to the noise. Lauren walks towards the lifts, she waves as she goes.

'Bye guys.'

'Bye Lauren,' Mark says, sarcasm dripping from his mouth. I go to wave then think better of it.

'Let's go,' I say.

* * *

SEX LESSONS

As we walk towards the bar my mind, being nothing if not consistent, replays the kiss in the closet. What the hell was that all about? First she's Hilter's daughter then she's a giggling schoolgirl in the closet? I do feel a little better about things but maybe that's what she wanted all along. Give him a kiss and that'll sort him out. But it didn't feel like that, there was passion and fire. So much fire. I could do with some serious advice. Of course, the person I normally turn to in these predicaments is Mark. Problem. Now I'm going to have to sit and listen to him babble on about how great she is, maybe even give advice on how to pull her for himself. Brilliant.

We arrive at The Wine Lounge. Jazz and soft blues float on the air. People sit in high-backed booths with cushions, occasionally this place has a live act but mostly it's just guys in suits drinking and the occasional lost tourist. We find a booth, I take my jacket off and throw it to the back. The waitress walks over, a big toothy smile on her face.

'Hi, can I get you some drinks?' she asks. She's got an accent, Dutch maybe, can't place it.

'Two beers please,' Mark replies, I glance at him, unsure if alcohol is such a great idea. He sees my look. 'That okay?'

'Sure,' I reply. The waitress walks away. Mark stares at me, grinning. 'What?'

'Nothing.'

'Come on then. What did she say?' I ask. So fucked up.

DANIEL GRANT

'Okay, so I walk in and she's fiddling around on the computer, she's got her glasses on. Have you seen her wearing glasses? Fucking hot.' I nod. 'So we talk about the ING deal for a bit and she says she's snowed under with all this paperwork, so I say you need to relax a bit. Then I just come out with it.' He pauses for effect. He's waiting for me to tell him to go on, I stubbornly refuse. He's staring at me. I give in.

'Yeah?' The waitress suddenly interrupts us and sets our drinks on the table. We wait patiently until she is on her way.

'So I say do you fancy getting a drink sometime. At first she's all like 'no, I can't I've got too much to do, blah-blah' then I say 'doesn't have to be today, how about Thursday?' she still doesn't want to. So I say 'It's not a date or anything, just two colleagues going over the figures.' He raises his eyebrows suggestively. I flash him a smile but it's the last thing I feel like doing. What I really want to do is throw up, but what am I supposed to do? Make a beeline for the Men's? He's in the middle a story.

'Didn't go for that either?' I ask.

'Well no, she said it wasn't appropriate for us to go on dates. So I said other people would come along.' I jump on this.

'Ha, I knew it. So it's not a date.' He holds up his hand.

'Hang on, I said other people would come along afterwards, we'll have about two hours before they get there. I reckon I can work my magic before then.' I fear he may well be correct. I know what Lauren said but women always find Mark charming. They don't even realise they're being pulled half the time.

'Where you taking her?'

'Jo Jo's of course. Be great if Jess was there this time. Can you imagine?'

'Yeah...well good luck,' I say.

'Man, this is the fucking best thing that's happened since that bitchbag got knocked up.'

'It's good news,' I say. Mark frowns.

'Be a little enthused.'

'I am. It's great. Good job.' He stares at me. I know I'm being crap but fuck him, I can't jump up and down about this.

'What's wrong with you?'

'Nothing, I'm tired you know...'

'Okay, well...this is a big deal James. Girls like Lauren don't come along every day.' No argument from me.

'I'm sure it will go great,' I reply. I can't hide it much more. Mark is staring at me, I don't want make eye contact. I stand up. 'Just going to the loo.' I can feel him watching me as I head to the gents.

I find a cubicle and sit on the seat, holding my head in my hands. This is a fucking nightmare and it's getting worse with every word he says. What to do? Maybe I should just be honest with him, sod what Lauren said. But if he blabs to someone, I'm screwed. No more Lauren and that is not an option. I flashback to the closet, kissing, biting. Fantastic. Although that fart was something horrendous. I breathe out slowly. I need to make excuses and get the hell out of here. I stand and walk out so consumed in thought, I almost knock over a tall guy in a navy suit.

'Excuse me,' I say. He grunts and carries on. I wander back to Mark. As I approach, I notice he's got a strange smile on his face. I squeeze into my seat and huff. 'What?'

'Who's Sarah?' he asks. My eyes widen and suddenly any food in my stomach rushes up my throat. I swallow hard and cough. Mark stares at me, the smile getting bigger.

'You dog, who is she?'

'How do you know?' He produces my Blackberry.

'It rang, I tried to answer it but don't worry, I think she left a voicemail. Just says missed call from Sarah.' How could I be so stupid?

'She's my cat psychologist.'

'You don't have a cat.'

'I was thinking about getting one.'

'You don't want to tell me, that's fine. But I'll find out, just have to do it the hard way.'

'She's just someone I met and...I'm taking it slow, okay?'

'Slow. So, is she pretty? You can tell me that.' AGGH!!

'Yes.'

'How old?'

'Mark...'

'Come on...twenties?'

SEX LESSONS

'Yes. Twenty-five maybe.'

'Maybe? You don't know? Brilliant. Hey listen, we can go out on double dates when I pull Lauren.' Something twangs inside my chest.

'Yeah,' I reply.

SEVENTEEN - WHAT GOES AROUND...

I open the door to my apartment and flick the light on. I walk into the living room and collapse onto the sofa. I take out my Blackberry and listen to the voicemail.

'Hi James, it's Sarah. I got your text, Thursday is good for me, maybe after you finish work? Text me when you're leaving and I'll come to yours. Bye.' It's weird, she sounds almost normal, like she's one of my friends or something. I toss the Blackberry onto the table and sit, pondering.

I've got too many balls in the air, I need to remove myself from some of this before they start dropping. Not sure how though. Can't drop Lauren. Maybe I could drop Sarah but she's pleasant and, in theory, she could potentially cure my various hang-ups. She is costing me a fuck load of money though, I could spend that on Lauren. A romantic weekend for two or some jewellery maybe. Also not sure how I declare it for tax purposes either. Worry about that in April. If I

SEX LESSONS

can keep Mark at bay until the end of the sessions, that should be okay.

Thursday after work, that's what Sarah said. That's when Mr. Pasty and Lauren go out on their big date. Of course it would have to be the same night Sarah's free. I'm not going to get upset about it, Lauren does what she wants. I have no claim on her, but if Pasty gets beyond first base I will have to break his kneecaps.

I pick up the Blackberry again and compose a text: 'Hi Sarah, Thursday sounds good I'll text you when I'm leaving. James.' I hit send and chuck it back on the table. I click on the TV. MTV is playing the Time Travellers video of 'Cheater'. The lead singer, Johnny Dougan, is in a pretend police uniform and is writing out a speeding ticket for a stunning blonde with an equally stunning boob-job. Their videos are always a bit weird. Such a good song though. I glance towards the French doors and Docklands beyond, wondering if Sarah's working tonight.

Thursday is on me before I know it and gloominess starts to linger around my thoughts like a Salt 'n Vinegar burp. I sit at my desk, constantly glancing over to Lauren's office, checking to see if Mark's in there with her. I can't see him, where is he? The biggest problem I have sitting here is the fact I can't see his desk. I need to stop this, just relax and let it be whatever it's going to be. I should communicate that sentiment to my stomach, it's doing cartwheels down there. Lauren is still sitting at her desk typing something. She's got her glasses on. Probably e-mailing him.

'Well Mr. Dark Horse.' Karen stands behind me. She makes me jump. Why can't people just come to the front of my desk, damnit?

'Hi,' I say.

'So when were you going to tell me?' she asks, one eyebrow raised slightly higher than the other.

'About what?' I feign ignorance, always best until we know what we're dealing with.

'Your new girlfriend?' She's got her cheeky smile on. Fuck, Pasty blabbed.

'She's not my girlfriend,' I snap. Karen holds up her hands.

'Easy. I'm just asking. Who is she?'

'No one. Just someone I met, it's nothing.'

'Is she pretty? What am I saying, of course she is.' I sit and say nothing. 'You may as well tell me.'

'Why's that?'

'Because nothing you do, when it comes to women, stays secret for long.' Now, I don't know about you but that sounds almost dangerous. Did Jenny tell Karen about my...problem? Oh God. I stare at her intently. 'What's that look for?'

'Did Jenny say something?' I blurt out. She's surprised at my question, a slight frown appearing on her forehead.

SEX LESSONS

'No. Why?' Damnit. Now she'll go and ask Jenny.

'Nothing, please just...'

'What did she do?' Karen asks. I shake my head and blink slowly.

'Nothing, let's drop it, okay?' She looks a little hurt.

'Okay. I was just teasing.' I go to say something but she has already turned and walked away, leaving me to feel like an arsehole. Christ, the stress is starting to get to me. Just another ball in the air.

I need to stop the date tonight but how? I see Gina sit down at her desk and begin unwrapping a chocolate bar. An idea forms. I walk over to her.

'Hi,' I say. Gina looks up surprised, a guilty smile forming.

'Just a snack. Diet can wait,' she says. I smile.

'You going tonight?' She swallows the chocolate.

'Tonight?'

'Yeah, Lauren and Mark and a few others are going down Jo Jo's.'

'Oh. What time?'

'Straight after work, I might see you there but I've got loads of catching up to do. But, you should go.'

'Yeah. I didn't know about it but I will go I think.' Bingo.

'Cool, maybe see you later then?'

'Yeah. Thanks Jams,' she replies. I walk away. That, as they say, is how you do that. I may get in trouble and it might just be a Band-Aid on a shotgun wound but sod it, it sorts me out for tonight. I feel like all the weight I've been carrying around has lifted. In fact I'm so relaxed, an hour later as I'm coming out of the toilets I do a little skip. Which, embarrassingly for me, Gina sees as she comes out of the Ladies. I flush red, then shrug.

'Oh, James. Can't make it tonight, my mother decide she's coming round. Next week maybe?' Before I can argue, she's walked away leaving me with an open mouth and a big fucking problem. I mosey back towards my desk. As I enter the trading floor I see Lauren's office is empty. Panic fires through me. I race over to my desk, yank my jacket from the chair which causes it to crash to the floor. I ignore the looks from my various co-workers and run out. I catch the first lift, trying to peer down to reception through the glass. I can't see blonde hair anywhere. I stand next to the lift door willing it to get there faster. The doors begin to open, I pull them apart, run through reception and out on to the street. I look left, then right. People are everywhere, it's the middle of rush hour. I stand on tiptoe. No sign of them. I jump on top of a pile of rubbish bags in the street and look around me. People stare but I don't care. The noise of traffic is overwhelming after coming out of the calm interior of the bank. It's no good, I can't see them. Fuck! Do I go to Jo Jo's? Make a complete fuckwit of myself. What's my plan anyway, tell them I'm coming along as well? Don't see why not, if others are joining them later then surely I can come along a little earlier? But what about Sarah? Can't cancel her now.

I stand amongst discarded refuse and honestly, I haven't got a clue what to do. I'm frozen with indecision. Do I?

    a) Go after them, cause a scene, create a situation?

    Or...

    b) Go home? See Sarah. Have her play with my balls?

It's not unappealing but it's Lauren I want tonight. Even more now Pasty's with her. Give it up James. Just let them get on with it.

I stumble down from the rubbish and catch my foot on one of the plastic bags. A guy goes to grab my arm but he misses and my knee scrapes the ground.

'You okay buddy?' I hear him call. I manage to right myself and head back into the bank, ignoring him. Yeah, couldn't be better.

EIGHTEEN - A TUTORIAL

You'd think, by the time Sarah arrived at my apartment, I'd have calmed down. I'd have had a good think and realised it was all out of my hands and I should just go with the flow. If only. When I do finally open the door, I'm wound up tighter than a Pharaoh in a bandage-wrapping contest.

Sarah's got her silver puffer jacket on again. Doesn't she have other clothes?

'Hi,' she says, smiling.

'Hi,' I grunt, leaving the door open as I head back to the living room. I know my behaviour stinks but I don't care. I sit down on the sofa, resuming Coronation Street on the SkyPlus box. Sarah steps into the room, her coat still on.

'You okay?' she asks. I don't take my eyes off the TV, just nod. 'So, are we going to do this then?' I glance at her. Sex is the last thing I want.

'Today's been shit,' I say. She walks towards me, stepping over my feet and sits down next to me, crossing her legs. She's wearing a short skirt, tights and black heels that look uncomfortable.

SEX LESSONS

'Shall we see if we can make things better?' she asks. I smile but it's another fake, I'm crap at pretending.

'I don't know,' I mumble.

'Talk to me.'

'It's nothing. Just...the girl I like...'

'The one at work?'

'Yeah. She's on a date with my best friend and...I dunno.'

'A date?'

'Yeah.'

'A proper date?'

'Well other people from work will turn up at some point.'

'So it's more like, work drinks?' Hmm.

'Maybe, I guess.'

'Does this girl like you?'

'I don't know, she says she does but, I keep getting mixed messages.'

'Okay, suppose you were on the date tonight and she wanted to get down to it, would you be comfortable?' I shrug.

'I dunno.'

'James..?'

'No, I guess not.'

'Then let's sort this thing out so when the time comes, you are.' I consider her words.

'What do you have in mind?' I ask almost begrudgingly, like she's going to ask me to do my seven times table. Which I can, by the way.

'Your first exercise.'

'What does it involve?'

DANIEL GRANT

'We're going to try something and I don't know if it will work or not but I think we should give it a go.'

'What is it?'

'You're going to take me through having sex.' I frown.

'What does that mean?'

'You and I are going to have sex and you're going to tell me every thought and feeling you have as we do it.' She taps my forehead. 'I need to know what's going on up here,' then she rubs my crotch, 'before we can fix what's going on down here.'

'Interesting theory.'

'You need to tell the truth. You were pretty honest in our talk before but this might feel a bit different. You think you can do that?'

'Yeah,' I reply, a little defensively. Feels like the central heating is on too high.

'Come on then,' she says.

'Now?' I ask. She tilts her head to the side, glancing at the paused Coronation Street episode on the TV.

'You can catch the omnibus on Sunday.' She takes hold of my hand and leads me into the bedroom. I'm suddenly starting to get nervous. I glance at her arse, firm and rounded. The image doesn't help. We arrive next to the king-size and I start taking off my shirt.

'Hold on there, Chucky,' she says. I turn around. 'Did I tell you to do that?' I shrug.

'I thought we were having sex...' I start to say.

SEX LESSONS

'We *are* having sex James, but the way this works is you don't do anything unless I tell you. This is my program, so we do things my way, okay?'

'Yes boss.' I give a mock-salute. She points to the floor in front of her.

'Stand here, facing me.' I walk to the middle of the room and stand in front of her. I can feel the warmth of her breath on my chin. I reach around her waist, she slaps the back of my hand.

'I didn't tell you to do that, did I?'

'Uh. No.'

'Then don't.' Weird. Never been dominated before, kinda fun and scary at the same time. I smile then try to remain serious. 'Close your eyes.'

'Should we have a safe word or something?' I ask instinctively. She raises her eyebrows.

'James. Do you want to do this or not?' I nod and close my eyes. Her voice becomes quiet.

'I want you to imagine I'm your date. We've just come back from an upmarket restaurant. We've had a nice evening together. I've been suggestive with you all night. You know it's going to lead somewhere. You're sitting in the restaurant paying the bill.'

'Oh I'm paying, am I?' I tease.

'Are you the man?'

'Yes.'

'Then you're paying. Now shut up.' I'm smiling but I force my face to behave. 'So as you're paying the bill, I lean forward and I say 'do you know what I'm going to do to you when we get back?' Her voice is hushed and sexy. 'Tell me what's going through your mind when I say that?'

'Uh, excitement I guess.'

'What else..?'

'I dunno...'

'You feel good about what I said?'

'Yes, but I'm also thinking...what happens when we get back to mine.'

'You're worried about things not working?'

'Yeah.' My heart starts thumping hard again. Not sure how much I like this. Her voice is warm and soft.

'Okay. We've just walked into your apartment. Tell me everything you're thinking in this next part, okay?' I nod, one eye opens slightly.

'Ah ah. Keep them closed,' she commands.

'Sorry.'

Suddenly, I feel her lips on mine. Tender and gentle at first, then more urgent. I feel her expertly prise open my mouth with her tongue, then I sense her hand on my arse. Any moment she's going to move to my groin, there's nothing going on. Do I need to impress her with a solid dick straight away? She'll probably not mind if it's not. Be nice if it was though. Come on little guy.

'James,' she whispers softly into my ear. A flash of Lauren with Mark hits me like a train. They are having drinks, laughing hard, utterly smashed together. Staring at each other. Kissing. I pull away, opening my eyes.

'Talk to me,' Sarah waits for my answer.

SEX LESSONS

'It's nothing.'

'What is?'

'It's not a big deal.'

'James...'

'I just had an image of my best friend kissing the girl at work.' She gazes at me then says

'What were you thinking before that?'

'The kissing was good, but in the back of my mind I was starting to wonder how I get through this without you finding out my dick wasn't hard. I mean, you know the problem but if you were a girl who didn't. I'm not making much sense.'

'No, you are. Let's carry on okay? See where it takes us.' I nod. She puts her arms around my waist. 'Close your eyes. We're back on our date. We've kissed, now you're going to fuck me.' She kisses me again, more powerfully this time. My hands move slowly down her body. God, she feels good. She takes a sharp intake of breath and speaks faintly in my ear. 'What are you thinking James?'

'You smell great...there's nothing happening downstairs though, that's what I'm thinking about.'

'Don't worry about that. Focus your thoughts on me. Do what you want, I'm giving you free reign.' My hand finds its way under her skirt, she moans again.

'Ahhh, good boy,' she says. Boy? Am I a boy? I guess I am. Her fingers move over my crotch, massaging. She unzips my fly and pulls him out. I'm not hard.

'Talk to me,' she says.

'I dunno. I'm wondering what you're thinking.' She starts to pull and push, up and down.

'I'm not thinking anything James. How's that feel?' Things start to happen.

'Good,' I mutter. My hand moves over her breast, I pull her into me. The other hand still lingers under her skirt. Her voice starts to quiver.

'Yeah...oh, James.' I'm rock hard. I don't understand why, but I'm not complaining. I move her onto the bed, yank down her tights and thong and move between her legs.

'Uh ah...condom,' she says, breathless. I reach over to the bedside table and pull out the rubber. My dick is still hard, surely he'll start to flag when I put this on. I peel off the foil and roll it down. Weird, I lose no rigidity at all. I turn back to her. She's looking at me, her eyes studying my expressions.

'Is it on?'

'Yeah.' I'm in before I know what's happening. It's warm and feels fucking amazing. Thrust after thrust, she's moaning. The condom doesn't affect the feeling, another rush of pleasure shudders through me. Shit, I'm going to come. I need to stop. Quick, think of something. You're screwing your grandmother. Yuck. It's working. But it still feels incredible. God. Must stop. I try to slow down but she's moving back and forth. More friction. It's going to happen. Please! Too late. My brain swims in adrenaline and feel-good juice. I lie on top of her, panting. I feel her tummy moving up and down under me, her balmy breath tickling my neck. I roll over and lie next to her. Silence fills the space between us. It's not uncomfortable but I'm still anxious. Like a gymnast waiting for the scores to come. I can't take the waiting anymore.

'Well?' I ask. She sits up and leans on her elbow, looking at me.

'How do you think it went?'

'I didn't have any trouble rising to the occasion, which is weird, because that's what the problem normally is. The premature thing has happened before but not like that. That was really quick.'

'Yes it was,' she replies with no hint of irony. Ouch! I don't expect straight tens, but a nine point five at least, come on. 'So you weren't worrying about getting hard?'

'I was at the beginning. But you were doing things that worked. Not all the girls are as…educated.' She chuckles.

'Here's what I think,' she says. I swallow involuntarily. 'This is obviously not representative of what normally happens in these situations. You said with…uh, Jenny was it?'

'Jenny, yeah.'

'You said you were hard for a bit then it stopped.'

'Yeah, I start to think oh my god, it's working! Keep going, doing good, then it stops.'

'You're overanalysing. Sex is best when it's spontaneous and creative. Your mind should be relaxed and focused on what you're doing in the moment. Not whether you're performing well enough. If you're constantly examining everything like that you're bound to fail.' She's balanced and positive but it still feels like an ego flogging. I nod but I feel like a failure. That was the word she used, wasn't it? Failure. She sees my expression and lifts my chin up slightly.

'Hey. It was good, but you're capable of so much more James. Really. I can feel it. I know this is hard, so to speak, I'm trying to be as even-handed as I can. Too honest?'

'No,' I reply, 'just need to get over the male thing of having to be fantastic every time.' She nods slowly.

'On the plus side you're foreplay was good, although that could have been longer as well. You got me going quickly though. We also need to get into oral, that's very important. You need to be able to control the urges and have them do what you tell them, not the other way around. Ideally I want you to be in a place where you can become hard and lose it and not worry about it not coming back. And far be it from me to stroke your ego too much but, you've got large equipment. It feels good inside me.' I smile slightly. Hear that, I have large equipment. Maybe I could go into porn, on a part-time basis.

She leans over and kisses me on the cheek. 'Good. But there's still work to do.' She stands up. I glance over her body. She has small, pert breasts complimented by her stunning arse. She picks up her tights and skirt and starts pulling them on.

'Quite good fun this, isn't it?' she says.

'You're leaving?' I reply.

'I've got Uni early tomorrow. Don't worry, we've got plenty of time. Listen I don't suppose I could get that money. Like a true student, I'm eating out of baked bean cans at the moment.'

'Sarah, have something here. I'll make some pasta or something.'

'Nah, I'll be okay.'

I go to the desk drawer and take out six hundred pounds in fifties. Fuck that's a lot of cash. I hand it over to her. She folds it and puts it in her bag. Money well spent, I think.

'Don't you want to count it?' I ask. She looks up.

'I trust you,' she replies, staring at me. 'And if you're short I'll just charge my typical thirty per cent APR.' I smile and nod. She puts on her puffer and grabs her bag. I yank my dressing gown on and walk her to the door.

'So I'm free Saturday daytime if you want to carry on?' she says.

'Sure,' I reply. She stares at me and smiles.

'You okay? Was I too harsh?'

'No, not at all. You were...great.' A flash of something in her eye, she leans forward and kisses me full on the lips. The happy juices rush through me again. She pulls away.

'Bye James.' She leaves. I listen to her walking down the stairs. I slowly close the door.

DANIEL GRANT

SEX LESSONS

DANIEL GRANT

PART 2

SEX LESSONS

NINETEEN - PUBLIC DRESSDOWN

Friday at work. It feels like the whole bank is getting ready for the weekend. Lauren is in her office talking with Darren Hargreaves about something or other. I haven't seen Mark yet but the day is young. The Blackberry rings, making the valid point that I should do some work. I answer it.

'James Kennedy.'

'Didn't feel like coming out last night then?' I glance over to Lauren's office, she's looking at me through the glass, phone to her ear.

'I was told it was invitation only.'

'You *were* invited James. I wish you'd come.' My ears prick up to her tone. I glance around the office for nosy neighbours.

'Why's that?'

'He's a bit heavy, isn't he?'

'Mark? Sometimes. He's never tried to pick me up though.' She smiles.

'I think he's still in love with, Jess is that her name?'

SEX LESSONS

'Jess, yeah. Did he talk about her?'

'He got a bit drunk and started telling me the whole story. She's pregnant with some other guy's kid.'

'Yeah, I know. He was pretty devastated when he found out.'

'I can imagine. But he sure doesn't beat around the bush when he likes you.' I smile. We stare at each other.

'I enjoyed our date James. You up for doing it again?' Excitement tears through me. I stare at her through the glass, her blonde hair is so bright when the sunlight hits it like that. She flashes me a smile. I turn back to my desk.

'Sure. When's good for you?' I ask.

'Saturday night?'

'Okay, I'll come to yours, we can go somewhere nearby.'

'Uhh, maybe we could meet in town. Might be better.'

'Okay. Where?' Suddenly the line goes dead. I look up. Mike (prick) Cartwell is standing in her office talking to her. Fuck. She nods her head, then she stands up. Did he catch her? She follows him out of her office and towards a conference suite. She glances over to me and nods. She's okay, didn't get caught. I breathe out. Jesus, that was close.

'You know you're not supposed to make personal calls at work.' The voice belongs to loudmouth Poppy, the girl who sits opposite me and never seems to do any work. I spin around to see her standing over my desk. She's got this weird matted hair that makes her head look suspiciously like a boiled egg. Bad teeth and a mild case of halitosis as well. I was going to write an anonymous note with the number of a good dentist I know and leave it on her desk, just never got round to it.

'Yeah but they called me.'

'You should really call them back in your own time. You've got a mobile, don't you?'

'Yes Poppy, I have a mobile. Don't worry, it won't happen again.'

'I just don't see why I should be disciplined for using the phone for personal calls when other people do it as well. Maybe I'll mention it to that Lauren girl, she seems like she's got her head screwed on. I won't refer to you by name, don't worry.'

'Let's just leave it and say I'm sorry. Come on, I know they disciplined you but you were unlucky. They're all fascists here, what's a little personal call here and there anyway, this company makes millions.' By the way, with Poppy, it wasn't a phone call 'here and there,' it was most of the morning then some of the afternoon.

'Exactly, that's what I told them. But you know, sometimes they need a fall girl and I guess I was it.'

'Dumb luck.'

'Yeah,' she studies me carefully then says, 'alright James, I'll not say anything. Just don't do

SEX LESSONS

it anymore, 'cos it leaves me with few options.' I nod with as much sincerity as I can muster. She sits back down. What a bitch, eh? You can see why I think it would be best for everyone if she was sent packing. I know she's got kids and childcare and whatnot, but it's not even that. She isn't very good at her job. And who talks like that anyway? 'It leaves me with no options?' She sounds like a manager. We go on courses to speak like that.

The morning progresses slowly. I have a big mess to sort out. A large fuckup by one of my junior traders. I saw him in Mike's (wank stain) office earlier being pummelled with swear words. The guy looked like he was going to cry. Tell you something, the day I'm financially secure I'm going to walk in there and tell that shit-for-brains exactly what I think of him. What a shitkicker he is.

Lunchtime. Still no sign of Pasty. Recently, he's had more time off than Santa Claus. I ask Sandra, the girl who sits in the cubicle next to him where he is. She says she hasn't seen him all day. I take out my phone and write him a text. 'Hey shitbag, where you at?' I hit send then walk back to my desk and have a seat. I've barely logged back on to the computer when

DANIEL GRANT

'Hi James.' I turn around. Jenny is standing next to my desk, down from finance. First time I've seen her since...*that night.*

'Jen. Hi. Uh, how are you?'

'I'm good. Listen, have you time for a quick bite to eat?' Honestly, I'd rather go hungry for a week.

'Um, okay.' She looks good, her hair's tied back. She's wearing a power suit like Lauren, but her lapels are bigger and somehow seem more stylish. I guess that's what comes from working upstairs. We leave the building together and head over to Pret. I grab my normal all-day breakfast sandwich and an OJ, she takes a pack of sushi. We stand in line together, it's uncomfortable.

'So how's it going?' I ask. May as well kick things off.

'Yeah it's okay. Listen James, I don't know if I ever asked before but are we seeing other people now?'

'Huh?' was my purely instinctive response.

'I've heard, on the grapevine (Karen) you're seeing someone else. Is it true?'

'Uh, hang on. I heard, on the same grapevine, you were sleeping with two other guys when you were with me. Apart from the obvious hygiene issues, what the fuck?' Two people in the queue in front of us glance around.

'I was not sleeping with two other guys, is that what Karen told you?' Jenny whispers. 'I liked you James. I know you've got issues but I figured we could sort them out. Together, you and me.'

SEX LESSONS

Easy tiger, we're in a queue where half the office comes to have lunch. Jesus.

'You walked out, left me a 'Dear John' note. And it's not like we've been in constant touch since then. What am I supposed to think?' James, keep your voice down.

'I had an early meeting that day. You know I've been in New York trying to sort out ING contracts, I told you that.' More people start turning around this time, I smile and mouth 'sorry' to them. I'm so confused, I swear I feel a tumour forming in my head. Remain calm.

'Keep your voice down,' I whisper, 'I assumed it was over.'

'Maybe you should speak to me first before jumping to assumptions. Who is this girl?' Honestly, I didn't see this coming, hot Jenny is actually a psycho. Here I was thinking she was all aloof and gorgeous when in reality she's neurotic, crazy and off the board. Let me tell you, as I stand here listening to batty Jenny slowly turning my nuts into Swiss cheese, I feel about as calm as the flight controller handling United 93.

'Look, I'm sorry, I thought it was over,' I say as softly as I can.

'Just because you couldn't get it up once, doesn't mean we cancel the whole thing.' Now, in her defence, she did whisper that last line. However, the fact she's saying it at all, let alone in a public sandwich bar are grounds for a firing squad as far as I'm concerned. I step back from the queue, throw my sandwich back on the shelf and walk out. Everyone stares at me, staff included. Jenny follows me. 'I really liked you James, but this tramp can have you, whoever she is. Hope she likes limp dicks!' She turns on her heels and walks off. Oh that's great, the whole street has stopped and is staring at us. On top of everything, now I'm going to have to find somewhere new to have lunch.

It was over, wasn't it? That letter she wrote was code for 'Go fuck yourself James.' Suddenly I'm overcome with an urge to hit back, how dare she speak to me like that in front of all these people I'll never see again.

'You broke my fucking coffee pot bitch!' I yell after her. I'm not sure what effect I was hoping to achieve with that classic. I ponder the reasons as I watch her walk away. She still has a great arse but Jesus, the girl needs to go on a program or something. Help her work through those issues. The passers-by start to move again, laughing with one another. Yeah, pretty entertaining, huh? Like a live episode of Oprah. Fuck you all.

As I walk back towards the office I only pray she doesn't tell anyone about my problem downstairs or I may have to seriously think about getting a new job.

My phone bleeps. It's Mark. It says 'I'm at your desk, where are you?' I reply saying 'Getting a sandwich, didn't go quite to plan. Meet by river in five?' He replies with a 'will do' and I start heading in that direction. She thought we were still together? After that God-awful sex? Why would any girl want to stay with me after that? Baffling. Then guilt starts to harrang me like a swarm of jungle mosquitoes. Now I feel bad for Jenny. I had no idea. I just assumed. But I do think what she said was, how would Poppy put it, 'not acceptable behaviour.' Definitely not necessary to tell the patrons of Pret about my current dick status.

I reach the river still mulling over what just happened. Mark's already there, he spots me and I head over to him.

'Where've you been?' I ask.

'Did Lauren say anything?' he blurts out.

'About what?' I've barely uttered the 'about' when I realise how dumb I'm being. Mark, by the look on his face, agrees with my assessment.

'What do you think? Last night?'

'She said she had a nice time.'

'Really?'

'No. She said you came on way too strong.' Mark mouths the f-word. 'What happened?'

'I got a bit drunk, I think. It's a little hazy actually.' I nod in pretend sympathy. 'I might have said I loved her.' I'm starting to enjoy this story.

'You just met the girl.'

'Yeah, I meant, I love the kind of person she is, I'm not *in* love with her.'

'You love her tits you mean.'

'Yeah...no. I like her, a lot. So what did she say?'

'That's it, she just said you came on a bit strong.' And she wished I was there, ha! 'Oh, and you kept talking about Jess.' He closes his eyes as if hit in the back by an arrow. 'Don't worry mate, there's plenty of others...'

'I'm not giving up. No way. Lauren is fucking gorgeous.' He stares at the river, with a slightly crazed look. 'I shouldn't have told her about Jess, fucking stupid.' He slaps his forehead in pretend self-flagellation. 'Amateur.'

'Maybe you should just leave it for a bit.' I suggest.

'Did she say that?'

'Well...no, but...I think she might just need a cooling-off period before you hit her again. You know?' Mark nods.

'Maybe.' He glances to me.

'So why was your lunch not what you planned?'

'Huh?'

'In your text, you said...'

'Oh...yeah. Jenny came over for a chat and we ended up having a thing in the middle of Pret.'

'Really? Why?'

'She thought we were still going out.'

'I thought you dumped her?'

'Yeah. Well sort of. But she got it in to her head we were still seeing each other. And somehow, she thinks I'm seeing some other girl,' I say with a degree of sarcasm. Mark pretends to think for a moment, then off my look he says

'Well she is a bit...' he spins his finger next to his temple then gives up the act. 'Okay look, I might have mentioned it to Karen.'

SEX LESSONS

'Why stop there? Why not start up a web site, send out a group e-mail to everyone with the link. Fuck, Mark.'

'Yeah, okay sorry. So you gonna tell me who Sarah is?'

'No I'm bloody not.' He offers me part of his half-sandwich.

'You want some?' I stare at him, an incredulous look etched on my face. My phone bleeps. I almost don't want to look at it with Pasty so close but what the hell. I take out the mobile and glance at it. It's from Lauren, I turn away from Mark. 'Meet you at 8 PM McArthur's on Gerrard St. L x.' I put the phone back in my pocket.

'Who's that?'

'Your mum wanting her money back.'

'I did tell her you were a crap shag.'

When I arrive home I find I have seven messages on my answer phone. Seven! Jesus, I've never had seven messages in my life. Of course, when I hit the play button things start to become clearer.

BEEP! 'It's Jenny, if I wasn't clear before I think the way you handled this whole thing was really crap. You just don't treat people like that.' BEEP! 'James it's Jenny again, look I've been thinking, maybe I was a little harsh before and maybe I owe you an apology for what happened today. Give me a call when you get this.' BEEP! 'Okay, so you're obviously ignoring me, very mature James.' BEEP! 'Pick up, it's Jen...James? PICK UP.' BEEP! 'I think your answer machine might be fu...' BEEP! 'James, you need to delete some of your mess...'BEEP! BEEP! Click! BEEP! 'AGGHHH!!!' BEEP! 'James I...' BEEP!

Un...believable.

SEX LESSONS

TWENTY - PHONE CALL

Dates for me, if you can call them that, always seem to come along at the same time. I must ensure this doesn't happen again, it's not great for the stress levels.

I make the bed nicely and down a cup of extra strong coffee from my new cafetière. It's great sitting here, reading a newspaper, enjoying the thoughts of the day ahead, quality cup of aviation fuel in my hand. I run through the day's schedule, it's like an itinerary from heaven.
A) I get to have sex with Sarah today, hot. Then
B) I go on another date with Lauren, triple hot!

This is going to be a good day, I can feel it already. I bet you're sitting there thinking 'it's all going to go wrong James, what are you doing?' Well, let me tell you that Sarah is coming over at twelve so I should be done and dusted by ten past. Just kidding, two o'clock at the latest, right? Which leaves me most of the afternoon to mess about until I go out with Lauren. See, got it nicely planned to avoid any potential nastiness.

DANIEL GRANT

The buzzer sounds at five to twelve. She's early. Not a problem, because I anticipated such a move and had tidied up by eleven-thirty. Ha! Stick that in your pipe and smoke it. I buzz her in and open the door. She appears at the top of the stairs. She's lost the puffer jacket and now has on a fetching pair of tight, worn-in jeans and a close-fitting t-shirt under a denim jacket. The high heels have been replaced by a pair of slightly scruffy white trainers. She has the same black handbag over her shoulder and smiles when she sees me.

'Hi. You should think about putting in a lift,' she says puffing away.

'I've thought about it many times. Unfortunately the architect, creative as he was, didn't consider lifts necessary to young professionals. Come in.'

'Thanks,' she replies, walking inside. I close the door.

'You're looking...nice,' I say playfully. She turns around, a cynical smile on her face.

'Thank you James.' She walks into the living room and sets her handbag down on the table, glancing around.

'Did you clean up or something?'

'Actually I did, yes.'

'I'm honoured.'

'So am I. Twice in one week?'

'Well, you're a special case James. You need...particular attention.'

'Is that right?'

SEX LESSONS

'Yeah.'

'Something to drink?' I ask.

'Tea?'

'Cup of tea,' I say in a silly posh voice. I wander into the kitchen.

'How's Uni?' I shout towards the living room, removing the kettle from the stand and filling it. She appears at the door.

'Painful. I have a dissertation that has to be in by the end of next week and I've barely started.'

'Uh oh. Which Uni are you at?' She pauses a moment, considering her response.

'University of London.' She looks at me for a reaction. I nod. 'Not that far from here. The club takes up more and more of my time. I just need to juggle better that's all.'

'Are you sure you're okay for today? We can reschedule if it's easier,' I say.

'Nah, I'm here now. This won't take long,' she replies, a twinkle in her eye.

'Right,' I reply. She raises her eyebrows playfully and runs her hand through her hair. A silence parks itself between us, only the sound of the kettle coming to the boil fills the kitchen.

'So...how did you get into this?' I ask.

'Get into what?' I suddenly feel embarrassed even bringing it up but I've started it now.

'The sex thing or...stripping?'

'I don't have sex with just anyone James.'

'No, sure...' I go to say but she interrupts me

'I mean it. I've never done this before.'

'Why me then?'

DANIEL GRANT

'I dunno. I had a good feeling, you're not offensive to look at.'

'Sounds like a compliment.'

'And I need the money.' I nod slowly. 'In answer to your question I tried a couple things here and there. But honestly, I think I'm just lazy. I don't really want a 'proper job', I earn far more at the club. I like talking to people, listening to their problems. Your predicament intrigued me. But this is definitely one of the more bizarre things I've done.'

'Did you think I was a psycho?'

'No. I thought it was an interesting dilemma and I'm a sucker for men with a problem they want to sort out.'

'So did you have like shitty parents or...'

'What is this, twenty questions?' I shrug.

'I just like to know the people I sleep with, this is new for me too.' I say.

'Yeah right,' she replies. I chuckle. 'My parents live in a nice house in Surrey. I'm not poor, I just chose not to take their money. I want to do this myself.'

'So you strip?'

'I don't expect you to understand. I'm not unattractive, I think I've got a good body so why not use it?'

'Fair enough.'

'I find it interesting how men on one level are all so predictable. They all say exactly the same thing at work but then someone different comes along and makes me think.' In case you hadn't cottoned on, the atmosphere in here is starting to get a little close. Maybe it's just the steam from the kettle. I pour the water into the mugs and dunk the tea bags, my back turned towards her. 'What about you, where are you from, originally?'

'I was brought up in Canning Town.' I stop there, considering whether to continue.

'What about your parents?'

'Divorced.' I turn to face her. She stares at me. Not sure how much I like all this probing.

'You prefer living here?'

'Duh, what do you think?' I reply, a little too sarcastically. She doesn't take her eyes from me. I need to think of something to ask her. An idea pops into my head. 'So, do you have a boyfriend?' She breaks eye contact. There's a pause before she answers.

'Yeah,' she replies. I turn around.

'Really? What does he think about all this?' Her body suddenly stiffens.

'He doesn't exactly know. I need to tell him, I just...I don't want to hurt him.' I nod raising my eyebrows. 'I know. I should tell him.' She glances towards the window, then breathes in deeply. 'What about your girlfriend? I take it she doesn't know about our little, meetings.'

'She's not my girlfriend, we've only had one date but...I dunno, I like her. I told you she's my boss.' Sarah smiles and shakes her head. 'Yeah I know.'

'Playing with fire,' she says.

'I know but...'

DANIEL GRANT

'She's a looker.'

'Yeah. That's not the only reason though…' I start to say.

'Sure, James,' she replies, grinning as I hand her the mug.

'So what are we doing today?' I ask.

'I have a few things in mind.'

We take our tea into the living room and wander over to the French doors.

'It's such a beautiful view, you're so lucky,' she says, staring out over the river. She puts her tea down.

'Yeah. Pretty much the main reason I chose to live here.' Suddenly her hand grabs my crotch, my tea nearly ending up over my front. I stare at her, surprised. She shoots me a 'what you looking at' glare. I put the tea on the mantle.

'Get hard for me James.'

'Come on,' I say, trying to laugh it off. I attempt to move her hand away. She shoves it straight back and starts massaging me through my jeans. Feels good but this isn't going to work. Sarah doesn't take her eyes from me.

'Take it out,' she demands.

'Here?' I ask involuntarily, acutely aware that most of East London can see me through the windows.

'Here,' she replies. I glance through the window, she seizes on my hesitation. Before I even know what's happening she's unzipped my fly and pulled him out. I'm nowhere near erect. I feel invaded.

SEX LESSONS

'How does it feel to have your dick out in front of your neighbours?'

'Maybe we could do this in the bedroom?' I suggest.

'No.' She grabs my dick and yanks it sending a little shock of pain through it. 'Are you ashamed of your penis when it's not erect James?' Interesting question. I shrug, giving no response. She gazes at me, her eyes piercing through me. She starts to gently massage it between her fingers. It feels tender under her touch. 'How's that feel?'

'Nice,' I reply, swallowing.

'When the pressure's off, you'll find things flourish all...by...themselves.' Sure enough as she rubs and kneads I start to become hard. I breathe out, giving myself over to the sensations welling through me. 'What are you thinking James?'

'Nothing actually.'

'Correct answer,' she replies, bending down and taking me in her mouth. I glance to the window again, suddenly it doesn't bother me. I imagine all the people out doing their flower boxes or walking their dogs along the Thames who might happen to look up and see me standing there with Sarah's mouth running up and down my dick. The thought makes me smile. I look down at a head of hair moving around my groin. The ripples start getting more intense. As though feeling it, she slows down, then stops altogether.

'Uh uh...not yet,' she whispers, standing. I start to move my hand down towards my groin, need to keep it up. She grabs it and shakes her head. 'Let it go. It'll come back when the time is right.' I'm unconvinced, she's got me to the point and now she's telling me to just leave it? I have a strange trust in her though, she speaks with such certainty and confidence. 'Your turn,' she says. I process what she means, then grab her hips and go to kiss her. She pulls away and pushes my head towards her abdomen. 'Not here...here.' She places her hands on her hips. I kneel down and pull at the buttons on her jeans. 'How often do you do this James?'

'Pretty often but...I normally lose the erection.'

'Don't worry about that.' I tug her jeans down. Her belly is flat, she must do like a hundred sit-ups at day or something. She's wearing a black lacy thong. I slowly slide it down and start to kiss inside her thighs, gently touching her skin with my mouth. She starts to move with me, I hear a moan escape her mouth, her hushed breathing becoming heavier. I feel her fingers move through my hair, her nails scratching along my scalp. Hairs on my arms stand to attention. I glance up, she tilts her head back, eyes closed. My erection has deserted me but I'm enjoying seeing her under my spell. She arches her back slightly, almost trying to get away. I respond by pulling her into me further. 'God...James.' She breathes faster and faster, her stomach starts to shudder. Suddenly the phone rings. It's so loud it makes us both jump.

SEX LESSONS

'OO...Jesus,' I blurt out. I stand up, my dick still hanging from my fly. I run to the phone and pick it up. 'Hello?'

'Hi, it's Lauren.' Fuck!

'Hi,' I say, glancing over to Sarah, who stares at me with a playful glint in her eye.

'I'm just checking we're still on for tonight?'

'Yeah, yep, definitely,' I reply.

'You okay? You sound out of breath.'

'Yeah...just been doing a bit of exercise.' Sarah slaps a hand across her mouth trying to stop herself laughing, I smile but it's not funny.

'Getting ready for later?' You have no idea.

'Uh yeah.'

'Okay well, I'll let you get on. You're not still feeling funny about Mark are you?' Sarah has walked over to me and is now kneeling down in front of me. I try to push her away but she grabs my legs and takes me in her mouth.

'No. I'm fine.' Sensations whip up through me.

'So where are we meeting James?'

'Uhh...' fuck what was it called again? Damn that feels so fucking good, 'it's uhh...'

'McArthur's, eight o'clock.'

'Yeah, exactly.' I'm hard again and Sarah is going full throttle.

'You sure you're okay? You sound...strange.'

'No I'm fine. See you at eight?'

'Yeah, see you then.'

'Okay, bye.' I put the phone down, then immediately knock it over as I try to grab on to something. I try to push Sarah away again but she digs her nails into my leg and continues as forcibly as she can. It's no good, can't stop the flood.

'Aggghh!' I almost shout as I come. My head feels squidgy. I'm floating. My body spent, I steady myself. Sarah slows down and stops. She looks up at me. I'm sweating, my forehead looks like a mirror. I smile then collapse on to the sofa, lying across it. 'Fuck,' I say. Sarah sits down on the sofa opposite, her bare legs squeaking slightly on the leather. She's staring at me.

'Did you like that?' she asks.

'No it was the worst blow job I've ever had.' I reply, a vague attempt at a joke, but as I glance at her it's clear she's not so sure. 'It was amazing. You know it was.'

'Good,' she says, 'did you notice how your erection came back quickly?'

'Yeah. Maybe you could have waited until I finished the phone call.'

'Why?' she asks, meaning it as a serious question. 'Was it that girl you like?'

'Lauren, yes. We're going out later.' She smiles.

'I'd try and avoid having sex if you can.'

'Yeah?' I reply. She thinks carefully and then says

'I just think you need a few more sessions before you try it properly. Not saying there's ever any guarantees but I'd like to know I've given you the proper benefit of my knowledge before we start field trips.'

SEX LESSONS

'What do you call this?' We look at one another and start laughing. She has a laugh you go out of your way to make jokes for just so you can hear it again. I haven't heard her laugh properly like that before.

'French oral?' she suggests, this cracks us both up.

'Good one,' I say. It's not really that funny but somehow it's the right joke for the moment. Suddenly I look at her and see only the beautiful girl studying psychology. Bunny is gone. This is the real Sarah. She sees me staring at her, her smile fades and it's back to business. 'Well that wasn't quite the structure I had planned, I wanted to show you some techniques which will drive your woman wild but...'

'Show me.'

'We can push it over to the next session if you want. No extra charge.'

'I might need a few minutes but yeah I'd like to know.' She smiles.

'Okay.'

TWENTY-ONE - A TALK AND A DATE

We don't have any more sex. Not sure how that happened, I was curious to see what these new techniques were Sarah was talking about. Instead, we sit and talk for most of the afternoon. It's strange, once we got chatting I started discovering all sorts of things about Sarah and I didn't want to stop.

She has a brother in the army, currently on a tour of Afghanistan. She has had both male and female companions. Her boyfriend is a gentle soul who she doesn't want to upset by telling him what she does for a living. Seems reasonable. She's also incredibly smart. I sit there listening to her babble on about the various things you have to do to get a psychology masters. Glad I didn't go anywhere near university, sounds like a pain in the gonads.

'What about your friends, do they know what you do?' I ask, munching on a biscuit and blowing into my cup of tea.

SEX LESSONS

'A couple of them do yeah. I don't go broadcasting it to people on campus.'

'What would they do if someone saw you?'

'Who? The Uni?' I nod. 'I don't know. Kick me off the course maybe?' she replies, matter-of-fact.

'Really?'

'I don't know. But I don't feel the need to find out,' she replies. I nod and sip my tea.

'Didn't you say you had a dissertation to write?'

'You want me leave?'

'No, not at all.'

'I can leave it for a bit.' She looks out towards the French doors, her eyes staring into the distance. Then, as if remembering something she says, 'tell me about this Lauren girl then. Is she blonde?' I smile and nod.

'Yeah.'

'Big tits?' I nod, my smile becoming a grin. 'Dumb as a fence post?'

'No, actually she's pretty smart. Keeps me on my toes.'

'Why'd you like her?' I think for a moment before answering.

'I dunno. She's beautiful, I mean...stunning. And the way she carries herself. Just...so much confidence. Like you...'

'Me?'

'Yeah, when you walk, you have this confidence that's...I dunno, it's just really attractive.' She raises her eyebrows and nods, a smile on her face.

DANIEL GRANT

'Thank you.' She glances up and catches me staring at her. I look away, self-consciously. 'Well, I'd better be heading off.'

'I'll get your money,' I say, heading to the bedroom. My sock drawer has become a temporary cash machine. I pull out the wodge of fifties and bring it back to her. She takes it and places it in her handbag.

'Thanks. Sorry there wasn't as much, teaching this time. Got sort of carried away talking. We'll do an intensive catch-up session next time.'

'An intensive session? What the hell is that?'

'All in good time, dear boy, all in good time.' I walk her to the door and pull it open. 'Text me when you're around and we'll fix another time.' I nod.

'I could come around yours if it's easier, don't know where you live but...' I suggest.

'...uh, probably best we keep it here. Not sure my room-mate would be too happy about you fucking me while she's trying to study Applied Cognitive Psychology.'

'Fair point,' I reply. I'm acutely aware that she's still standing next to me. Suddenly everything feels awkward. Does she want a kiss goodbye? We stare at each other, suddenly intense. I consider moving in towards her but I leave it a fraction too long.

'So I'll...see you soon,' she says, starting down the stairs. 'Good luck with Lauren.'

'Yeah. Thanks,' I reply.

SEX LESSONS

'Remember...no sex.' She shoots me a fleeting look. I hear the downstairs door open and slam shut. I stand in the doorway, lost in thought.

I find McArthur's tucked away in a little alleyway off Gerrard Street. Okay, I admit it, I got lost. Soho is so bloody confusing. All the streets look identical, have the same people and are always packed to the nines. I only found the place by chance as I was retracing my steps back towards Old Compton Street. Could she have picked anywhere more obscure? Of course saying that, when I walk in, the place is heaving. I tell the maître d' I have a table reserved under the name Bates and I'm waiting for my partner. He checks his list and tells me to wait at the bar. I push through the small crowd waiting for a table and head over in that direction. I find a stool to perch on and try to get the bartender's attention. He's a big, bald guy with a tattoo of a lion on his arm. Looks scary, don't think I'll fight with him tonight.

'Yeah?' he growls, glancing at me.

'Uh, lager please.'

'What kind, Heineken, Groslch...'

'Heineken.' He nods and wanders over to someone else to take their order. As I sit there, unconvinced he can remember more than one thing at a time, Lauren arrives. She sees me and forces her way through the throngs of people. She looks hot in a short red mini dress, red heels and a long black jacket over the top.

'You look lovely,' I say. She smiles, leans in and kisses me on the cheek. 'Busy huh?'

'You can't even have a drink in here without a reservation,' she replies. The bartender places my drink down next to me, then sees Lauren. I watch his body language change immediately. He's suddenly aware of his behaviour, a smile appears as if back from a long holiday.

'Hi there. What would you like?' he asks. More polite as well. She glances over the bartender's shoulders to the choices behind him then down to my beer.

'I'll have one of those,' she replies, pointing to my glass.

'No problem,' he says and gets to work. She sits down next to me.

'Have you been here long?'

'No, just arrived.' She checks her watch.

'It's ten past eight James.'

'So? You're late too,' I reply. She smiles.

'What have you been up to today then? You sounded distracted on the phone.' I cough and hiccup. Composing myself quickly I say,

'Oh, you know, just watching TV. Cleaning. Normal stuff.' Definitely not being blown by a stripper in front of half of East London.

'Cleaning?' She looks surprised. 'You don't have a cleaner?'

'No I like to do it myself.' The bartender sets her drink down.

SEX LESSONS

'Thanks,' she says, smiling at the bartender. I'm not sure why, but it makes me feel uncomfortable. She takes the bottle in her hand and takes a gulp.

'So the date with Mark didn't go...'

'Stop calling it that, it wasn't a date.'

'Okay, the evening with Mark wasn't what you thought?' A group of women start singing along to George Michael at the end of the bar.

'No. You should have come along and saved me.'

'Didn't have to say yes,' I reply, sipping my beer.

'I don't want dramas at work. If I piss him off, it will come back to haunt me in some form or another. Better he thinks it went well.' I gulp.

'Yeah. So...been in any more closets recently?' I smile as I say this but I do genuinely want to know. She gives me a cheeky grin.

'I don't know what came over me. You know when you just have to have someone. After your little moan in my office, I just sat there thinking, what would really blow you away? The closet was the best I could come up with in the time available.'

'Good effort,' I say. Her eyebrows dart upwards as she takes another sip and looks over to the singing women. They're so loud they're almost screaming, the waiters faces are classic. They have no idea what to do. I glance at Lauren. She is so damn gorgeous. Her eyes return to me, catching me staring. I look back to my beer and take another swig.

'Where did you work before this?' I ask.

'UBS in Singapore and before that Nat West.'

'You lived in Singapore?'

'Yeah. I wanted a change, get out England for a bit. It wasn't the best year I've ever had.'

'No?'

'No.' Her eyes drift away from me. I'm not sure if she wants me to keep on this topic but I elect to carry on regardless.

'What happened?' She looks up at me, the slightest hint of pain in her eyes. She sighs.

'My mother died. Cancer.'

'Shit.'

'Yeah.' Her eyes glaze over as she considers her next words. 'That wasn't the worst part. Four months later, my father killed himself.' Holy shit.

'God. Lauren.' I move my hand over hers, she pulls away.

'It's fine. It happened four years ago, I don't think he could live without her so...'

'Were you close?' I ask. She sighs again and looks at me mulling over how to continue.

'Look, this is supposed to be a nice evening. Let's not talk about it, okay?'

'Sure,' I say. I think she does want to talk, maybe now is not the time. I watch her sip her beer again.

'You're so beautiful, you know.' I say, smiling slightly. She returns my smile.

SEX LESSONS

'Thank you,' she replies quietly. 'I'm not used to talking to guys about this stuff.'

'I understand.' A waiter clears his throat behind Lauren.

'Excuse me, Miss Bates? Your table is ready.' The waiter sounds like he's got something stuck up his arse.

'Thank you,' she replies, standing.

We move across to our table and make ourselves at home. I order two more beers, I think we both need to keep ourselves well-oiled tonight. We talk about Mark and the job. I learn she gets on with Mike (todger) Cartwell and thinks he's 'okay.' I resist the urge to have an argument about it right there in the middle of the restaurant. But she moves quickly onto other subjects, starting with,

'I heard you ran into Jenny.' My eyebrows nearly hit the ceiling. 'I told you, it's my job to know what's going on with my staff.' Somehow that doesn't make me feel better. 'Beautiful women like that aren't always what you expect them to be.'

'Thanks, I kinda worked that out when she started ripping me a new arsehole in Pret.' This, Lauren finds hilarious. Okay it's not exactly original but she apparently hadn't heard it used before. I smile, enjoying her laughing at my joke. Her laugh is a strange thing to listen to, not what you'd expect at all. Almost like a snort. She calms down then says

'So what was she saying?'

'Just...you know, I was a bastard and...how could I do this to her? I'm like, you walked out on me! Anyway...'

'Oh dear...' she's still laughing. Her little grunts getting more rapid, quite sweet. 'Sorry, my laugh...' she puts a hand in front of her mouth.

'I love your laugh,' I reply, putting my hand on hers again. She smiles and looks at me, a flicker in her eye.

'James...' she says smiling and rolling her eyes. Got her. We sit there, staring at each other.

That's how the rest of the evening goes. Longing looks and lots of smiling, sprinkled with the occasional piggy laugh. I know I shouldn't call it that, but I don't know how else to describe it. It's cuter than I make it out to be. The bill comes and I put down my Amex card.

'I'll get this,' she starts to say.

'No you bloody won't.'

'James, I make more money than you.'

'Are you trying to insult me?'

'No.'

'Good, then shut up and let me pay.' I pick up the silver plate and signal for the waiter to collect it, which he does, surprisingly quickly. I turn back to Lauren who's staring at me, a slight smile on her face.

'What?' I ask, not sure what that look means.

'You're a really nice guy James.' I shrug away the compliment. 'You are. Jenny's obviously not a smart girl.' My blood suddenly races to my head, my heart shifting from first to fifth in seconds.

SEX LESSONS

She places her napkin on the table. 'Take me home.'

'Okay,' I reply.

DANIEL GRANT

TWENTY-TWO - IN AND OUT

'It's just here,' Lauren calls to the cab driver. The taxi pulls over to the kerb and we stumble out. I pay the driver and walk her up to the front door. She lives in an old Georgian apartment block in Pimlico. White stone with large bay windows protrude towards the street. I feel the first droplets of rain on my shoulder then a rumble of thunder. Lauren pulls out her keys and glances up at the sky.

'Oh no. Thunderstorm,' she says, opening the door and going inside. I hesitate slightly, unsure what I'm supposed to do. She turns around. 'Come on, I don't want to be here by myself in a storm.'

'Ahh, is little Lauren scared of a few raindrops?' I ask, teasing in my voice.

'Don't call me little. I'm not scared either...,' another rumble of thunder echoes around the sky, '...but I think you should come in now,' she says. I smile and go inside, hiking up the first flight of steps. I take note of the creepy abstract paintings on the wall. Of what, I have no idea. The first floor has a modern kitchen and living room, neutrally decorated with matching cream sofas and chairs. To the left is a floor-to-ceiling bookshelf. I spot some Helen Fielding in there. In the corner is a TV with a wooden cupboard next to the sofa. A pile of logs lay beside an enormous stone fireplace.

'Make yourself at home,' she says, taking off her coat. I catch a glimpse of the shape of a butt cheek under her dress. I walk over to the window and peer out. Rain is starting to splatter the glass, I look up at the orange haze of London's skyline as a flash of lightning crackles in the distance. Lauren wanders back in and opens the wooden cupboard, revealing a small hi-fi unit. She takes out an iPod and inserts it. Norah Jones' mellow tones fill the air. A deafening clap of thunder booms around the apartment. She suddenly leaps towards me, throwing her arms around my waist.

'Oof! S'okay,' I say, moving my arms around her.

'I'm not really scared, just felt like a hug.'

'Sure,' I reply, smiling down to her. She seems so vulnerable and burning urges suddenly swell through me. She stares straight at me. My smile disappears. She leans in and kisses me gently. My heart soaks with excitement. Dizziness swirls through my head. It could be just be the alcohol. I pull her into me, our bodies grinding up against each other. We sway to the music, my hands move under her dress. '*No sex.*' I suddenly hear Sarah's voice say in my mind. I unintentionally pull away, letting my hand slip from under her dress.

'What's the matter?' Lauren asks. Uh James, what are you doing?

'Maybe we shouldn't...' I reply. Jesus Christ, it's like dialogue from 'Titanic.' Lauren, judging by the look on her face, is equally perplexed by my sudden change of heart.

'James..?' Her voice is stern and full of doubt.

'No look, I want to. But...' Fuck, look at that expression, you'd better say something fast or you're going to lose her. 'I want this to mean more than one night.' She takes in what I've said. 'Why wouldn't it?' She glares at me, a frown appearing on her forehead.

'I don't know, I just wonder whether we shouldn't wait.'

'It's funny because you gave the impression you liked me.' Her words drip with hurt.

'I do, God. I just, want to make sure it's special. Sorry I...'

'Why wouldn't it be special James?' Now what? I'm out of ideas. She pulls away.

'I really like you Lauren.'

'Yeah? Strange way to show it.'

'I'm saying I don't want it to be just one night.'

'You know how that makes me feel? You're basically saying you think I go around having one night stands.'

'No, I'm not...'

SEX LESSONS

'Yes you are.' She suddenly storms over and turns the music off. I'm out of things to say. I'm becoming an observer to events unfolding before me. The internal flagellation has begun. I try to move my arm around her, she slaps it away. 'No.'

'I'm not trying to hurt you.' Say what you're feeling you moron, she doesn't understand!

'Then next time, get on with it. If there is a next time.' Of course, what I want to say is I'm afraid I'll disappoint her, that when we get down to it I'll more than likely fuck it up just like I did with Jenny and the others. And we'll go from something with promise to almost strangers in one night and that is the last thing I want. Sarah's right, why fuck it up? But I guess, by doing this, haven't I already done exactly what I feared? God. What's the answer? I don't know and in my typical male way, I don't have any way to communicate any of these thoughts so I remain quiet. We stand in silence, the only sound in the room, breathing.

'Maybe you should go,' she says eventually. I have no response. Reluctantly I pick up my coat and walk to the door. 'I don't believe you,' she says, before I get to the top of the stairs.

'What?'

'I don't think you stopped because you didn't want this to just be one night. It's an excuse.'

'Maybe you're right,' I reply, aching to tell her the truth. Her expression changes slightly, now there's anger in her eyes.

DANIEL GRANT

'You're so full of shit, James.' That one finds the mark. I stare at her. I can't tell her.

'I am so crazy about you Lauren.' I want to say more but I can't seem to slot the words in the right order. I shake my head, beaten and start down the stairs. I feel her watching me go. I open the door and step out into torrential rain.

I'm soaked before I cross Grosvenor Road. I walk East along the Thames, shoving my hands in my pockets, a hopeless attempt at keeping some part of me dry. I try to maintain a brisk pace to keep myself from letting go. Rain batters me from all sides and the droplets soon mix with tears. The old wallowing fully kicking in. I can't help it. I'm such a screw-up. What is the matter with me? Other blokes can just do it, no problems. I keep hearing how common this erection stuff is but I don't see any evidence. None of my friends have it, they can all satisfy their partners perfectly and brag about it down the pub.

I wander along deserted streets towards Westminster. My pace slows and I come to a stop, my body shaking. I support myself with the stone railing next to me, nuzzling my face into my jacket. I glance around, a clap of thunder roars above me. There's barely a car on the road. I look back towards the river; the disturbed reflections of streetlamps pave a golden pathway before me.

I sniff.

Alone.

SEX LESSONS

I want to tell someone but I can't think of anyone who'd understand. Not Mark for obvious reasons. Don't want to involve Karen or Gina. I'm ashamed. Sarah...I don't know. Maybe she'd listen. She's probably working down at the club entertaining some other guy. You're on your own James, deal with it.

I carry on walking, fighting the rain with every step, going over the same familiar material in my head. My Blackberry rings, I feel it vibrating in my jacket. I yank it out. It's Lauren. I pause to consider my options. Quickly realising I have none, I answer.

'Hi.'

'James, come back here, it's pouring.'

'I'll be fine.'

'No you won't. Turn around and walk back.' I glance back towards Pimlico then over to the river. Cold rain streams over my hair, face and nose. I'd barely noticed but I'm already starting to shiver. Fuck it, no more than you deserve.

'I'm sorry.'

'Just walk back, okay? Are you walking?' she asks. I give in and start in her direction.

'Yeah.'

'Good.'

I cross the road, the phone still on my ear and head back towards her building.

'Where are you now?' she asks.

'Grosvenor Road,' I reply.

'Okay. Keep walking.' I get to her street and turn down it. As I approach her apartment I see her standing at the door. I stop.

'Come on,' she says. I do as I'm told, no point in arguing any more. I can't think, numb in body and mind. She closes the door and I start up the stairs.

'Wait...you're soaked. Take some of these clothes off. I'll get a towel.' She walks back upstairs. I don't bat an eyelid, I just do what she tells me. I remove my shoes and peel off my shirt and trousers. I'm shivering even more now. She appears at the top of the stairs and walks down, giving me the towel. I rub myself down, zoned out, unsure what's what. I finish, I'm still damp but not dripping. She peers at me, a concerned look on her face. I catch her eyes and look down.

'Come on,' she says. I follow her up in nothing but a pair of boxers, watching her arse moving above me.

She pulls out a large fluffy blanket and an enormous leather beanbag and sets it next to the crackling fire. I sit down, the beanbag enveloping me. She makes hot chocolate, putting it on the table beside me. She sits next to me, the beanbag scrunching around her. I stare at the fire.

'I'm sorry. I overreacted,' she says.

'No you didn't,' I reply.

'I misunderstood what you were saying. I thought you were saying I was some slut who just slept with people willy nilly.'

'That's not what I meant.'

'I know. I thought about it after you left and...realised maybe I took it the wrong way.'

'Sorry,' I say. She leans in and kisses me softly on the lips. Nothing sexual, just warm and simple.

'I can be a little, short sometimes. I've had so many relationships go wrong, I guess I'm always on the lookout for the next screw up.' I nod slowly. 'It's not even funny how many mistakes I've made. When I feel someone not being honest I just want to run because I know, further down the road he's just going to break my heart again.' I nod. Feels like we're back on the same page. She lays her head on my shoulder and cuddles up next to me. 'At least I know you won't do that, not intentionally anyway.' Guilt rises through me. Maybe this is the point I should tell her about Sarah. Is this classed as a relationship? We haven't even had sex. I decide that's more than enough justification for not saying anything. We snuggle together in silence watching the fire spit and splutter before us.

DANIEL GRANT

TWENTY-THREE - TRYING TO HELP

Saturday morning. I'm woken by my mobile ringing. It's like a claxon against my ear. I sit up, brushing Lauren's back with a searching hand. She groans as I find the phone and answer it.

'Hello?' I growl.

'James?' asks a voice.

'Yeah, who's this?'

'It's Billy. Did I get you up?' I find my watch and look at the time. It's eleven-thirty.

'No. I'm up.'

'Sounds like it's a bad time. I'll call back.'

'No, it's okay. What's up?'

'I just wanted to get your advice on something.'

'Sure.'

'Well, maybe we could meet up somewhere if you have time?' I glance at Lauren who's now turned over and lying on her back, a wrist hanging over her eyes.

'What's the problem?'

'Nothing, I just...okay I met this girl and I dunno. I just need some advice on things.'

SEX LESSONS

'Uh, okay. Where do you want to meet?'

'Somewhere central is good for me, but seriously James, if you can't make it...'

'South Bank, in an hour?'

'You sure, it can wait?' I glance at Lauren, her stomach moving slowly under the covers. Damn.

'See you in an hour.'

I arrive five minutes late. I couldn't stop kissing her, I know it's pathetic but I feel so much better this morning. She seemed genuinely pleased to have me there which is a bonus. I'm trying to keep myself in check, don't want to go flying off to love world without the proper precautions. It did feel like we broke down some barriers last night. Okay, it was all a bit dramatic but when I woke up this morning I felt like a new man. She seems to have accepted me more. Now all I have to do is finish my sex lessons so I can ice the cake. I've decided not to tell Lauren about Sarah, I don't see the point. They are two different situations and ultimately I'm doing this for Lauren so in theory she will be benefiting from my practising. Okay, it's lame but in my mind it all works.

In stark contrast to last night, today has blessed us with bright sunshine and not a cloud in sight. I pay the cab driver and wander past the bland concrete Royal Festival Hall and over to the South Bank. There are hundreds of people out

DANIEL GRANT

enjoying the weather. A busker plays a violin, boys on skateboards clap and scrape down ramps next to an old seventies block staircase. A temporary book market stands under Waterloo Bridge; I wander along the isles looking over the tattered second-hand spines.

'James.' I look up and see Billy waving. He is sitting at one of the many tables and chairs arranged outside. I walk over to him and shake his hand.

'Hey man,' I say, 'how goes it?'

'Good. Have a seat, want a drink?' he asks. I hold up my hand.

'I'm okay thanks, just had my second cup of coffee.' I sit down next to him. 'So...Mr Strachan, tell me everything.' Billy looks away sheepishly.

'Well...I've liked her for a while and, I just thought she wasn't really interested but, well...' I note he isn't making eye contact with me as he speaks, '...she had a boyfriend, about two years ago, you remember, Jonathan something?' My mind does a one-eighty. Jonathan?

'Wait a minute, Karen?'

'Oh...yeah. Sorry, didn't I say that?'

'Uh, no. That's an important detail.'

'Yeah I guess it is.' He chuckles, I can hear how nervous he is. His breaths are short and fast.

'Mate, that's brilliant. So you asked her out or...?'

'Well, no...we all went out for drinks about a week ago and she was quite flirty but I just thought it was the alcohol. She had a lot...'

SEX LESSONS

'Whoa...back up now. Quite flirty, what does that mean?' I love this. Little Billy and Karen, an item? This is huge.

'Well, you know...she was saying suggestive stuff...'

'Like what?'

'Like, I helped her up after she tripped over a bar stool. She said she always thought I was sweet.'

'Classy,' I say. He giggles like a girl then stops, probably realising how he sounds.

'Yeah well. Anyway she said a few other things and I thought, you know, maybe she likes me...' his face becomes more animated as his excitement builds, 'and last night we went out. Gina was supposed to come as well but she had to pick her friend up from the airport or something. So it was just me and Karen. We went to Jerry's in Blackheath, do you know it?'

'Jerry's? Oh, with the red door?'

'Yeah, she tells me about Gina, so now I'm like suddenly really nervous. But she's being friendly and everything and we start ordering drinks and, I got so drunk. I can't even remember half the stuff we did. But I do remember...' he stops abruptly. I wait patiently.

'Yeah? What?' I ask. He glances away, shyly.

'She kissed me.' I smile. 'She's amazing. The problem is, I think I love her.'

'Uh, okay. It's one date...'

'I know but, she said I was the only guy she could be herself with,' he replies, beaming. I don't know why but something jumps inside me. Alright, you may as well know I had a little thing with Karen about four years ago, it never went anywhere. It was just for a few weeks and we both decided to leave it. I think we confused being close friends with sexual chemistry. No one knew, not even Mark.

'Still, no reason to throw caution to the wind and end up in a hole you can't climb out of. So when are you going to see her again?'

'Tonight. I just...I'm a bit worried about the...?' I know what he's going to say but I wait for him to say it.

'What?'

'Sex,' he whispers.

'Oh. Why?'

'You won't tell anyone this, right?'

'I promise,' I say. His voice lowers to a whisper.

'I'm a virgin.' He stares at me, a worried expression on his face, waiting for my reaction. Honestly, it doesn't come as a surprise. Billy's always been a private guy, so I never knew if he'd had girlfriends or not.

'That's okay man. Karen will love it...'

'I can't tell her!' he whispers sharply. 'What do I do?'

'What'd you mean?'

'What *do* I *do*? What position should I do? What if I can't...you know, get it up? Suppose I...you know, too soon?'

'You'll be fine. Don't worry about it.'

SEX LESSONS

'I am worrying about it. I can't think of anything else. She's been with loads of guys James and she'll be expecting me to be...good. I don't know if I am. I tried asking an ex but my right arm didn't respond.' He sniggers to himself. I smile. The busker playing the violin stops and the crowd around him clap and start to scatter.

'Well you can either tell her the truth or you can try and fake it. If you want my advice, just talk to her.' Oh the irony. Billy shakes his head.

'Can't. It's too embarrassing.'

'Honestly. I'd be surprised if she didn't already suspect.' Billy glares at me.

'What do you mean?'

'I mean, I've never seen you with a girl. You've never spoken about any girl.'

'So?'

'So, my advice mate is to just talk to her.' He considers my words.

'Yeah? You don't think she'll think I'm pathetic?'

'Karen's with you because she likes *you* mate. You guys have known each other for a few years now. Just trust that.' He nods slowly.

'Maybe you're right.'

'Normally am.'

'Thanks James. Sorry to get you out, I just thought, you know more about this than anyone.' I raise my eyebrows. 'No, I mean you've been with lots of girls so you know how they'll react if you tell them certain things.' I nod, forcing a smile.

'Yeah.'

DANIEL GRANT

I catch a cab back to my place and jump in the shower. I hear my phone ring as I stand under the water. It can wait. I finish and rub myself down. I wander into the living room, towel around my waist, and pick up the phone. One missed call from Mark. I click 'Return Call,' it rings over and over then goes to his voicemail.

'Hi this is Mark, sorry you missed me. Leave a message after the beep.' BEEP

'Hi it's James, you called me? Call me back dipshit.' I hang up and chuck the phone on the desk. The buzzer sounds. I glance over to the intercom and walk over to it, lifting the handset. The LCD lights up, Sarah stares into the camera. Shit!

'Hi,' I say, surprise in my voice.

'Hi. I was, in the neighbourhood and thought I'd say hi.' I glance down at the towel covering me.

'Uh okay, hold on a sec, I'm not dressed,' I reply.

'Don't bother,' she says smiling into the camera, 'you'll only have to take it all off.' I smile. There's something different about her, can't put my finger on it. I buzz her in. I feel vulnerable like this. A knock at the door followed by a giggle. I open it to find Sarah standing there. However, next to her is another girl. Sporting short, cropped, dark hair she is also the proud owner of a pierced belly button.

'James. This is my good friend, Kate,' Sarah says. I hold on to my towel as I shake her hand. They walk inside, I close the door behind them.

SEX LESSONS

'Uh, so what are you doing here?' I ask.

'Well, we were just walking by the river and I thought, I know someone who lives just up here so...' Kate wears a lot of makeup, especially around her eyes. I try to smile but this is uncomfortable. 'I thought we'd continue the lessons.'

'You told Kate?' I say, suddenly trying to keep the small alarm going off in my head from getting any louder. She hears the tone in my voice; the smile disappears from her face.

'I thought this might make a good lesson,' she replies.

'I know loads of men with a similar problem. Come here, I'll show you what to do.' Kate's accent is husky and sharp but her words only boil my blood faster.

'I don't need 'showing' what to do,' I say, my voice now louder. Sarah holds her hands up.

'Okay. Calm. It was just an idea, we were in the area...'

'No, this is private. You can't just go telling anyone. I'm not some freak show...'

'I never said you were. There are things I thought you could learn from being with two girls. I'm sorry.' I'm trying not to explode here but my heart is thumping like trance music at an illegal rave. Sarah turns to Kate.

'Could you...give us a minute?' Kate sneers and brushes past me on her way out, slamming the door behind her. I turn to Sarah.

DANIEL GRANT

'I'm sorry,' she says, maintaining eye contact, 'my mistake, okay. I thought it'd be a bit of fun and maybe give you some confidence.'

'I've got plenty of confidence,' I snap. She frowns.

'Look, I'm here because I want to be...'

'No, you're here because I pay you!' Sarah blinks then shakes her head.

'Fuck you.' She turns and walks to the door. I've gone too far but I'll be damned if I'm now supposed to say sorry. Do I try to stop her? No, she should be apologising to me. For the second time in as many minutes the door slams shut. I stand in the same position, unable to make a decision. My eyes find the window, I move towards it and look out. I watch them walking down the road, I can't hear what they're saying but it's definitely high-pitched bitching. Sarah glances back towards the apartment, I hit the deck. Don't know if she saw me or not. I stay on the floor, listening to their echoed voices getting fainter and fainter. Okay, what have you done James? You need Sarah, remember? Shit!

I stand up and stare out the window. I can't see them. Have to sort this, right now! I run to the bedroom, pull on some jeans and a t-shirt. I find one trainer. Where the fuck is the other...there! I pull it on, grab my keys and dash down the stairs, two at a time. I run along the street, parked cars racing past me. I get to the end of the road and look left then right. Nothing. I guess they're heading towards the tube. I turn right and start running again. They're probably going to Canada Water. I cross the road and run as fast as I can. I have to stop and pull up, panting. I bend down, hands on my legs, trying catch my breath. I need to join a gym or something. There's burning in my lungs but it evaporates instantly as I spot them entering the tube station. I break into a run again, through the entrance and inside the modern concrete structure. I sprint down the escalator. I can hear the sound of a train screeching to a halt down below. I get to the barriers. I don't have a ticket or one of those stupid Oyster things. Shit! I peer over the barriers, searching for them. Can't see anything. I rush over to the ticket machine and buy a single, it seems to take forever to print. The ticket drops, I snatch it and insert it into the ticket barrier which opens slowly. I hurry through, down another escalator and on to the platform. My lungs burn. A train is sitting at the station. The doors start to ring. I glance over to the opposite platform, can't see them. The glass doors slam shut and the train pulls away. I bang the doors with my fist, still wheezing.

'FUCK!' I shout. The people on the platform stare at me.

TWENTY-FOUR - HIGHS AND LOWS

As I wander back towards my apartment I take out my Blackberry and dial Sarah's number, then hit stop immediately. I suddenly realise I have no idea what I'm going to say. Sorry for being a fuckwit? I was out of line? I don't know, I need to get her back though because now I'm halfway through the 'program.'

So...what, she wanted a threesome with her and that Kate girl? Very original. Just to clarify James, you not only turned down a threesome, you got angry when she even suggested it? What the hell's the matter with you? And the question is not rhetorical. WHAT WERE YOU THINKING? Honestly, the only thing I felt at the time was betrayal. Like she'd told her friend my deepest secret and fear, had a good giggle about it all then brought her over to have a laugh at my expense.

Anyway, what's done is done now. I look down at my phone again, then go into the settings and click 'Hide Own Number.' I call her number again. It rings. She doesn't pick up. The rings carry on,

SEX LESSONS

then click! The sound of busy traffic in the background fills my ear.

'Hello?' Sarah's voice says.

'I'm sorry,' I reply quickly. She says nothing, I carry on. 'I was totally out of order and I took it out on you.'

'You were fucking rude James. I'm trying to help you and you practically call me a hooker.' My mind immediately interjects with 'but you are a hooker.' I keep the thought locked away.

'I know. I'm sorry. I need you Sarah, I behaved really badly. What can I do to make it up to you?'

'Leave me alone.'

'Please, I said I'm sorry. You just showed up with this strange girl I don't know and you just expect me to just...perform. The whole point is I don't have any confidence, I thought you understood that-' But the line goes dead.

I dial her number again, this time it just rings out and goes to voicemail. Damnit. I'm about to place the phone back in my pocket when it rings. Excitement races through me until I see it's Mark.

'Hi,' I say.

'Ah good, you're alive,' he replies.

'You called me?'

'Yes, fancy a beer?'

'I do actually.'

'Great, be over shortly.'

'I'll be here. On the edge of my seat.'

* * *

DANIEL GRANT

Even though the beer fridge is three-quarters full, I stick some more in anyway. I have a feeling this might be a heavy afternoon.

Mark arrives fifteen minutes later, parking his red Alfa Romeo up on the side of the kerb, abandoned-style. I buzz him in and pull out two cold ones.

'So what's the matter with you?' he asks.

'Nothing,' I reply.

'Are you happy?'

'Yeah,' I shrug.

'You should tell your face about it.' I force a smile.

'Pretty funny.'

'Uh huh.'

'You hear about Billy and Karen?' I ask. He swallows a gulp of beer and shakes his head, belching. 'They're going out.' His eyebrows rise.

'Really? When did that happen?'

'Last night, he told me this morning.'

'Billy and Karen. Wow, didn't see that coming. This is perfect, we are going to have to wind her up something rotten.'

'Yeah.'

'Want to hear my breaking news?'

'You're gay? No wait, that's not breaking news.'

'Funny. No. I'm going on the mother of all dates with Lauren.'

'What?'

'Yep and the best part is, she called *me* this time.' Alarm bells crash inside my head.

SEX LESSONS

'When was this sorted out?' I ask, a vague attempt at hiding the panic in my voice. He checks his watch.

'I dunno, maybe forty-five minutes ago.' What. The. Fuck? The colour drains from my face, anger rushing through me again. 'Did you see what she was wearing last Thursday, tight little suit, buttons undone so you can see just enough.'

'Yeah,' I say, menace rising in my voice.

'You okay?'

'Fine.'

'I think she wants me James. The girl wants to get it on and you can't blame her, I am a sex machine afterall...'

'Fuck you!' Mark stares at me, shocked at my outburst. It's just all a bit too much. First Sarah, now Mark and Lauren I can't deal with it. I feel like I'm going to explode. Need to get out, get some air.

'What's your problem?'

'Nothing, I'm just sick of hearing about it,' I reply, trying to reign in some of my rage.

'Okay well...sorry, I won't bring it up again then.' Jesus James, calm down. We sit in silence for a minute. It's unbearable. I'm so angry and consumed in jealousy. 'I don't understand you sometimes. You should be happy for me after all the crap with Jess. You know I don't sleep at night? And even when I do, all I see is her fucking face and that bloody bump on her stomach.' He glares at me. 'Fuck James, I'm trying to do something here.' I have no answer to this. He shakes his head. 'Maybe I should go.' When I don't respond he stands. I stay seated, saying nothing, staring at the TV. 'See you later buddy.' Even when I hear the door slam and his car start up outside I still don't move. I glance towards his half-empty bottle of beer as I listen to his car pull away. I lean back into the sofa and sigh. Sorry mate. I take out my phone, staring at it. Do I call Lauren now or leave it? Fuck it. I click previous numbers dial, find her number and hit 'Call.' It rings once...twice...three times...click!

'Hello?' People are laughing and shouting in the background. Her voice is different.

'It's James,' I say, trying to keep my anger from boiling over.

'James, please leave me alone.' It takes a split-second to realise I've dialled Sarah again. Bollocks.

'Sorry, I meant to call, someone else. I'll let you go.'

'What's the matter?'

'Nothing, everything's great.'

'I don't like it when you infer that I'm some sort of hooker. I'm a stripper James. You're the only guy I have sex with, understand?'

'Fine, but do you get why I was mad?' A long pause ensues, I go to say something but she speaks first.

'Yes. I shouldn't have sprung that on you. I've been sitting here feeling like shit, okay?' Join the club. I pause to consider what I say next.

'Where's here?'

SEX LESSONS

'Browns near Shad Thames.'

'Oh,' I reply. Another pause before

'You want to meet us?'

'I dunno, I just found out the girl I like is dating my best friend as well as me.'

'How'd you know that?'

'He just told me, he doesn't know I'm seeing her as well. So fucked up.'

'You spoken to her?'

'I was about to. That's who I was trying to call before I got you.'

'Call her, be calm. It may not be what he says it is. If you want to come down, we'll be here for a bit.'

'Okay. Thanks.'

'You can buy me a glass of wine to say sorry.'

'I will.'

'James?'

'Yeah?'

'Stay calm, okay?'

'Yeah.'

'Bye.'

I hang up and take a long, deep breath, letting it out slowly. I find Lauren's number and dial it.

'Lauren Bates.'

'Hi, it's me.'

'Me?'

'James.'

'Darling. Missing me already?' My guts are churning.

'Mark just came over.'

DANIEL GRANT

'Ah. Okay, I know what you're going to say but it's not what you think.'

'What is it then?'

'It's a business meeting next week with some of the brass for Hutchinson in Hong Kong.'

'Hong Kong? You're going to Hong Kong with him?'

'He set the deal up. It's not a date, it's business. Honestly James, you have nothing to worry about with Mark. Do you understand?'

'Why didn't you tell me before?'

'I got the call two hours ago, I was going to tell you tomorrow at the office, or maybe we could find another closet and I could tell you there.' Her offer does nothing to settle me. 'James, we're going to have to trust one another. I have to trust you as well.' I nearly blurt out 'I didn't go for the lesbian three-way Lauren, give me some credit.' I decide not to. I consider her point and realise it's a good one. I guess, technically, I am being unfaithful.

'I guess so.'

'It's for four days. I have the day off on Friday, why don't you try and finish early and come round mine.'

'Okay.' I want to be enthusiastic but that's nearly a week away, I need to see her now. Somewhere inside I feel like I've already lost her.

'Got to go, the other phone's ringing. I'll call you tomorrow,' she says.

'Okay. Bye.'

* * *

SEX LESSONS

After umming and ahhing about whether to go to Browns I decide I have nothing to lose. I feel shit about Mark, I feel shit about Lauren.

Browns is packed when I arrive. Saturday afternoon and people are chatting noisily. Glasses clink as waiters clear away empties. People stand impatiently at a long wooden bar waiting to be served, ten and twenty pound notes in their hands. Some people sit outside, it may be sunny but it's still too cold for me. The imposing Tower Bridge stretches out to the left. I look around, quickly spotting Sarah and Kate. They've got a table near the window and look up as I approach. To my surprise Sarah smiles. Kate, on the other hand, doesn't.

'Hi,' I say. I'm nervous.

'Hi,' Sarah replies, standing. She kisses me on the cheek and puts her arms around me. It's exactly what I need. Her warm body against me. I close my eyes, enjoying the brief closeness. When I open them Kate is staring at me. I smile.

'I'm sorry for before. There's no excuse, I just...it's been a strange day. What are you drinking?' I ask, looking at the half-empty glasses of white wine.

'Don't worry, I'll get my own,' Kate replies, standing and walking to the bar. I turn back to Sarah.

'Sorry,' I say.

'She's just like that. In twenty minutes you'll be laughing with her.'

'I'm sorry for what I said.' She shakes her head.

'Let's not dwell, you're sorry, I'm sorry. Did you talk with Lauren?' I nod.

'She said I had nothing to worry about.'

'Well, there you go.'

'Yeah. Except for the fact she's going to Hong Kong with him next week.'

'With who, your best friend?'

'Mark, yeah.'

'Look if she says you have nothing to worry about then you're just going to have to trust her.' Yeah right. 'Does she know about me?'

'God no.' I blurt out. Sarah gives me a 'well then' face. I sigh. I know she's right but none of this makes me feel any better. I notice her glass is empty.

'So, what would you like?' I ask, taking my wallet out.

'How 'bout a sex sandwich?' I do a double take. She bursts out laughing. 'Sorry, your face.' I smile. Her laugh is infectious, it starts me off. 'James, what are we going to do with you?'

'I don't know,' I reply and I mean it.

'I'll have a white wine if Kate hasn't already got me one. When you get back we'll talk about what you should do about Lauren.' I nod and walk to the bar, passing Kate who's carrying two glasses of wine. She ignores me and carries on. Whatever.

Afternoon soon turns to evening and the bar gets more and more packed. Sarah listens and gives objective advice on what I should do. She says Lauren is in to me but she's also nervous about being hurt. I need to give her space. It's strange but listening to her advice is like hearing the truth from your mum. She just knows what to say.

I discover Kate and Sarah are old school friends. Kate works in the 'entertainment' industry but doesn't elaborate further. I small talk with her but it's when I'm speaking to Sarah I realise how easy it is to be with her. We chat about how we met, and the strange circumstances of our first 'lesson.' I talk about my job and more about Lauren. Kate pronounces that Lauren will end up having sex with Mark, which winds me up no end.

We get more and more drunk as the hours fly past. Kate's volume control is stuck on high which, I suppose, in any other setting would be annoying. Luckily the bar is so loud, she blends in. I catch Sarah looking at me a couple of times when Kate is talking. She holds my stare then slowly turns back to Kate. She has so much confidence, it's unbelievably sexy. She keeps putting her hand on my arm as well. I pretend not to notice but when Kate makes a joke, we laugh and I feel her fingers wrap around my arm. I'm still not sure about Kate but she's growing on me, sort of.

By eleven-thirty we're wasted and staggering around next to the Thames. I'm sure they've missed the last tube.

'Do you guys want to crash at mine?' I suggest. They both give me a look. 'Not like that. Just use the beds. I've got plenty of room.' They speak quietly to each other. I wait as patiently as I can, given how much I need the toilet.

'If you don't mind...' Sarah says.

'If I did, I wouldn't offer,' I reply.

I hail a cab and before long we're dumped outside my building. I fiddle with the keys in the lock and yank it open.

'Second time lucky, right?' I say.

'Exactly,' Sarah replies.

SEX LESSONS

TWENTY-FIVE - WILD IMAGININGS

I wake at five in the morning, checking the clock quickly before relaxing once I see the time. I feel movement next to me and turn my head slowly. Kate has her arm around Sarah, they're both fast asleep. Sarah has her mouth open slightly, deep, warm breaths stroking my nose as I look at her.

I study the contours of her face. Her soft, high cheekbones, long nose with a slight crease in her brow. Her long, shiny hair draped around her eyes. I glance over to Kate who also looks striking when she's sleeping. Her closed eyes make her appear like a stone statue or waxwork. As if not alive. I consider how all the events in my life have brought me here, to this moment. Lying in bed with two beautiful girls. I haven't had sex with them in case you were wondering. I think we were all a bit too wankered to do anything. In fact, now I think about it, I can't remember even going to bed. I do know there's a pulsating in my skull that will be with me the rest of the day. Kate

DANIEL GRANT

suddenly moves off Sarah and turns away, snorting a little as she does. I glance at Sarah whose eyes suddenly flick open. We stare at each other. She gives me a cute smile, closes her eyes and yawns before returning her gaze to me. She leans forward slightly and we kiss. Her hand moves over my ear as she strokes the side of my head. Her lips move carefully over my mouth. Lightness balloons inside me. Our lips break contact and she leans back, still staring at me. A whole conversation is going on between us, silently. This girl is in to me, like, not just for the money. I feel it through every pore in my body. As if sensing my realisation, she suddenly turns away and cuddles up to Kate. What does that mean? I spend the next hour or so trying to work it out until we get up. It's awkward, Sarah doesn't make eye contact with me as she picks her clothes off the floor. She gets dressed in the bathroom. Kate goes with her. I offer breakfast and/or coffee. They both decline. I make a pot anyway and sit at the kitchen table, reading the newspaper when they walk in.

'I made coffee, sure you don't want some?' Kate shakes her head.

'No thanks, better be going,' says Sarah, still not making eye contact with me.

'Anyone seen my coat?' Kate asks, suddenly looking around.

'It's in the living room, on the sofa,' I reply. Kate leaves to retrieve the jacket.

SEX LESSONS

'You okay?' I ask. Sarah looks up, feigning surprise.

'Hmm? Yeah. Great. How you feeling?' I nod and shrug.

'Been better, I think I'm still a little drunk.' Sarah grins.

I put the coffee down and walk over to her, placing both hands on her shoulders.

'Thank you,' I say.

'What for?'

'I don't know...just being there,' I reply with a smile.

'Any time.' Our eyes meet again, her confidence returned. I go to kiss her when my phone suddenly rings. I turn and grab it from the table. It's Lauren.

'Hi.'

'Hi. I just thought I'd call before I get on the plane.'

'Oh, yeah. You're at the airport?' Sarah nods and points towards the door. I hold up my hand trying to stop them.

'Yeah, flight leaves at eight.'

'Is Mark there?'

'He's getting breakfast. You okay?'

'Yeah, yeah, good.'

'What did you get up to yesterday?'

'Went down the pub with a few friends,' I reply. Sarah gives a small wave and goes to the door, opening it quietly. They step out then suddenly slam the door shut.

'Shit!' I say, involuntarily.

DANIEL GRANT

'What's wrong?' asks Lauren.

'Nothing, wind blew the door shut.' I'm a bad man. If I were made of wood, my nose would be touching the wall.

'Oh. Are we still meeting up on Friday when I get back?'

'Definitely. Yeah.'

'Okay. So, see you then. No messing around with other women now.' I laugh nervously, trying a bit too hard.

'Yeah, okay. Have a good trip.'

'Bye James.' She hangs up.

'Bye.'

I stand in the kitchen and glance over towards the closed door. I throw on some clothes and head out.

On my way down to the car I check my post box and see I have a box from onlinepharmacy.org. I open it, pulling out the trays of blue bills. So many. Jesus, did I really order all these? Fuck, I could stay erect for a year. I stare at the small diamond shapes of blue. My saviours and jailers. Maybe I don't need these afterall. Things went well with Sarah the last time we shagged, sort of. I decide to keep them anyway. Just in case.

The week at work drags painfully. I spend most days thinking about Lauren and what she might be getting up to with Mark. They've

SEX LESSONS

probably got connected rooms so they can sneak between them. I see her riding him slowly first, then faster and faster. Her face contorted in ecstatic pleasure. I see how long he lasts, he doesn't need any sex lessons. No Viagra, nothing. The man is just that good. Fuck. I should have tried to stop them, maybe offered to come along. Now he's got her bent over a walnut desk whilst enjoying a Hong Kong harbour view room at the same time. I grab a Coke and a Mars bar from the machine and chomp away but images fly to me faster than a Japanese Bullet Train. Now they're in a noodle house feeling each other and laughing, trying to master chopsticks. I shake my head, I can't take this.

I hear an advert on the radio for new 'nasal delivery technology for men who need an extra lift.' Nasal bloody delivery bloody technology. Yeah right. I take down the number anyway.

The only brief distraction comes when I see Karen walk into the trading room. I'm up like a shot and marching towards her. She spots me and immediately starts walking in the other direction, pretending not to have seen me. I catch her easily.

'Hi Karen,' I say. She sighs. 'How's it going?'
'It's going fine thanks James, how about you?'
'Oh...great.' I stand there, big grin on my face.
'Come on then, spit it out,' she says.
'So...you and Billy...'
'Yes, me and Billy. We're seeing each other, it was supposed to be a secret but Billy went and

blabbed to you and now, strangely, everyone bar the janitor knows about it.'

'No, he knows too.'

'Great,' she says, 'look, James I'm actually quite busy.'

'Ohhh no. You and I need to sit down. I want details.'

'You got them from Billy,' she replies.

'Well, I want to hear them from you.' She sighs again, dramatically.

'Fine, early lunch at twelve?'

'Perfect. You have a nice morning now.' She shakes her head and carries on. For the smallest of moments, all thoughts of Lauren and Mark leave me. However, by the time I'm back at my desk, a new image of Mark and Lauren using sex toys on each other has found its way into my mind and suddenly lunch doesn't seem so appetising.

I find a seat next to the window at Pret and check my watch. I glance around nervously, watching out for anyone that might recognise me from my spat with Jenny. Luckily, it's only twelve so it's not that busy. I stare at the sushi rolls before me and start to wonder why I chose these instead of a sandwich. I bite into one and immediately want no further part. I place the roll back in the packet and take a sip of orange juice. I watch the world going about its business

SEX LESSONS

outside. So many people in suits with places to be, people to deal with. I check my watch again and figure Mark and Lauren are probably just sitting down to have dinner about now. I hear Sarah in my head saying how I should trust her. I can't help feeling I'm being fucked with. Look I know I can hardly complain given I was in bed with two girls last night but stay with me on this. I need to get this sex thing sorted out as soon as possible so if I bed Lauren, I won't constantly be worrying about whether things will go South.

I pull out my phone and start texting Sarah, then think better of it, considering the possibility of a reply whilst I'm talking to Karen. See, I can learn from my mistakes. As I put the phone away, Karen walks in. She glances around and spots me. I give a little wave, she walks over and sits down next to me. She's wearing a strong perfume. It's a little overpowering. The suit she's got on is nice and accentuates her figure but I don't like the shade of grey, too dark for her I think. Jesus, I'm starting to sound like a girl.

'So Billy...' I say, grinning.

'Yes, Billy. I like him James, always have. Newsflash over.'

'I think it's great. I'm really happy for you both.' She eyes me suspiciously.

'Yeah well...after Wesley I thought, never again. But Billy's perfect and he's got a massive cock.' She suddenly bursts out laughing. I open my mouth in shock.

'Je-sus, Karen...' She's giggling hysterically, trying to stop herself but she quickly starts up again. I glance around, people couldn't care less. I smile at her, she eventually composes herself.

'Sorry. Ah dear.' She takes out a tissue from her handbag and dabs her eyes.

'So you guys have...' She glances at me.

'None of your business,' she replies, 'but no, not yet. We're taking it slow.' I'm unsure whether to mention Billy's anxieties then I figure he'd never forgive me.

'Well, honestly, I think it's great,' I say.

'Thanks. So what happened with Jenny? She came up the other day fuming. Did you have a fight or something?'

'Hmm, Jenny. Yes. When you got us together, you never warned me she was uh, A FUCKING PSYCHO! Jesus. She's saying *I* dumped her!'

'You said you did.'

'No. Well, yes. It...didn't work out and she didn't call me so I assumed it was over. She went nuts, starting ripping me to pieces in front of everyone.' Karen starts laughing again.

'She can be a bit dramatic sometimes.'

'A bit? No it wasn't a bit Jen. You should hear my answerphone. The girl's insane.'

'Ah James, what are you like?' she asks.

'Fucked if I know.'

'So you gonna tell me about this new girl, Sarah?'

'Nope.'

'Come on, who is she?'

SEX LESSONS

'She's none of your business.'

'I told you about Billy.'

'No you didn't, Billy did.' She pretends not to hear me.

'Well, we know she's pretty, James doesn't go out with unattractive girls.'

'I'm not sure what you mean by that but I'm going to ignore it.'

TWENTY-SIX - KISSING AND NEAR-MISSING

On the drive home, I come within a split-second of killing myself and a bunch of pedestrians. The lights ahead were green, I was speeding up a little to catch them before they changed when for reasons best-known to herself, this woman decides red is not her colour and floors it across the box junction I'm approaching. I slam on the brakes and swerve left. The tyres make this awful screeching sound, the pungent smell of burning rubber fills the car. I fly past her, seeing utter horror in her eyes. I match her fear with my own, too terrified to scream. The second I realise I will live, my fear mutates into unrestrained fury. I yell words I've never heard, my mouth spewing a torrent of foul language and hatred. Well she nearly fucking killed me! Stupid bitch. I spend the rest of the ride home catching my breath and replaying the incident, pondering whether I could have handled it better. By the time I enter my road I'm actually feeling guilty. What is that about? I pull into my garage and find my space.

Walking out, I notice someone sitting on the step outside my front door. As I get closer I realise it's Sarah, she has her head in her hands.

'Sarah?' I say, approaching her. She looks up, her eyes are moist, trying not to cry.

'Hi. Sorry to just show up like this.'

'Don't be silly, what's the matter?'

'Can I come in?'

'Of course,' I reply. She stands as I unlock the door. We walk up the stairs. She sniffs twice on the way. I'm trying to work out what could be wrong. Maybe something to do with Kate, I never trusted that girl. Trouble at Uni, perhaps?

I let us in and close the door. She turns around, looking for direction.

'Let's go to the living room. Do you want a drink or...?' I ask. She shakes her head. We sit down on the sofa. She looks up to the ceiling, trying not to let a tear roll down her face. Giving in, she brushes it away. I place a hand on her back and rub slowly.

'Jason and I broke up. He found out about the strip club.'

'Ah,' I reply. She sniffs again, trying to hold it together.

'So stupid. I knew it would happen. Kept telling myself, he's going to find out Sarah. Just be honest with him. One of his friends saw me on a stag do. We just had the biggest fight. I know

DANIEL GRANT

why he's upset, I don't have any excuse but...I really liked him James.' Her head drops and she starts to cry softly. Tears drop onto her top, creating dark spots.

'I'm sorry.' I move in and hug her, she wraps her arms weakly around my back and we sit in silence holding each other.

'Sorry to just turn up like this. I just...I didn't know who else to talk to. Most of my friends don't know what I do. Guess they will now.'

'Don't be silly, you came to the right place.' She starts crying on my shoulder. Dejected, she gives up trying to hold it in and allows herself to fall apart. I hold her as she shakes beneath me. Wave after wave. She stops for a moment, then starts again.

'I've really fucked this up. What am I doing?' I'm struggling to come up with any helpful advice. The guy just found out his girlfriend is a stripper, I mean, you can't blame him for being a bit miffed.

'These things all happen for a reason. You didn't want him to know because you knew this would happen, totally understandable. You were protecting him.'

'Yeah but I should have just been honest with him from the start. He's in the same class as me. By now the whole university will know.' She starts to cry again. She's not wrong, this is a bad situation. I run my hand through her hair, it smells of honey and oatmeal.

SEX LESSONS

'It'll be fine. Why would he tell everyone at the university? It makes him look bad as well.' She looks up at me and frowns. 'Okay that was pretty lame, sorry.' I don't know what to say. 'They won't kick you off the course.'

'Well I'm two years in, I'd have to start from scratch.'

'Really?' I ask. She nods.

'I'm a mature student. I went travelling for two years before.'

'So you'd have to do it all over again someplace else?' I ask.

'I don't know.'

'Look I don't know either because I never went to university but I'd be amazed if they kicked you out for something like this, really.' A thought hits me. 'Does Jason know about what you've been doing with me?' She nods.

'Yeah. I figured once we started talking he deserved to know everything.' Now that wasn't very smart. Jesus, the poor guy was probably already on his knees when he found out she was getting her tits out for other men. Then she tells him she was shagging a complete stranger for money. Whichever way you look at it, it's not good.

'I have fucked this up properly, haven't I?'

'Well, you know, it's nothing that can't be repaired.' She glances up at me again, makeup streaming down her face. 'Okay, yes it's not good but you wait, this will end up being a blessing.' She snorts.

DANIEL GRANT

'How?' Yeah James, how? Ummm...

'Well, we need to make sure your course is safe first. Maybe you should just talk to the Dean or whoever's in charge.'

'And say what? Hi Mr. Hughes, I want to confess I've been whoring myself to pay my tuition fees this past year, that's okay, isn't it?' Hmm, not an unreasonable point. I'm out of ideas.

'I'm going to get us some alcohol,' I say. It's about the only positive thing I can think of. I pull away, she falls on to the sofa and lies on her side, feet still on the floor. I bend down, pull her boots off and lift her ankles gently to the sofa. I brush her hair away from her face and touch her cheek. Then I go into the kitchen and straight over to the wine rack.

We're going to need something special to sort this out. I pull out a two thousand and one Ribera Del Duero I'd been saving for a special occasion. No time like the present. I grab a corkscrew and open the bottle. Grabbing two glasses, I walk back into the living room. She's closed her eyes. Fuck that, I just opened a hundred pound bottle of wine.

'Here you go,' I say loudly. Her eyes flick open and she sits up slowly. I pour the wine, it makes a fantastic glugging sound. I hand her a glass and pour myself one. 'Here's to a new chapter in your life.' She manages to eke out a smile then sips the wine. I look to see if she notices how good it is but she just places the glass back on the table.

SEX LESSONS

Unbelievable. I should have just gone for the ten pound Wolf Blass. I know she's upset, but Jesus.

I take a sip, it's like liquid ecstasy, going down easily and leaving a lovely after-taste.

'That's good,' I say in a vain attempt to cue her. She just nods, her mind elsewhere. I head towards the TV.

'Thank you James.' I turn around. 'For being here. I know we haven't known each other for long but, I feel like I trust you more than most of my friends.' I nod, a sympathetic smile creeping across my face.

'Any time. Mi Casa es su Casa.' She grins. 'Was that a smile? I think it was. Well, good to know I haven't lost my touch.'

'You have a very gentle touch. This Lauren girl is very lucky.' I elect to ignore that comment, flick on the TV and sit down next to her. She leans in and rests her head on my shoulder.

Now I know you're going to think I'm taking advantage with what happens next. In my defence, I will say she started it and made the first move. We polished off that hundred pound red, see the empty bottle sitting on the table like a used condom. We also managed to consume half a bottle of port and two shots of tequila. I know I have work tomorrow but friends have to help friends out, right?

So here we are, in the bedroom. I'm just taking off my shirt when I feel her presence behind me. Before I can turn she reaches around my waist and pulls me into her. She hurriedly spins me round and kisses me. I feel her fumbling with my trousers. I move my hands under her top to her bra. She yanks my trousers down, rapidly followed by my boxers. She doesn't wait to get them off properly, before I even know what's happening she's dropped to her knees and has me inside her mouth. I have no rigidity at all. I start trying to think erotic thoughts. For some reason images of my granny keep popping in. So I'm like 'hey gran, fuck off out of my erotic thought, it's wrong and it's inhibiting my erection.' Gran doesn't leave without a fight. Meanwhile down there, as I'm having it out with granny, Sarah is sucking and licking. I want to be hard, surely I should be by now. It feels great but I need to be hard, right now. Come on, damn you. What is your fucking problem? She starts taking my undercarriage in her mouth now. I'm exhausted and I haven't done anything, ripples of pleasure oscillate through me, twisting and turning. He's not reacting. Everything feels so good but the arsehole won't stand to attention. COME ON, DAMN YOU.

As if hearing my mental arguments, Sarah suddenly stops and looks up.

'James?' I don't want to look at her but I guess I have to.

'Yeah?'

'What's wrong?'

'Nothing, I just…nothing.'

'Sit down, over here.' I do as instructed, with very small steps as my boxers and trousers still hang around my ankles. She crawls over to me and rises between my legs. 'Relax. Clear those thoughts. Close your eyes.' I shut them. 'Focus on the feeling. How good it feels, okay?'

'Yeah. I'm not sure if this is a good idea, feels wrong somehow.'

'I need to feel better about things.' Well, who am I to say no when she's patently decided what's best for the both of us. She starts once more. I sit tight, eyes closed, feeling the warmth of her mouth and graininess of her tongue.

'Relax,' she whispers. I feel her fingers under my scrotum then suddenly things are happening. Sensations whoosh through me. Damnit that's good. I feel myself become hard. Sarah straightens her back slightly. I open my eyes, she glances up to me and smiles. She pulls her top off and jerks her bra up, revealing her pert breasts. I move my hand over one of them. Feels soft in my hand.

'See,' she says. I nod and smile. 'We're going to have sex now James.' She pulls out a condom from her handbag, rips the foil and pulls it down. Then, slowly she lowers herself on top of me, closing her eyes as she slides down. Up, then down. Up and down. Her breasts circle round and round. I take deep breaths, trying to control myself from coming.

'Don't think about it, just relax,' she whispers, arching her back. My breathing is regular, I feel at peace. I don't need to come, everything is working. Sarah's moaning. It feels the way I always imagined it could. I'm in control. She stops and wiggles her waist around me. Then she lifts herself off and gets down on all fours, grabbing on to the head of the bed. I need no other cue. I clutch under her stomach and enter her from behind. In and out, faster and faster. Her back glistens under the light. This is what normally gets me. I last about fifteen seconds in this position.

'Just relax, go at your own pace,' she says. I slow down and continue trying to control my breathing. Everything still works, although more feeling is fluxing through me, I can control it.

We change positions again and again. I'm lasting longer than I ever have. In the end I can't help myself and I come hard inside her. I collapse on top of her, panting. She clings to me. Normally I want to get off almost immediately but this is different. This time, I just lay there, holding her tightly in my arms.

SEX LESSONS

TWENTY-SEVEN - WAITING

Sarah leaves early. We don't say much to each other but perhaps surprisingly it's not awkward. She grabs her clothes, gets dressed, says thanks to me again and leaves. I lay in bed mulling over last night. For the first time in ages I feel like I have a chance of beating this problem that has been with me since…forever.

The clock on the wall ticks. I hear the neighbour's cuckoo clock sounding five. Fucking thing. I swear to God I need to buy something that goes off every hour and nail it to their bedroom wall. Only problem, it would wake me up as well. I have a strange feeling about Sarah, we're getting very close for two people that are supposed to be just screwing. She didn't ask me for any money either which is strange. I'm grateful for the freebie but there's always a cost to these things one way or another. I wonder what Lauren's doing now. It's the middle of the day in Hong Kong, maybe they're shagging in the meeting room of some flash high-rise building. I don't want to think about it. Pointless torturing myself. The space where Sarah had been is still warm. The pillow has her smell. I breathe it in, savouring the memory. What's wrong with me? I should wash these sheets, can't remember the last time...nevermind. I pull the covers off, cold air hitting every part of my body. I run to the shower and turn on the water, shivering as I wait for the water to become warm.

I drive to work, having spent ten minutes trying to prise out a piece of burnt toast caught in the toaster without electrocuting myself. Yes, of course I unplugged it.

The rest of the week goes by so slowly, I think I'm starting to gain days. Mike (jerkoff) Cartwell is being a major irritation. He starts giving me the run down on this Nat West project. Some deal we're doing with them, closer ties etc. He speaks to me as if I wasn't the man that put the bloody thing together. Man, if I were to ever meet him on the street and I didn't depend on him for a job, I would so kick his arse. Okay, for clarity, I've never kicked anyone's arse. Had mine kicked many times but I'm sure I could kick fat Mike's any day. Just have to get in shape and learn a martial art or something.

Neither Lauren nor Sarah makes contact for the rest of the week and I start to feel down again. Anyone else would be happy with this situation. Two beautiful girls, one guy. Every man's fantasy, no? The urge to text Lauren is so great, it feels like I'm on some compulsive drug, the only cure

SEX LESSONS

for which is shoot-up text. I resist, however, knowing the consequences. I've been there so many times, you send a text, then spend the rest of your life waiting for a response and when they don't reply, you start to read all sorts of nasty things into it. No thanks, I'd rather be stuck in ignorance and make the visions up myself.

When I wake on Friday I spend fifteen minutes in the bathroom staring at the packet of blue pills. I could be seeing Lauren tonight. Deductive reasoning thus far leads me to conclude sex may well be on the menu. Unless Mark got her knocked up, of course. But just in case he didn't, I need to seriously consider the pills. I know it all went well with Sarah before but...you never know. I stare at the white box, the 'Viagra' logo stamped on the front. Come on, I don't need these. Do I? Maybe I just need to have a little faith in myself. Trust in what I've already accomplished with Sarah. Can you imagine though, Lauren and I get down to it and...God I'm hyperventilating just thinking about it. I break off a line of blue boys and shove them in my pocket. In case of emergency, break foil.

TWENTY-EIGHT - RAIN DOWN

It's 15:30 and I'm sitting at my desk ever-so slowly going out of my mind, wondering if Lauren will get in contact. Suddenly my phone bleeps. I almost drop it in my flustering to open the text. It reads: 'Hi, just got in. Bit tired but if you still want to come over I could cook something? L xx.' Damn right I'm coming over. I hit reply and type 'Sure, I'll try and get away by five-thirty, see you at six?'

She replies in agreement and the date is set. I'm not going to ask her about Mark or anything else. It's pointless, if they've been shagging non-stop for four days what's the point in me knowing about it? Just gets me annoyed and jealous. Let's just pretend that nothing happened and everything she told me is true. Ah, the world is a beautiful place when you come at it from a standpoint of denial.

Five-thirty comes and I'm packing my bag to leave as discreetly as possible when Mike (wankstain) spots me and asks what I'm doing. I

SEX LESSONS

invent some excuse about my grandmother being sick and how I need to be by her side. He doesn't buy it and questions how convenient it is that my grandmother happens to get sick on a Friday afternoon. I feign both indignance and outrage that he should suggest that my sick granny, who may not make it through the night by the way, would conveniently fall ill on said Friday afternoon. He backs off and walks away mumbling something. What a crackerjack fucker, eh?

I rush to the car and hightail it out of there, faster than Batman out of his cave (or as previously suggested, the Boy Wonder.) I get there in record time. Of course, what I haven't considered in all this is the absence of parking in Pimlico. It's a fucking nightmare. I need to stop swearing so much. Okay from now on, I'm going to have a swear box and if I say a swear word I'll put a pound in the box, okay? Remind me, because I'll forget. So, eventually I find a space, about ten minutes from where she lives. I hate walking when I have the car.

I get to her door at a quarter past six and ring the bell. I wait for a moment or two then hear a click and the door opens. Lauren stands in front of me, wearing a revealing, tight-fitting cream dress. Damnit, I should have worn something smarter.

'Sorry I didn't realise it was a smart thing,' I fumble. She glances down.

DANIEL GRANT

'This thing?' she says, a glint in her eye as she turns round and starts up the stairs, her bum waving at me from its superb vantage point. Okay, I know I'm being manipulated but that's fine. It's okay if you're aware of it, isn't it? I follow her, like a puppy dog.

She's set out the living room with candles and low lighting. Duffy is playing quietly on the stereo. Doesn't Duffy always sing about heartbreak and splitting up?

'Wow, this is nice. You look amazing,' I say, suddenly wishing I'd brought flowers or chocolates or wine or anything.

'Thanks. Champagne?' she asks, pulling the bottle out of the ice water bucket.

'Great. Want me to open it?' I say. She glances at me.

'I've got this one James, you just sit down and relax.' I wander into the living room, faking interest in her framed photos and weird paintings. I notice a photo of Lauren with an older man and woman, her parents at a guess. The woman is just as beautiful with long flowing blonde hair. The man is older, rough shaved, but a glint in his eye. They smile at the camera, happier times. I glance over to her, she's having trouble with the cork. I look back to the fireplace. Hearing a huff, I turn back.

'Sure you don't want me to...?' She shoots me devil eyes, then, realising she won't be able to do it, gives in and hands me the bottle.

SEX LESSONS

'Thanks. So, how was Hong Kong?' Uh James, I thought you weren't going to ask?

'Busy, we didn't stop from the time we got there to the time we left.' Didn't stop doing what?

'Oh. Was it a nice hotel?'

'Shangri-La, very nice. Not that I saw much of it.' What, too busy shagging in the conference suites? 'But we got it done and I think Mike's (tossa) going to be pleased.'

'What was the deal?'

'We don't have to talk about work, James. How are you?'

'Yeah, good,' I reply, guilt starting to harrang me.

'What have you been up to?' she asks.

'Nothing.' I blurt out. I try to recover. 'Nothing much. Pretty dull really.' An idea forms. 'I have some interesting news though. Karen is now seeing Billy.'

'Really? That's great. Billy's a nice guy.' Nice bit of redirection.

'Yeah.'

'I'm just going to check on the food, two ticks,' she says.

'Sure.' I watch her walk away. That dress is smokin'. Seriously, it barely covers anything. Maybe that's the point. Don't be so dumb James, of course it's the point. I wait patiently, listening to the sounds of dishes clanking. Her paintings are very strange. I'm not sure what she's trying to convey about herself by hanging them on her wall. They look like the work of a schizo. Maybe she bought them from Jenny. Duffy's singing about being dumped for the third track in a row, she's got an amazing voice, just needs to find a man that won't fuck her over every two minutes. Bollocks. Yes okay, pound in the box.

I walk to the window. Gloomy street lights illuminate the parked cars below. In the distance I can just make out the edge of the Thames.

'Damnit.' I hear Lauren's whisper carry from the kitchen.

'You okay? Want a hand?' I shout.

'No, I'm fine,' she replies. What is she doing in there, sowing the potatoes? She comes out a few minutes later with flushed cheeks, I smile.

'Everything alright?' I ask.

'Yeah, just a bit tired,' she says.

'You didn't have to cook. We could have just got a take-away or something.' She rolls her eyes.

'*Now* you tell me. Just kidding, I wanted to cook. I guess I underestimated how much time this recipe would take.'

Eventually, after more frustrated whisperings to the oven, we sit down and eat. I stare at the meal before me, vegetables, steak, chips, sauce and mushrooms. The woman's cooked enough for six people. I have to ask if anyone else is coming. She glares at me, I decide not to bring it up again.

'So. Miss me?' she asks, glancing up from her plate.

'Yeah. Well, you know, yeah, maybe, a little. Did you miss me?'

'Yes,' she replies and carries on eating. This might be the night James, hope you're ready. I think I am. Like an Olympic athlete who trains for years to get themselves in to peak physical condition for one race, I feel pumped and ready to go. Of course, on the way, there's always a few hurdles. Here's a classic line I came out with to jutter the moment.

'So, how was Mark? Did he behave himself?' She smiles and nods.

'Yes, he was the perfect gentleman. You have nothing to worry about.'

'I know I don't. I just wondered if he made a move.' I study her face, searching for any betraying expression. The smile dies and she looks at me. Uh oh.

'He made plenty of moves.' Fuck. Damnit, one more pound in the box, maybe I should just buy credit or something.

'Yeah?' I reply, nonchalantly.

'Nothing happened. He got the message.'

'Oh?' I say, raising an eyebrow. She sighs faintly.

'Look, I don't want to have to keep going over this so I'll say it once and hopefully you can absorb it and take it as read. I'm not interested in Mark. If I were, I would be with him. I like you, but every time you bring this up it makes me...'

'What?'

'I don't know, uncomfortable. Relationships should be about trust James. I don't understand your insecurities, you come across so confident in the office. And yet just scratch the surface, you get all this other stuff.'

'Sorry. I feel insecure because...' Why James? Totally out of your league? You're with a girl most guys can only fantasize about? You have dick issues? 'I don't know...' She grins.

'You're cute when you get all serious, you know? This little wrinkle forms on your forehead when you talk like this.'

'I've had it mentioned before, what do you want me to do, have surgery?' Suddenly she puts her knife and fork down and stands. She walks over to me and sits down on my lap. My dinner, half eaten, remains in front of me. It's strangely distracting. She puts her arms around my neck and leans in to kiss me. Her bum feels warm on my legs, her perfume floats through me. I close my eyes as I feel her hands run through my hair. She tugs it gently, pulling my head back. I feel a hand on my crotch. My eyes open slowly.

'What about dinner?' I ask in a hushed voice.

'Sod it, we're moving straight to dessert,' she replies and leans in to kiss me again. That was cheesy, don't you think? It's weird when someone actually says something like that to you. I almost had to check over my shoulder and make sure I wasn't living life in some dodgy rom-com. Let's look at it again, 'we're moving straight to dessert.' Lauren, that is truly awful. I make a mental note to have the dialogue doctor come have a chat with her as soon as this session is over. I'm trying not to giggle at this point, the line stuck in my head. She pulls back.

'What?' she asks. I shake my head, trying to cover my smile.

'Nothing,' I reply. Since we're moving in the realm of cliché and for reasons best-known to me, I reach around her waist in an attempt to turn her more towards me. What I end up doing is allow my sleeve to brush against my glass of wine. It rocks then falls almost in slow motion. The wine tips along the glass then out, free, suspended in midair before crashing down onto Lauren's dress. She's off me in a flash.

'JESUS!' she says, glaring at her dress before running to the kitchen.

'God, I'm sorry.' I stand, feeling like a naughty schoolboy who's now going to get the bollocking of his life from the headmistress. I wait. Should I follow her or wait here? 'You okay?' I ask.

'It's ruined,' I hear her reply. Uh oh. 'Fuck James.' I think she might have to start contributing to the swear box too, luckily I have the presence of mind to keep that sentiment to myself.

I watch as she walks out, a big wet patch on her dress where she's tried to clean it.

'Have you got any white wine?' I say. She tilts her head, eyes burning. 'No really, it cancels it out. You put white wine on a red wine stain and it gets rid of it.' She eyes me suspiciously.

'Yeah?' she asks.

'Yeah. Let me get some.' I wander into the kitchen and open the fridge door. There's a bottle with the cork in. I pull it out and walk back. 'Take it off,' I say.

'No, just...' she stares at me, '...okay, fine.' She pulls her dress off and hands it to me. Except it falls to the floor because my interest in the dress has vanished. She's wearing a black lacy bra and thong. Holy...crap. Her breasts must be like D's or maybe high C's. She's got a perfect hourglass figure, with skin so smooth I figure she must moisturise every hour.

'What?' she asks. Yeah, like you don't know. I shake my head, unable to move my eyes away. Christ I want her, right now.

'Nothing,' I say, still gawking.

'It's rude to stare.'

'Yeah. So people tell me.' I prise my eyes away and kneel down to apply the white wine to the stain. I glance back to her. She has her arms on her hips and catches my glance. I look up at her remarkable body. She stares at me, I can see her breathing faster.

'It just needs to dry out,' I say, standing. I offer her the dress. She takes it, her eyes locking on to mine.

'Would you...' my voice is hoarse, I cough and try again, '...would you have any objections to me kissing you?'

'I might,' she replies, taking a step towards me. 'But I guess you'll just have to find out for yourself.' I lean in slowly, the dress falls from her hand.

DANIEL GRANT

TWENTY-NINE - TAKE HER FOR A SPIN

Right champ, this is it. This is your dream come true moment. Don't fuck it up. DING! Yes okay, I think I'll lose the swear box now, going to end up costing me more than a night with Sarah.

Lauren and I transfer seamlessly to the sofa, kissing and stroking each other. Every time we have a breather I open my eyes and take in the sight before me. I just can't believe it. She's here, in front of me. So damn beautiful. Christ knows what she sees in me. Doesn't matter James, you got her duped, go for it before she figures it out. Good advice from the Mind there.

Her bra strap feels tight on her shoulder. The touch of her skin is as achingly smooth as I imagined. She tastes even better than the hundred pound bottle of wine. Her hand massages my groin. Okay, don't think. Remember, just relax. Enjoy the sensations. Okay. Yes, that's nice. She moves her hand a little

SEX LESSONS

faster, I squirm under her touch. I move my fingers along her leg, she breathes fast and heavy in my ear. Going good so far, James. Stop thinking about this, just focus on her. I move the bra strap down and lean in, gently kissing her neck. A moan escapes.

'Ah,' she says, more to the ceiling than me. She undoes my flies and pulls him out. He's at his midway stage, neither erect nor unresponsive. I pull her bra down, revealing two more-than-a-handful sized breasts. Absolutely astonishing. She slides down until her mouth is next to him. Adrenaline crackles through me, my breathing rushed and uneven. She moves her mouth over him, her head beginning to move up and down. Slowly at first. A warm pleasure-cave. I reach down and unclasp her bra, throwing it to the floor. My hands enclose her breasts, kneading and rubbing, soft and delicate in my hands. Things are working, I'm hard. Oh YES! Thank you Sarah! Thank you. Lauren's moving faster now. Jesus, I hope she slows down because at this rate I'm not going to last two seconds. I try to hold on to her face to slow her but she's taken some kind of blow-job speed and won't quit.

'Wait...hold on...' I attempt to splutter out. She ignores me. 'Fuck, stop...stop,' I whisper, trying to reason with her. I see her glance at me. She knows what she's doing. 'I'm going to come.' Suddenly she spits me out. I'm nearing the edge, don't want to do anything for about fifteen minutes. Let him calm down, regain his composure. I stand, catching myself in the reflection of the one of the framed paintings. Jesus, I look like a coat-hook. He's still shiny, a chilly draught whistling over him. Lauren lies down on the sofa. I move my head between her legs as little sighs start to drift from her mouth. She pulls my head in closer. I stay focused but I can feel my erection waning. Now what? What did Sarah say? Am I supposed to be okay with it deserting me? I try keeping it up myself whilst carrying on. It's no good, I can't do two things at once. Panic enters my mind for the first time, I don't want to lose my hardness. Need to just get him inside as soon as possible.

If I don't go in now, I'll lose him. I move up her body, kissing her belly and breasts as I go. I try to move inside her but my erection has lost more rigidity than I thought. FUCK. Not again, come on. Please.

'Hold on,' Lauren suddenly says, seemingly detecting my alarm. She moves down and starts on me again. It doesn't seem fair but it worked the last time. It has to work now. Nothing's happening. Come on. She's sucking a dead cock. Please, it feels so good. It's been a minute already, in thirty seconds I'll get the first of many concerned looks. In a minute, she'll stop and ask if everything's okay. And I'll give her that look and she'll know it all.

Twenty seconds. Twenty-five. I close my eyes. I don't want to look at her. Just keep going, it will rise eventually. It has to. She stops. God no.

SEX LESSONS

Don't stop. Please Lauren, don't stop. I keep my eyes firmly shut, this can't be over already. It's barely begun. I should have taken the pill, should have excused myself and taken the bloody pill. I open one eye when I feel her arse in my groin. Her back faces me as she wiggles her butt around my cock. Then she bends over, her hips swinging left to right.

'Teach me a lesson James,' she whispers. I don't know what that means. What lesson? She slaps a butt cheek and rubs it playfully, climbing on to all fours on the sofa. She bends down again and shoots me a devastatingly sexy look.

'Are you going to punish me or what?' she asks. Well this is different, but sure okay, why not? I move up behind her and gently slap her arse. 'UHH!' she moans arguably a little theatrically but what the hell. I rub my fingers around each cheek, then spank her again. She cries out. Bizarrely my erection is starting to return. Okay Lauren. Now we're talking. 'Harder,' she says. I slap again, the cheek is starting to redden. Her head falls to the cushion, a moan hissing from her. Shit, hope I haven't killed her. That would be bad. She waits on all fours.

'Condom?' I ask, glancing around. She shakes her head.

'Come on,' she demands. I don't need asking twice, I'm inside before you can say 'Viagra, what Viagra?' In, out. Mustn't come too fast. Try to keep a steady pace like running a marathon, just keep focused on the goal. 'Yeah, fuck me James.

DANIEL GRANT

Fuck me.' I'm trying darling, I'm trying. She moans, breathless. As I grind with her I take stock of the situation in front of me. All is well, I don't need to come...yet. Her arse is red but that's a good thing, I think. She seems to be enjoying it, saying 'fuck me's' and groaning in the right places. I am the sex god. Look at this. Look at me! A sudden rush of urgent sensation fills my groin and I slow accordingly. Careful James, don't want the party to end just yet. I move slowly now. In and out. Leisurely. We have all the time in the world. Suddenly the stresses and strains aren't there any more, just me and Lauren. Sarah was right. This is how it's meant to be. Two people enjoying being with and inside each other, as close as human beings can get.

I pull out, Lauren repositions herself, lying down on her back. I move between her legs and go in. It's...love. That's the only word I can find. Pure love. Of course, desire and urgent need is there too. It feels as if I might burst. A sudden wave of gratitude flows over me. Thank you God. Thank you Sarah. I'm on the home straight, I've done enough but I'm still going. We're both glistening with sweat. I thrust harder now, my body is ready and somewhere inside I feel she is too. Faster and faster. Her arms rise above her head as if strapped by invisible handcuffs. I kiss her lips, her breasts, her neck. She moans with every thrust. I'm coming, oh God! Her arms suddenly lock around me, her nails scratching into my back. Giddiness deluges through me.

SEX LESSONS

Swells of raw pleasure rise and fall within me and move through her. Our energies combine for one perfect moment as I hold so tight I never want to let go. Everything stops. Stillness and silence as we cling to each other. I dare to breathe out, she follows. Eyes shut, my mouth feels sticky. Our clammy bodies warmly entwined. I breathe again and cock my head back to look at Lauren. Her hair is a mess on the pillow, knotted and scraggly. Beads glisten on her forehead. Her breathing is sharp, her breasts rising up then down, trying to keep up. How did I do this? I almost cannot process what has just occurred. I have not only just had sex with the girl of my dreams, but I didn't lose my erection or come ridiculously early. Has Sarah made me a God in bed? You know, I think she may just have.

Lauren opens her eyes and watches me, a smile growing on her face. I smile back. We lie there, just smiling, I don't even know for how long. The happy drug flows through my veins so fast my heart struggles to keep up.

'That was...' Lauren whispers unable to complete her sentence. I frown, confused.

'Good?' I ask, suddenly unsure.

'Perfect,' she replies. Before I can say anything else she reaches up and pulls me towards her.

DANIEL GRANT

THIRTY - OFF

I'm conscious before I open my eyes. Warm memories and hazy dreams drift around inside my head. So much has happened. The problem I've nursed and suckled through my entire adult life is no more. I feel deeply contented. Joyful even. My eyelids flick back revealing Lauren's dimly lit bedroom. The sun strives to make the most of the slender break between the curtains.

I roll onto my side and into a mane of blonde hair. It tickles my nose. I brush it away and watch Lauren's chest moving evenly up and down as she sleeps. I stare at her face. As I look, I start wondering who was the girl that grew up to be this beautiful woman? Was she always the one in the front of class, putting up her hand to answer any question the teacher asked? Was she the devious, popular girl who bullied the ugly girls? Was she the brace-lined loner who never hung around with anyone? Who are you Lauren Bates? I want to know it all. I want to know everything there is to know about you. What really happened to your parents? Is that why you're so tough now?

I move lightly stroke her hair, careful not to disturb her. Feels like threads of silk, shimmering through my fingers. A snore escapes from her mouth, then another. I smile and extend my hand, brushing her forehead. She draws in a deep breath and turns onto her front, facing me. She puts a thumb in her mouth. I smile. So, Miss Bates, still sucking your thumb? This will be classic when I bring it up later.

I move the pillows around and lean up against them, waiting. I'm in no hurry, content just to be next to my girl. I can't remember ever being so relaxed. So calm. She stirs next to me, looking up with sleepy eyes. I smile.

'Morning,' I whisper.

'Hi,' she replies, yawning. I carefully place my arm around her and go to kiss her. She pulls away covering her mouth. 'Bad breath.'

'I don't care,' I reply and move in again. She's tense for a moment, then gives in to the kiss. Our lips break contact.

'Do you want me to make some breakfast?' she asks.

'No hurry, I need a shower first.'

'Yeah. Me too.'

After we're both done fooling around in the shower we go back to the bedroom to dress. She starts to dry her hair. I pull on my clothes, suddenly feeling the packet of blue pills in my pocket. I look towards Lauren and wander back to the bathroom. The sound of the hairdryer drowns everything out as I close the door. I pull out the bent packet and stare at it. See, I didn't need you guys afterall. In fact, you know what, I don't need you ever again. The pills say nothing, seemingly unconcerned with my change of heart. Slowly and deliberately I pop each pill out, one by one in to the toilet. The last one plops into the bowl. I peer down at the little pile gathered at the bottom. Adios. I flush the toilet, watching the water churn around until they disappear. Feels strange, almost sad. I've needed them for so long, relied on their power to fix me. But deep down it was me. It's always been me. My mind. My thoughts about me. Thanks for the memories guys, but our relationship is done. I'll bin the rest when I get back home.

Lauren finishes drying her hair and we head out for breakfast. As we walk, she puts her arm in mine. Feels like we're a proper couple. It's a little cloudy and the wind has a nasty bite to it. Lauren takes me to a small cafe up the road called 'Maggie's.' It's a simple but classy affair. The thick wooden tables and chairs give it the feel of a country pub. Everyone seems to be wearing a tracksuit and halfway through walking their dogs. We find a table and settle in. The waitress who takes our order looks like she's wearing two goldfish bowls in front of her eyes. It's a little scary. I have the full English, Lauren has muesli and won't hear my objections.

'So, how do you feel?' she asks, picking up her cup of coffee and sipping it slowly.

'Great,' I reply, 'how do you feel?' She looks at me and nods slowly, smiling.

'Good,' she says, placing her cup down.

'Last night was amazing,' I say.

'Yeah. It was good fun.' I don't know why, but bells are ringing in my head. Maybe it was the way she used the past tense there.

'You were bad,' I say. She chortles and nods again.

'Yeah, I can get a little too into it.' I take her hands in mine.

'I loved it,' I reply, still smiling. She fires a smile back then withdraws her hands. It's nothing. She just wants another sip of coffee. Amy Winehouse is playing on the cafe speakers, it seems deeply inappropriate for the moment. We sit in silence, suddenly having nothing to say to each other. 'You okay?' I eventually ask.

'Yeah.'

'You sure?'

'Yes James, I'm fine.'

'Okay.' This is weird. It's not a cold-shoulder but it sure feels chilly in here all of a sudden. Our food arrives. I wait patiently as the waitress places the plates down. I study Lauren's face, she's trying not to make eye contact. I tuck in to a large sausage, then a little hash brown. It tastes good. Lauren has two spoonfuls of muesli and

DANIEL GRANT

leaves the rest. I don't mention it. I glance out of the window, people sit at tables chatting and laughing. They're nuts, it's cold and looks like it could rain at any moment.

'So what do you fancy doing today?' I say, with half a mouthful of French toast.

'Don't know,' she replies. What is this? Last night was all lovey-dovey, now she's all withdrawn and ominously quiet. I put my knife and fork down on the place, it clangs on the china. She glances up at me. Something in her eyes that wasn't there before.

'What is it?' I ask.

'Nothing.'

'Lauren...'

'James, I said everything's fine. I'm just a bit...'

I wait.

'What?' I ask. She shakes her head. 'Scared?'

'Overwhelmed. I haven't been with anyone for six months and the last guy I was close to really screwed me over.'

'I understand.'

'You don't James, trust me,' she replies, picking up her spoon and stirring her museli.

'Help me understand then. Talk to me.' She sighs as she ponders her next sentence.

'He was Johnny Dougan.' Uh...what?

'Johnny Dougan from the Time Travellers?' I ask, trying to cover my shock.

'Yes. We knew each other at university. We got together last year and dated for like...well, it didn't work out.'

SEX LESSONS

'What happened?' She looks away as if trying to figure out a way of not telling me, then seems to give in.

'He caught me in bed with someone else.' Whoa! She's staring at me, analysing my face for a reaction. Unfortunately I'm rubbish at hiding my surprise. 'He was drunk or on drugs or something and ended up saying some crappy things about my mum and dad and...I was too weak to dump him then. I thought I couldn't live without him. Of course then he goes and writes all these songs about it and the album is played in every bloody club and radio station from here to Yemen. Can't get away from the bastard.' Oh no, I love the Time Travellers, now I'm going to have to hate them. That's fucking annoying. I hate finding out celebrities you thought were cool are actually dicks.

'So 'Cheater' was about you?' I ask. She nods.

'And Stab through the Heart, and Lies, Lies, Lies. The whole album. I even had photographers outside my house for a time.'

'Well, don't worry I promise I won't write any songs about us if we don't work out,' I say. She smiles and takes my hands again.

'Just...be patient, I know I come across as a bit harsh sometimes but inside, it's all a bit fragile.'

'I hear you.'

We spend the rest of the day just walking, stopping off in pubs and talking. She tells me more about how devastated she was when her mum died and then how she found out her dad committed suicide only a few months later. She tells me more about Johnny and how she would stand in the wings watching him perform to an ocean of people. How insecure she felt being with him and how she'd tried to get him off a lethal cocktail of amphetamines with no success. She talks about how she lost her virginity when she was fourteen with a boy four years older than her. Her voice trembles as she explains how much it hurt and how he never spoke to her again afterwards. By the end of the day I feel so much closer to her. It's strange though, she looks at me with such affection then I see the fear glazing over in her eyes and she turns away.

It's a good day, as if we're getting to know each other again, except this time I'm not seeing the hardened trading manager. This Lauren Bates is vulnerable, has a past with issues and is obviously still trying to deal with the death of her parents and break-up with Johnny Dougan.

The time approaches five when we come to say goodbye to each other. We walk to her door and kiss gently and tenderly, careful with each other's hearts. We stand looking at each other, neither saying anything. I'm always the first to look away in these moments but with Lauren I hold her gaze. As we do a new, hidden, more powerful conversation starts between us.

'I had a really nice day James,' she says.

'Me too,' I reply.

SEX LESSONS

'You're sweet. I hope I can live up to what you expect from me.'

'I don't expect anything,' I lie.

'We'll see,' she says, kissing me on the cheek. 'Safe drive home, call me when you get in.'

'It's only up the road.'

'I know. Call me anyway.'

'Okay,' I reply and with a quick wave, I start back towards my car. I turn around after twenty paces, she's still watching me. I blow her a kiss and do a silly little skip on the pavement where I trip and nearly end up in the road. She laughs but seriously I could have hurt myself. I pretend it was deliberate and turn the corner. As I walk, I replay that last conversation. What had she said at the end? 'We'll see?' What does that mean? She's already planning our downfall? No, maybe she means 'will I see' when she goes off with someone else? Fuck, I don't know what it means. Did something happen with Mark afterall and she means 'we'll see when I tell you I fucked Mark?'

I get to my car having worked myself into a state. I open the door and get inside, inserting the key in the ignition but not starting it. I sit and consider the possibilities. 'We'll see.' What will 'we see' Lauren? What surprises lurk just around the corner for us?

As I walk through my front door, my Blackberry rings. I glance at the display, it's

DANIEL GRANT

Mark. I briefly consider not answering then quickly decide that's a ridiculous idea.

'Hi,' I say.

'Hi,' he replies. I find myself surprisingly pleased to hear his cheery voice. 'You calmed down?'

'Yeah...' I say. A silence descends between us. It's uncomfortable. I take a deep breath. 'Look, I'm sorry for going off at you before. It's none of my business who you see or what you do with them.' Although, between you and me it bloody well is.

'Mate, nothing happened. I tried it on a few times but she kept knocking me back. Look, I don't want this to come between us.'

'Me neither.'

'The thing is, I think I'm still a little screwed up about Jess. I can't stop thinking about her and any excuse to focus on someone else...'

'No, sure.' Another silence before he finally says,

'I was a shit to Jess. Just took her for granted. She put up with it for so long. I dunno. I don't know why I did that. I was fucking crazy about her.'

'Sometimes we do stupid things. Maybe you weren't happy with yourself? I know what that's like.'

'Yeah. I know I can be a bit loud or whatever but Jess just saw through all that, you know?'

'Yeah. But look, it ended for a reason. You don't have to know what the reason is, just that you will end up with someone probably more suited to you.'

'Don't think it's going to be Lauren.'

'Maybe. Maybe not.'

'Yeah. So what are you doing now, fancy grabbing a beer?' He asks. A beer is exactly what I need.

'Yeah, where and when?'

'How 'bout Browns near Tower Bridge?' he says.

'Sure, in...' I check my watch, 'what, an hour?'

'Sounds good.' Maybe it's time to tell Mark the truth about a few things.

THIRTY-ONE - DOWN THE PUBLIC HOUSE

I want to call Lauren. She said to give her a ring when I got home but I'm hesitant. I'm doing all the running and I know she's screwed up about, well take your pick, but I don't want to be too eager. I s'pose I could warn her I'm about to tell Mark about us. Can't hide it forever. Fuck it, she'll be happy she didn't have to do it herself. Mark will just take it on the chin, I'm sure. Unless, of course, he did shag her in Hong Kong, then we may have a little problem. Let's worry about that when we come to it.

I decide to walk to the bar. I've got time and the sun looks like it's considering coming out. Yeah okay, I need the exercise as well. I start off along the Thames pathway leaving Canary Wharf behind me. It takes longer than I expected and I end up being ten minutes late. I get to Browns a little sweaty and wishing I'd just taken a cab.

SEX LESSONS

As always, it's rammed full and I have to stand on tiptoes to see where Mark is. I spot him at the bar, trying to catch the barman's attention. He's got a new haircut and he's used way too much gel. I clamber through people to reach him.

'Watcha. Nice haircut...not,' I say, slapping him on the back. He turns.

'Mate, what do you want, it's taken me fifteen minutes to get served,' he replies, flustered.

'Beer please.'

'Which one?' he replies, shouting above the din. I glance at the frankly outrageous choice.

'Budvar will do me,' I say.

'Okay, see if you can find a table before we drown,' he says.

'Sure.' I wander away. It's standing room only, this is a nightmare. I can't see a single empty space. People are chatting, laughing, drinking. I see a couple stand in the far corner but three guys, all in leather jackets are closer and nab the table. Fuckers. I start to move around, maybe I'll get lucky. I accidentally bang into a table as I try to move between them. A sharp pain throbs through my upper leg.

'Sorry,' I say automatically, although I think we know it should be them apologising to me for arranging the tables like that. The two women sitting at the table, both of whom look nastier than the Wicked Witch of the West, barely acknowledge my presence. This is impossible, I'm never going to- wait a second. That looks like...Sarah? She's sitting alone, drink in hand. I push past some people and stand over her. She glances up, surprise appearing on her face.

'James? What are you doing here?' she asks, hurriedly glancing around.

'Drinking. Isn't that what you do at bars? What are *you* doing here?' I reply.

'I'm...drinking also,' she says, forcing a smile. This is bad. I glance over to the bar, Mark has disappeared. I scan the crowd for him then look back to Sarah who's also looking around.

'Expecting someone?' I ask.

'Look, James can we speak another time...' I frown, 'I can't talk right now.' I look at the table and notice there's a half-pint of beer next to her glass of wine. Shit. I stare at her, she struggles for the words.

'Excuse me.' I spin around. In front of me is a large, buff guy with wire-frame specs and the remnants of acne on his face. I glance at Sarah and move out of his way, he shuffles past me and sits down opposite her. She shoots me a momentary look then faces him.

'Sorry,' I say, moving away and straight into...

'Careful,' Mark says, behind me. He's got two beers in his hands. 'There's a table right there, grab it.' I look over to where he's talking and head in that direction. My mind is spinning. What the hell is going on?

We take our seats, just as another couple gets to the table. They wander away with disappointed faces.

SEX LESSONS

'Nice,' Mark says. From my seat I can see through the gaps between people to Sarah. She faces me but is looking at him. Who the hell is he? Jason? Friend from Uni? Another guy? I sip my beer, never taking my eyes off her. She glances over to me, then quickly back to him.

'...which was fantastic. Have you ever been there?' Mark says, I tune in to the last bit and look at him.

'Sorry?'

'To Hong Kong?'

'Uh, no.'

'Strange place, I like it but it's a bit...' Mark carries on talking. I glance over to Sarah again. She's talking with the guy. Her hands reach over to his. My heart crashes to my feet. Do I go over there? What am I supposed to do? My breathing gets faster and faster. I swallow. Her eyes dart to me, she removes her hands from his. Suddenly he looks over to me. Shit. I look down.

'Hey, you even listening to me?' Mark asks.

'What?'

'You're not. What's up, you look weird.'

'Nothing,' I reply. My eyes find hers once more. They look like they're arguing now, she's shaking her head. His gestures are more erratic. He leans back in his chair, her eyes stare down at the table. Neither talks. I suddenly realise Mark has stopped talking and is glaring at me.

'What?' I say.

'You gonna tell me?'

'Tell you what?'

'What you're staring at...?' He leans into me, trying to see where I was glaring. He spots Sarah.

'Ahhh, okay. She's hot. Want me to distract the guy?'

'No. God, don't do anything,' I say, fast. He eyes me suspiciously.

'You know her?' he asks. We both stare in her direction. She glances to me then suddenly the guy turns again. He sees me and Mark both staring at him. I hear him shout something like 'it IS him, isn't it?' Sarah shakes her head and reaches for him but it's too late, the guy is already up. Uh oh. Now he's walking towards us. Uh, look at your beer. The guy appears at our table. I await some sort of physical harm to come to me. Nothing happens. My eyes dart left and right but I'm looking down so I can't see what he's doing. I chance a look up. He's standing right next to me, just staring.

'Can we help you?' Mark says in a cocky voice. The guy glances at Mark then back to me.

'Your name James?' He growls. Mark frowns and says

'Good guess, you should read palms.'

'Yes,' I reply. Here it comes. I stare at him. His face suddenly changes from anger to almost, sadness. He sighs quietly then says

'Next time you want a girl, get your own.' I stare at him and nod slowly. He goes to say something else, then looks like he changes his mind, 'hope you two are happy together. She deserves to be happy.' His finger taps the table

SEX LESSONS

next to me then he walks away, disappearing into the crowd. Don't I feel like the arsehole. Think I would have preferred it if he'd just punched me. I glance back at Sarah, she's seen the whole thing and is already on her feet walking out.

'That was weird, who was that guy, gym instructor?' Mark asks. I barely hear him as I stand and start pushing through the crowd towards Sarah. I can hear Mark yelling behind me but I don't care. I see her thrust open the door and head outside. She's twenty metres away, near the river, I accelerate towards her.

'Hey,' I call as I catch her up. 'Hey!' I grab her arm.

'What?' she replies, as I turn her towards me, tears glistening in her eyes. I let go quickly.

'Nothing, I just want to make sure you're okay.'

'I'm great James. Just fucking up my life.'

'It's not your fault...' Uh James...

'Of course it's my fault. It's not his, is it?' Very true. 'God. He was so...nice about it. I'm such a bitch.'

'No you're not.'

'Yes I am. He never did anything to make me unhappy or miserable, he just cared. That was his crime, he cared too much. What do I do, throw a fucking swing ball through his heart. Jesus.' She starts to cry, tears rolling down her cheek. I put my arms around her and pull her in to my chest. She thinks about resisting then gives in, sobbing into my shirt. I say nothing, just let her cry.

'I'll take you home.'

'I'm fine,' she sniffs, wiping her eyes.

'Sarah. Let me take you home.'

SEX LESSONS

THIRTY-TWO - AIR JUGGLING

In the cab on the way back to mine I get a text from Mark saying 'Uh dude where'd you go?' I don't reply. I feel a twinge of guilt but frankly if I'd taken him with me, there would be too many uncomfortable questions.

We arrive at my apartment, I pay the cab driver and we go inside. Sarah plonks herself down on the sofa.

'Tea or coffee?' I ask. She shakes her head. It looks like she's gone into shock. She barely said anything in the cab. I sit down next to her.

'How you feeling?' I ask. She shrugs.

'I just wanted to make it right with him. Explain why,' she says.

'About me?'

'About all of it. Now everyone will know.'

'Well, hang on, you don't know if he's told anyone anything.' She glances at me as she considers my words.

'Yeah, but Jason will probably blab to everyone now,' she replies, 'and why shouldn't he? I deserve it.'

'He may not, he seemed to be strangely accepting about it.'

'Come on James, we both know it's going to come out.'

'He *was* making you unhappy?'

'No...I dunno. I wasn't unhappy. I wasn't happy either.'

'If it's ended, it's ended for a reason.'

'Yeah, me taking my clothes off for money.' I smile. She suddenly chuckles through her tears.

'You're going to be okay. You're a smart, sexy girl.'

'Yeah...thanks. You've got to say that now the waterworks have come on. Christ, I hate being such a girl about it.' I give her another hug.

'You are a girl Sarah.' She nods with a 'guess so' look. 'Sure you don't want that tea?' She thinks for a moment then nods.

'Yeah, actually tea would be great.'

Poor Sarah, not sure what I can do to help her. My Blackberry rings. It's Mark, I reject the call. It rings again.

'Can't talk mate.'

'You don't get to call me mate. You left. Just up and walked away, didn't say anything. I sat there thinking it was a joke.'

'Sorry but I needed to get away.'

'To that girl? Is she there now?'

'Yes,' I whisper getting closer to the noise of the kettle boiling to hide my voice.

'And this is that Sarah you've been banging?'

'No.'

'Uh-huh. I don't blame you mate, she's a looker. Bet she's a screamer in bed.'

'Gotta go man.'

'Yeah right. Do me a favour, next time you want to go AWOL give me a heads up?'

'Yeah, sorry.'

'Wanker.' I hang up and put the phone back in my pocket, I turn to see Sarah standing in the doorway. My mind reruns the conversation I just had. I don't think I said anything...

'Sorry,' she says, 'was that your friend?'

'Yeah. I kinda left him there.' She pulls a sympathetic face.

'James, does he want to come over?'

'No, it's fine. He's a big boy, I'm sure he can find himself a taxi.'

'Shit, I'm sorry. Now I feel bad.'

'Don't.' I reply, walking over to her. I put an arm around her and kiss the top of her head. She leans into me and starts to kiss my neck. It's uncomfortable.

'Sarah...' I say, moving away slightly. She sighs.

'What's wrong?'

'Look, I'm seeing this girl now and...I just, don't know if we should, you know...?' She nods slowly, not looking at me. 'Is that okay?' I ask.

'Yes. Fine. Things seem to be working better for you now.'

'They are. Because of you. You've done so much, I can't even begin to tell you. I saw Lauren last night and we had sex for the first time...Sarah, it was perfect. Nothing went wrong at all. I lasted ages and...'

'That's great,' she says, turning away from me. 'Look, I'd better go. Face whatever music there is to face.'

'Can I give you something, for what you've done?' I ask. I go to my wallet and take out five hundred pounds. She turns to face me and looks down at the money sitting in my hand. Then slowly her eyes return to me. The instant I see her reaction I know I've done the wrong thing. But my hand is out there now, too late. I can't exactly withdraw it, then I'd look like a cheapskate as well as an arsehole.

'Keep it,' she whispers. She walks back to the living room to get her purse. I move quickly, dropping the money onto the table and cutting her off at the door.

'Wait Sarah, you don't have to go. I'm sorry, I just thought it might help with, whatever.'

'I appreciate it. Really. Goodbye James.' She leans around me and opens the door. I take a step away and watch her leave. Okay, this isn't exactly how I planned it. I go to the window and watch her walking away. Do I go after her? It was a business thing, like a contract. She helped me to sort out a problem and I paid her money. Yes we got close but, come on. You think I should go after her? I'm with Lauren now, Sarah was only ever my...teacher. I like her though and I care deeply about what happens to her. I hope we can still be friends. I'm sure when I call her up again everything will be fine. She's just upset about her boyfriend, that's all.

I don't know why but the Sarah thing bugs me for the rest of the evening. It continues to bug me in the car on the way to work the next day. The office has a sprinkling of Christmas decorations. I don't know who puts these things up but you'd think with all the money this company makes they could spend more than one pound fifty on paper chains and tinsel.

I find it difficult to concentrate sitting at the computer. My mind keeps wandering back to Sarah. I talk with people who have no manners. It's all I can do to stop myself from shouting at them. We need these people though, they bring in lots of money to United and they know it. Fuckers.

I feel like I've lost something. Like I'm never going to see her again. I know it's ridiculous but the thought makes me sad. I consider calling her but I can't bring myself to dial the number. It doesn't seem appropriate somehow.

DANIEL GRANT

In the office kitchen I get myself a cup of tea. I'm a million miles away when I hear

'Hi Jams.' I look up to see Gina. She's cut her hair shot and looks completely different.

'Hi, oh my God...' I splutter, trying to recover.

'You don't like it?' she asks, the smile suddenly disappearing from her face.

'No I do, it's just...it's so different.' I reply. It looks terrible by the way. I'm not a short hair guy at the best of times but it makes Gina look like a boy.

'Yeah, well I wanted a new look to go with my new job.'

'New job?'

'I got a job at Santander in Madrid so I'm going back to Spain.'

'Oh. Congratulations. That's great news.' I say stepping forward to hug her. 'When do you leave?'

'Two weeks, I was going to have a leaving do but the Christmas party is next week so I guess we can do both? Are you going?'

'If I wasn't before, I definitely am now. I'm so happy for you, Gina.'

'Thanks Jams. And if you're ever in Madrid, you always can stay with me.'

'Damn right I will.'

SEX LESSONS

THIRTY-THREE - BAD DREAMS

You know what, I'm starting to realise how much I don't like my job. All this corporate bollocks, I look around my office and all I see is misery and stress. It's like we sat down one day and came up with the worst possible conditions for the human body to endure then created a system in which we could live by them. Okay I earn loads of money, an obscene amount really but am I happy? Well okay, I'm happy about Lauren but that's not to do with work, is it? Other than the fact we work together and I wouldn't have met her if I hadn't been working here, so...umm what's my point? Dunno, I guess I just undid my argument there.

I barely speak to Lauren the rest of the week. I watch her all the time, the way her lips move when she's on the phone. Her posture in her chair as she types. Those sexy glasses. We catch each other staring every so often and that always makes me smile. I feel alive when I'm anywhere near her. Still, in the back of my mind, Sarah's still there. I know, I know. I should just pick one and be done with it. Lauren is so...I don't know, beautiful and intelligent. Okay, she's got her issues and she's a little high maintenance, but who isn't? Thing is, with Sarah I don't feel like I'm trying, everything's so easy. There's no crap, just honesty and there's something freeing about that. No, Lauren is who I want. I fell for her the second I saw her. She knows it as well. I know she manipulates me a little but girls do that all the time, don't they? And if it means I get to go home to her, it's a small price to pay.

Don't ask me why but I check my phone almost every hour to see if Sarah's called. I text her a few times as well. Just chatty stuff like 'hope all is well' and 'how's it going?' but she doesn't respond. Strange, feels like I've lost my best friend or something.

Lauren stays at my place on Thursday. She's distracted, we end up watching TV. I go to put my arm around her but she moves away, placating me by kissing my cheek. I glance at her. She's staring at the box, absorbed. I sigh and turn back.

When we go to bed, Lauren has a shower. I offer to join her, she makes some excuse about wanting to shave her legs. I sit on the bed, listening to the water hitting the floor. I wonder if this is how it will be. When she walks back into the bedroom she's wearing my dressing gown and a towel on her head. She sits at the end of the bed and pulls the towel off. I watch as she runs a

SEX LESSONS

comb through her hair, staring at herself in the mirror.

'You okay?' I ask eventually, having not tried to bring it up for most of the evening.

'Yes,' she replies, her back to me. The air is thick with atmosphere. What the hell is this? My heart thumps. I want to have it out, whatever this is. I go to say something but she switches on the hairdryer. Noise fills the room and I shy away, climbing under the sheets. My eyes move between the ceiling and Lauren. I don't know what I think anymore. I keep trying to tell myself this is what I wanted. I'm sleeping with the girl of my dreams. Yet somehow, this isn't what I imagined the dream would be. I glance over to her again. Her eyes stare at the floor as she tugs and pulls at her hair with the brush. She's a thousand miles away. I wonder what she's thinking. I feel sure it isn't about me. When her light is on me it feels like the most exhilarating thing in the world. But when she's like this, all that warmth turns cool and suddenly I feel, strangely alone in this relationship. If that's what this is. Maybe she's just having an off day or week. She is so pleasing to the eye though, it's like watching a piece of art. Her golden hair dances around her shoulders in the hot air.

She finishes and puts the hairdryer down on the table. Slipping out of my dressing gown she pulls the sheets away and slides in next to me. We lay together, neither saying anything. The light is still on.

DANIEL GRANT

'You going to turn the light off?' she asks. I sit up, leaning over towards the light, then pause and turn back.

'Lauren...?'

'Please James, I've got to be up early tomorrow.'

'Okay,' I flick the light off. Darkness engulfs the room, but sleeping is the last thing on my mind. I stare at the nothingness in front of me. I feel our souls communicating to each other, having the argument for us. My heart is still racing, I need to calm it down if I'm going to have any chance of going to sleep.

'James?'

'Yeah?' I reply, waiting for her. She takes forever to respond. Eventually she just says

'Nothing.' I consider the implications. She wants to tell me something but can't bring herself to. It's got to be she's shagging someone else, hasn't it? Maybe that Johnny fucker. Wouldn't surprise me. I should start buying Heat magazine, see if the paparazzi get a snap of them both. I need to calm down. It's probably nothing, I was wrong about her and Pasty, I'm wrong about Johnny too. I close my eyes.

I have strange dreams, all about Lauren. I see her on top of a hill, tied to a long post. She's shouting at me to save her. I run towards her as fast as I can. I'm out of breath but I keep going, faster and faster. She doesn't get any closer, I'm running, the ground is moving beneath my feet but she stays exactly where she is. Then suddenly, fire engulfs her. She's burning and screaming and I can't get to her. LAUREN!

I wake. Sweaty and out of breath. I inhale deeply, drawing in as much air as my lungs will take. I look over towards Lauren. She isn't there, just the space in the bed where she slept. I check the time, it's six-thirty. I sit up, listening.

'Lauren?' I call out. No reply. She's already gone.

DANIEL GRANT

SEX LESSONS

DANIEL GRANT

PART 3

SEX LESSONS

DANIEL GRANT

THIRTY-FOUR - WALKING ON A BROKEN SKY

I don't get it. I just don't understand her. I'm not being stupid, right? Tell me you're as confused as me? I mean, okay she's got stuff on her mind but to leave without even saying goodbye is a bit crap. Surely we're beyond that. Bet you ten pounds her excuse will be something like 'I didn't want to wake you.'

Isn't being in a relationship supposed to be pleasurable? I know that's a little naive but you're supposed to get something out of it. Aren't you? Or maybe this is the sacrifice I have to make for picking such a knockout. They're not all like this though. Sarah's hot and she's vaguely sane.

I pull on some clothes. I feel thoroughly miserable. Didn't someone say 'Thank God for Fridays?' Well he, clearly, had not met Lauren Bates. I know I need to snap out of it and I will. Maybe I should just make some coffee.

SEX LESSONS

I do exactly that, and you know what, it does lift my spirits a little. I sit in the kitchen, sifting through moments with both Lauren and Sarah as I sip my coffee. Where did the dream go?

I grab my keys and head out. The sun is just starting to peak out over the horizon, the light hitting everything with an intense orange glow. It's cold. I can see my breath but somehow the sunlight takes the edge off it. I sit in traffic in the Blackwall Tunnel trying not to think about Lauren or Sarah and failing spectacularly at both.

Maybe I need a holiday. Sarah was talking about going to Argentina before. That sounded cool. Come on James, get real. When the hell am I ever going to get to go to bloody Argentina? Don't they speak Spanish there? Fuck, I wouldn't make it past arrivals.

Having cheered myself up with the coffee, I arrive at work thoroughly depressed. I walk out of the lift and on to the trading floor. I'm early, there's hardly anyone here. Lauren's in her office. I walk over to the door and knock. She looks up, her face softening when she sees me.

'Hey.'

'Hi. You left.'

'You were sleeping, I didn't want to wake you.' Brilliant, I just won ten pounds, from myself. I smile at the irony.

'What?' she asks, smiling back.

'Nothing,' I reply, the smile draining from my face. 'Is there something wrong? I'm feeling a little strange about last night.'

DANIEL GRANT

'Can we talk about this later?'

'NO,' I say suddenly, closing the door. She glares at me, surprised at the force of my response. 'If there's something wrong, or you're not happy then talk to me, maybe I can help. Don't shut me out.'

'Jesus James, you sound like a blubbering girl,' she says with abrupt venom. Bloody hell. Easy tiger.

'Sorry for being concerned about you,' I say, hurt weaving between my words. She sighs.

'Look, I'm sorry. There's a bunch of stuff going on- '

'What stuff?' I say. Through the glass I spot Poppy walking in and sitting down at her desk. Poppy early, that's a first.

'Please James, let's talk later. Are you coming to the party tonight?'

'Is it tonight?' I ask.

'Yes. It's Gina's leaving do as well.'

'Yeah I know.' We stare at each other. She doesn't say anything and for lack of a better idea I go to open the door.

'Johnny's going to be there.' What?

'What?' I say, turning around.

'They wanted a band and Mike (buttscratcher) knew I used to go out with him.'

'So you convinced your ex-boyfriend, the one who fucked you up, to play at the office party?'

'We're still friends, we can speak to each other civilly. Mike (cockmuncher) asked me for Gina

SEX LESSONS

because she's a massive fan of theirs.' I can't believe what I'm hearing.

'This is a joke, right?'

'Come on James.'

'Come on James what?' I snap. We stare at each other. I can't take it anymore, I thrust open the door and I'm away. Poppy glances up from her desk, I barely register. I'm so angry I can scarcely contain myself. I make straight for the toilets. I burst in and slam the cubicle door shut behind me. I'm shaking with rage. I start talking to myself.

'What the fuck is going on?' I say out loud. This is ridiculous, absolutely fucking ridiculous. I lower the toilet lid and sit down. My head falls into my hands. I need to stay calm. I need to just...try to focus. Emotion courses through me like lava surging up a volcano. I'm angry, I'm upset, I'm jealous and I'm utterly insecure. Calm down James, just calm the fuck down. Take a breath in. Okay, now breathe out. Easy does it. Why would she do this? Why would anyone invite their ex to a party even if he is a famous rock star? Why would you want to be in the same room as said ex unless you still had feelings for him? I remind myself to delete all the Time Travellers songs off my iPod. I sit there for maybe forty-five minutes. I can't bring myself to go out there. I feel trapped, maybe I could fake being sick or something. Death in the family. I think I may have used that before, damnit I can't even remember my own excuses. I hear the door to the gents open.

'James?' Mark's voice echoes around the toilet. I glance up at the sound of his voice, then sit silently, hesitant to answer. The footsteps walk inside, he's right outside my cubicle.

'James?' His voice is quieter, more soothing.

'Yeah,' I reply eventually.

'You okay in there buddy?' he asks. I try to keep my emotion in check, sucking it in.

'Yeah, can't a guy take a shit any more without being interrogated?'

'Hey, I'm just checking if you're okay, Lauren said I should come find you. I thought you were praying to the porcelain god. Take your shit man.' The footsteps start to move away.

'Wait, Mark?' The footsteps stop.

'Yeah?' he says. I breathe out and stand, opening the cubicle door. We look at each other, then I quickly look away. Don't like these intimate man moments.

'What happened? Bad deal go down?' he asks. I walk over to a basin and start the cold tap. I splash water on my face. Mark waits. I wish I'd just let him go now. Save myself the Pasty Gestapo. He pulls down some paper towels and hands them to me.

'Thanks,' I say and wipe my face.

'So?' he asks. I scrunch the paper in my hands and throw it into the bin.

SEX LESSONS

'I had an argument with Lauren.' I try to say it calmly but the emotion in my voice is there and gives me away.

'What about?'

'About her ex playing at tonight's party. Did you know about that?'

'No, who's her ex?'

'Johnny Dougan.'

'No way!' Mark replies, suddenly excited. He reins it in when he sees I'm not smiling.

'So?' he asks, assuming his serious face again. I look to the ground trying to form the right words.

'You're banging her, aren't you?' he says. I look up. 'Are you?' I nod slowly. He looks up and shakes his head, breathing out loudly. 'How long?'

'Couple of weeks. I wanted to say something but it was complicated.'

'Complicated. Why? Because you're fucking this Sarah girl too?'

'No...well, yeah.' Mark nods, everything slowly clicking in to place.

'So all the time I was asking her out and flirting, you were already...' I nod again.

'It's not how it looks though,' I say.

'Oh? Tell me?' Mark replies sarcastically. He has a strange look in his eye. Disappointment.

'Sarah was helping me.'

'How? By sitting on your cock?'

'No. Come on.'

DANIEL GRANT

'Come on what? You've been lying to me for the last month mate. That sucks.'

'I know but my reasons actually made sense...'

'What are they then?' I want to tell him everything. I want to tell him how I'm not the bloke he thinks I am. I'm not the womaniser. I'm not the guy that shags around whenever I feel like it. I want to tell him I couldn't get it up and I needed to pay someone to help get it sorted out. I want to tell him that sometimes I come faster than a McDonalds Happy Meal. But when I open my mouth, nothing happens. I'm just too ashamed.

'I take it Lauren doesn't know?' Mark says eventually.

'About what?' I ask, confused.

'Sarah?'

'No.'

'You gonna tell her?'

'I don't know.'

'I'm not going to lecture you on being faithful James cos God knows I've made enough mistakes myself. I've kept secrets from people I care about. You know what happens? You lose them.' We stare at each other for a moment longer then he turns and walks out. He's right. I have let him down. I stand, staring at the door. Then I glance to the mirror and see myself glaring back. Except it's a me I don't recognise. All this time, I've been trying to sort myself out. Trying to do something about this fucking thing I've been carrying around since forever, rather than just keep acting as if I

SEX LESSONS

don't have a problem. I should have been honest. Should have just told Lauren what I was doing. I guess she can shag whoever she wants, it's not like I'm any better.

I walk back to my desk, my mind numb. I sit down. My phone rings off the hook. I ignore it, letting out a deep sigh.

'Hey,' Lauren stands next to my desk. I look up. She's tied her hair back in a ponytail and is wearing a concerned look on her face. Fuck, I don't deserve her. What was I thinking?

'Hi,' I say, uncontained misery in my voice. She sits on the side of my desk. Her voice is quiet and soothing.

'I understand why you're upset. I should have told you we were still in touch.' Oh man, don't start with this. Make me feel worse, why don't you? 'You don't have anything to worry about, okay? In fact, I've been thinking about you and I sneaking around and...maybe we should just tell people? What do you think?'

'Tell people what?' Poppy pipes up from the opposite desk. Lauren looks over.

'That the canteen is giving away free muffins today.' Lauren says, without batting an eyelid.

'Really? Oh my God.' Poppy's up and off like a flash. We watch her go. I smile and look up at Lauren who's got a mischievous grin on her face.

'So?' she asks, her eyes studying me for a reaction.

'I think...there are some things I need to tell you.'

DANIEL GRANT

'Sarah?' she asks. A million things shoot through my mind in a flash, none of which I can decipher. My eyes register the shock. She continues, 'You think I don't hear office rumours?'

'I...' Any ideas for what I say at this point gratefully received.

'Is it serious?' she asks.

'No, no it's not serious, that's the whole point...'

'I don't have any right to be jealous, James. I just want to know where we stand with one another.' What the hell does that mean?

'Why don't you have a right to be jealous?'

'We never discussed exclusivity, did we?'

'I thought it was implied.' I'm in a strange place. Jealous but not allowed to be jealous. Happy about being honest about this but at the same time not liking what I'm hearing. Doesn't she care I was screwing around with Sarah? What does that mean?

'Implied for me but not you?' she says. I shrug, unsure how to answer. 'James, I'm a funny girl when it comes to men. I want them but I don't want them. I hate the fact I need someone to be happy with myself but at the same time I love being with them. Close to them, being held. It's stupid really but I guess I'm just like every other woman deep down.' I'm confused, are you getting this?

'So...are we together or...?'

'What do you want, James? Sure you don't really want to be with this Sarah person? Who is she anyway?'

'She's...I met her in a club,' I say.

'I see,' she replies, her eyes searching me.

'What about you, sure you don't want to be with Johnny?' She sighs and raises her eyebrows.

'Johnny is too much hard work for me. We're friends, who have a past.'

'Okay. Why the cold-shoulder the last few days?'

'I have issues which are personal to me James. I don't expect you to be there for me because I'm used to being dumped at the exact moment I start to open up. So if we're going give this a chance I guess we both need to decide what we want.' I consider what she says. She's right, of course. Do I want to be with Lauren, she's pretty high maintenance even on good days? Sarah, I don't know. I get on so well with Sarah. Peas and carrots as Forest Gump might say. As if sensing my dilemma, Lauren rests her hand on my shoulder. 'Have a think. Let me know.'

DANIEL GRANT

THIRTY-FIVE - RUNNING FOR A FRIEND

I want to sort things out with Mark. I feel like such a shit for not telling him. I spot him walking out of the office, a gym bag over his shoulder. I leap from my chair and hurry towards him.

'Hey,' I say. He turns and sees me. I catch up to him. 'You going to the gym?' I ask. He glances at the gym bag then back to me.

'Yeah.'

'Do you mind if I join you, I think I need to start working out.' His sceptical look tells me everything I need to know.

'James, when was the last time you went to a gym?'

'I can run and stuff.'

'You got anything to wear?'

'Actually...no.' I wait as Mark thinks about it. Finally he says

'Come on, they sell stuff there.'

* * *

SEX LESSONS

The gym is packed. This is obviously what most of the company does in its lunch break. No wonder I never have anyone to go to lunch with, they're all down here. It's brand spanking new, the whole place is lit by those sunlight bulbs each of which probably use as much power as a small town. There are rows of running and cycling machines. Dance music blares out of the speakers and a headband-wearing, frizzy-haired gym instructor is trying to get a bunch of girls to cycle faster. She looks like she could have a coronary any moment. Think I'll keep away from her, I don't know CPR.

Oh and for the record I look ridiculous. I'm wearing tight shorts because they ran out of medium and large. I mean, who runs out of medium and large? These would be perfect on a nine-year-old. As it is, they will have to do. I'm also wearing a stringy vest. Like a T-shirt with no arms. This too, is also laughably tight, I look like a white Mr. Motivator. I hate gyms, what am I doing here? I look around and see perfect bodies everywhere. These are people who come here every day. Look at those posers on the weights, Jesus. Well done, you can lift the big one, what do you want, a gold-plated Lucozade?

She's quite fit though, that one on the running machine in the leggings. This music is getting annoying, I wouldn't even call it music, just noise with a beat. I fucking hate gyms. Mark appears from the changing rooms, he looks like one of these guys and just fits in.

DANIEL GRANT

'Right, so what are we doing first?' I say jumping up and down, pretending to look like I know what I'm doing.

'Always start with cardio. Running machine or cycling,' Mark replies.

'Pah! Cycling's for girls,' I reply and we walk over to the running machine.

'You ever used one of these?'

'Not this exact model but I know what they do,' I reply. Mark steps on to one. I follow, onto another. I look at the display and wonder if I've stepped on to the bridge of the Starship Enterprise. How many buttons does one bloody machine need? Jesus, I could time travel with this thing.

'You don't need to know what most of these do. But here's the start and stop button and these arrows make the machine go faster or slower. Okay?' Mark says. I watch where he's pointing and nod. I press the button. The belt starts moving. I walk in time with it. Okay, good. 'Remember, press this one to make it faster.'

'I know,' I reply. I press the button, the belt picks up speed, I start to jog. This is fine. I press more speed, now I'm running. This is easy. And before you say anything I'm not going to have any mishap. My legs hit the belt one after the other, bang, bang, bang, bang. I glance at Mark, he's flying. I don't look anything like that at all. I can feel my belly bounce every time my feet hit the belt. I'm not overweight okay, just have a small

SEX LESSONS

set of love handles. Extra layering to keep me warm in the winer. Fuck I hate to run.

'Don't go too high because you won't be able to do it,' Mark says. Well that sounds like a challenge to me. So being male and competitive I ignore him and press the up arrow. I can handle it. I have to run faster. I'm nearly at Mark's running speed. 'Slow down James, you won't be able to keep up,' he says, giving me a fake concerned look. I hit the speed button again, now we're matching each other stride for stride. Only problem is my legs are done and are having a teensy bit of trouble keeping up with the pace. I feel myself slowly moving back, I try to keep up but the belt's too fast.

'How do I stop it?' I shout. Mark glances at me, then reaches over to my machine but it's too late. My feet have slipped off the edge bringing my entire body down, chin first. I smack the belt and roll to the end, landing with a thud on the floor.

'AGGGHH!!' I shout. Mark slams the emergency stop button and the machine stops. He jumps down.

'You okay?' he asks, trying to lift my head. My chin and chest hurt and I think the belt burned a hole in my head. Damnit.

'No,' I say. Two instructors are on top of me before I know it. Then a small crowd gathers, no doubt revelling in my misfortune. Not only am I dressed absurdly but I'm bruised and my chin is bleeding all over my new stupid outfit. Fuck. The frizzy-haired woman tries to wipe my chin with

Detol or something. It stings with an unholy pain every time she touches it and I yelp like a lame dog.

'Don't be such a baby, it's just a scratch,' Mark says. I glare at him.

'I hate you.'

When I get back to my desk I have a large plaster on my chin and a big bruise on my chest which hurts when I breathe. Of course, when I suggest the idea that maybe I should go to hospital to get checked out Mark comes out with

'Don't be such a big Jesse, suck it up.' Great. I look like I've been beaten up or 'walked into a door.' Lauren strolls out of her office carrying some folders and spots me at my desk. She walks over.

'What happened to you?'

'Mark Pasty is what happened to me.'

'Did you have a fight?' she asks, touching my cheek as she examines my face. I flinch at her touch.

'No. I went to the gym.'

'Ah,' Lauren says in understanding. She shakes her head and smiles.

'I'll kiss it better later,' she whispers. I flinch again, this time accompanying it with an 'OW'. This just makes her giggle and she saunters away. I don't think it's funny but there we are, we always did have a differing sense of humour.

SEX LESSONS

Of course, this is exactly the look I wanted to go to the Christmas party with. I look like I've been in a ten car pileup. Damnit, why do I do these things? Mark finds me at my desk.

'How you feeling?'

'You mean other than my broken face and busted chin?'

'Yeah, besides that.'

'Great, couldn't be better. I want to do it again tomorrow.' I reply. Mark starts sniggering. 'What?'

'Nothing, just...you when you fell,' he starts laughing properly now.

'Oh that's great,' I say.

'You were like...bump, WHACK, OWW!' he says, doing the sound effects.

'I'm glad you had a good time,' I reply. He's still laughing, tears are rolling down his cheeks. The laughter eventually slows and he wipes his eyes.

'Uh, dear,' he says, 'too good.' I nod, waiting for him to come back to his senses. 'But listen mate, I kinda know why you did it and...well I appreciate it.' I turn to him, sudden warmth between us.

'You're my best friend,' I say. He nods slowly.

'I know.' We hug. It feels good to have my friend back. I slap his back and he slaps mine. And almost as soon as it started, we move apart. That's more than enough girly stuff.

'So I'll see you at the party?' he asks.

'Definitely.'

'For an audience with the Time Travellers.'

'Yeah, great,' I reply.

SEX LESSONS

THIRTY-SIX - OFFICE CHEER

The party is at Tower Bridge. I arrive at seven-thirty on the dot. I did consider trying to make myself fashionably late but after wandering around St Paul's Cathedral for the fifth time I figured I may as well just get there. Lauren was still working when I left the office. I tried to make eye contact as I was leaving but she never looked up. I walked out, struggling to ignore the slightly disappointed feeling in the pit of my stomach.

St. Paul's is lit up like a Christmas tree. I never get bored seeing it. The magnificent dome, the grandiose entrance. They've done such a good job in the lighting to make it stand out amongst the other buildings in London. The air is crisp and alive. I've got my long black coat on. I do a brilliant impression of a brooding George Clooney in this coat. I wander around with a taut face on.

Tower Bridge is another fantastic sight. People are out walking along the Thames. Somewhere I hear voices of carol-singers floating through the air. I stare up at the two bridge walks at the top of the bridge, disco-coloured lights flashing through the windows.

When I walk in, a man in a tux hands me a glass of Champagne. Good man, I like his thinking. I give my coat to the bored cloakroom attendant and wander through. At the top of the stairs I have a choice. There's a left and right bridge walk. I go for the right. 'Santa Claus Is Coming To Town' is thumping from a base system at the far end. People talk to each other in raised voices. It's not that crowded but I guess I am early. I look around for someone I know. I hate this part, Mr. Billy No-mates. There's no one I recognise here. Seriously what do all these people do? That guy there with the moustache and the Vulcan ears, I don't think I've ever laid eyes on him in our building. Freeloaders. Maybe I should ask who he is and what he does? Fuck it. Company money. I walk further along the bridge walk. The view of London is breathtaking. From this side I can see the Houses of Parliament, the Eye, the river running under me, reflections of street lights winking off the dark water. I glance around again. Still no one I know. Okay seriously, where is everyone? Then I spot Karen and Billy strolling in. Thank God. I stay put but make sure I'm visible. They're looking around now, any second...

'James,' I turn around to see...Jenny. She's wearing a short, low-cut sparkling dress. Her hair is in ringlets and she's got more makeup on than

SEX LESSONS

I've seen before. She wouldn't look bad at all...if she wasn't such a schizo.

'Hi Jen. You look, nice. I got your messages.' I couldn't help it with the last comment there. She looks down.

'Sorry James. That was a bit crazy.'

'It's okay.'

'You look nice in that suit.'

'Thanks. You too.'

'So, can we be friends, do you think?'

'Yeah. I'd like that.'

'Me too. Sorry about your coffee pot.'

'Don't worry about it.' She gives me a simple smile.

'Well, I'd better go get myself a drink.'

'Sure.' She goes to leave then turns.

'I've had a lot worse. You know?' I nod slowly, suddenly embarrassed but at the same time appreciative of the sentiment. She smiles slightly then turns and walks away leaving me to watch her go. Guess I'll have to reassign the pigeon-hole I'd put her in.

Karen and Billy have finally seen me and walk over.

'Hi James,' Karen kisses me on the cheek.

'Karen,' I lower my voice for Billy, 'Billy.' He chuckles and shakes my hand.

'Having fun with the ex again?' Karen asks.

'Oh Jenny's a scream.'

'She's in a strange place,' Karen replies. I shrug.

DANIEL GRANT

'She's alright, I think we've come to a truce,' I say. Billy laughs.

'Where do you find them?' Billy asks. I shrug again and shake my head.

'This is an amazing venue,' Karen says, taking in the cityscape before us.

'The view is better from the Wheel,' I reply. Karen rolls her eyes. We stand and stare out through the glass, pointing out London landmarks.

'Have you been to the other side yet?' Karen asks.

'Nope. We should definitely go over to *the other side.*' I reply, trying to be funny. It receives a polite chuckle. We get refills of Champagne and wander over to the second bridge walkway. This one looks east towards the tall, glittering buildings of the City and the Tower of London. We stand there for a while, taking in the beauty of it all. I hear a symbol crash and glance over to the source of the sound. I figure someone is having a laugh at my expense but I quickly realise it's the roadies setting up the drum kit for the Time Travellers, the logo plastered over the bass drum. I watch another bunch of guys moving a keyboard in place.

'You're joking, the Time Travellers are playing here?' Billy says.

'Yeah, Lauren knows them, apparently,' I reply.

'Good effort,' he replies.

SEX LESSONS

'Never heard of them,' Karen says. Billy and I both turn to her.

'You've never heard of the Time Travellers? Karen, come on.' I say.

'What?'

'They only had the number one album slot for the last month,' Billy interjects.

'Cry On My Shoulder? Leave Me The Hell Alone? Cheater, come on everyone knows Cheater,' I say. Karen shakes her head.

'You will when they start playing, you'll recognise it.' Billy says.

'Okay darling,' Karen replies, smiling. They kiss each other. I look away, pretending to be staring at the view. I sneak a peek at them. They look at each other the way new couples do, all smiles and teeth. It's cute, I guess. Karen glances over to me, I smile at her. I'm glad she's happy. They both deserve it. I love it when two of my good friends hook up, makes me think that maybe life isn't such a shitcake afterall.

'Ah, here you are!' I turn to see Mark standing next to me, a massive smile on his face. He looks like he's half-drunk already.

'What took you so long?' I ask.

'Well, strange you should mention that. I just popped around to our mutual friend,' he nods at me, tapping his finger on his nose. 'She sends her regards by the way, she'll be along later. Had a couple of things to finish up in the office,' I nod, smiling. 'Anyway, I got a little waylaid and lost track of time.'

DANIEL GRANT

'What's that, you got laid?' Billy says.

'Billy cracked a funny.' Mark wraps his arms around Billy's shoulders, instantly causing Billy to flush red. Karen rolls her eyes.

'More drinks anyone?' Karen asks. I look at my half-empty glass and hold it up. Mark looks at his full glass. You can see the cogs turning as he wonders if it's inappropriate to ask for another.

'Yes please,' Mark says, smiling. Karen takes Billy's hand and walks away. I turn to Mark.

'Look at the views here man,' Mark says, staring out towards the City.

'Yeah, pretty cool.'

'I just saw Johnny Dougan walking in.' He turns to me. 'You okay with that?' I shrug.

'I guess. Can't really be too upset about it, can I?'

'No. You can't,' he replies, 'but I'd understand if you were.'

He slaps my back. I feel the sting deep in my spinal cortex and stretch a little to shake off any permanent damage. Maybe I take Mark for granted a little too much and okay, he's nothing like me but he's what a mate should be. Always there when you need him and always ready to tell you the things no one else will. I guess I'm pretty lucky. All this time and effort trying to sort out my issues, maybe I could have just spoken to Mark about it from the start.

'So what do you reckon about Billy and Karen? Think he can get it up for her or do you think they just sit around talking about doing it?' he

SEX LESSONS

says. I smile. Then again, maybe things are exactly as they should be.

Hours go by and I get drunker and drunker. The Champagne is making a beeline for the pleasure centre of my brain. I laugh louder and even throw some moves on the dance floor with Karen and Mark. Billy stubbornly refuses to join us, preferring to watch from the sidelines. Then, the main highlight of the evening. For some. The Time Travellers start their set piece. Everyone is boogying and dancing. When they play Cheater, even Billy can't stop himself from joining in. They are great live and to be so close is fantastic, even if I can't stop staring at Johnny and imagining him with Lauren in compromising positions. His perfectly grown stubble and couldn't-give-a-shit wardrobe. Even his moppy hair somehow comes off as cool. I can appreciate talent even if they are a bunch of arseholes. Look you wouldn't want to try having a conversation with Liam Gallagher would you, but you can't argue with the quality of his music.

Johnny is a born performer and gets everyone to the perfect place. I watch him sing and move. He's pretty talented, I s'pose. I can see why Lauren would find him attractive. Apparently he writes all the band's songs and when he sings he does it with such emotion and power, I can't really compete with that. Not that I think I'm

DANIEL GRANT

supposed to. We're two very different animals. I have talents as well, like being able to eat three double choc-chip muffins simultaneously. You never saw that trick? Oh I'll have to show you it someday, it's a classic.

The band play to the interval, finishing on 'Lies, Lies, Lies'. Everyone cheers and whistles. Johnny waves as he walks off, grabbing himself a pint of beer next to the makeshift stage.

'That was fucking awesome,' Mark says, his voice hoarse from the shouting.

'Yeah, okay they're pretty cool,' I admit. Mark puts me in a headlock and rubs my head. It fucking hurts.

'He's good mate, but he's nothing on you, remember that.' I nod slowly.

'Cheers,' I say, suddenly feeling almost emotional. Must be the drink. 'I need a piss. You stay here.'

'I'm not going anywhere,' he replies. On my way, I bump into Gina.

'Hey, how's it going?' I ask.

'Jams,' she kisses me on the cheek. 'Is good. I love this party. Strange this is the last time I see everyone.'

'The place is not going to be the same without you. I mean that.' She smiles.

'Thank you. Is going to be strange leaving here. I have good friends. Like you Jams.' Gina says.

'Not sure how good a friend I've been.'

SEX LESSONS

'Don't always be putting yourself down. You are a good friend. And a good man.'

'Thanks.'

'I hear you and Lauren got together?'

'Uhh. I don't know. Maybe not,' I reply. She tilts her head. 'She's a great girl but...'

'High maintenance?' Gina asks. I laugh.

'I was going to say maybe not for me, but I guess she is high maintenance.'

'Nice tits though, right?' I glance at Gina and smile.

'Yeah,' I say. She puts an arm around me.

'Everything happens for a reason Jams,' she says, kissing me on the cheek and heading off for the dance floor. I watch her go then look around for the toilets.

I walk away to the end of the bridge and down a flight of steps. It's suddenly quiet. I can still hear the din upstairs. My ears are ringing but that will go. I get to the bottom of the stairs and look for the 'Gents' sign. I wander along the corridor, there's a slight draught coming from somewhere down here, giving it a chill. That's fine, I'm still hot from dancing. I pass another corridor and stop suddenly as I see Lauren and Johnny at the far end, talking. He is smoking a cigarette as he strokes her hair. She sits on a wooden box and pulls a cigarette from him, taking a drag. I can hear them speaking but I can't make out the words, just soft echoes. Then there's no speaking, just two people at ease in one another's company. He says something to her and she laughs, heartily and loudly. Her strange but infectious snort makes me smile. I watch them, spying on something quite intimate and yet strangely unthreatening. It seems so obvious now I see it before me. She's not meant for me. She's intended for someone else. She may not be meant for Johnny either but somehow, it doesn't matter. I know what I want and what I don't want. I feel strange. Scratch that. I feel...happy. Actually happy for her. This is how it's supposed to be. How it was always meant to be. Just being able to let someone be who they are. Not keep fighting for them to be how I want them to be.

I smile as Lauren suddenly glances over in my direction and spots me. She stares, saying nothing. Johnny takes the cigarette from her and inhales. He hasn't seen me. Lauren and I hold each other's look for maybe ten seconds but the silent conversation we have is more clear and defined than any we've had before. As if we both understand what has happened and where we must now draw the line. She gives me a simple smile then glances back to Johnny. When she looks back towards me, as I'm sure she will, I will have already gone. There's nothing more to say.

SEX LESSONS

THIRTY-SEVEN - TRY

Waves of excitement charge through me. Of course it's Sarah. She just fits. We love one another's company, I don't worry all the time, I'm sure she's in to me. Just need to get to her.

I'm sitting in a taxi staring at a red light ahead of us. I never went back to my friends. They're probably starting to wonder where I am. I send Mark a text 'Had to leave, speak soon.' A bit general I know but I'm not sure what my plan of action is. I tell the cabbie to take me to the strip club. It's the only place I can think of to try to find her at this time of night.

There are hardly any cars on the road and yet here we sit, at a crossroads on Embankment. I look over to the Eye across the river, the massive wheel lit with blues and yellows. I glance at the meter ticking over, the lights don't change. Come on, Jesus. Finally they flash amber and the taxi floors it. We drive along Embankment and turn right towards the West End.

DANIEL GRANT

I'm dropped at the main entrance. It's now past One in the morning and I can't see any sign of life. Maybe this wasn't such a great idea. Fuck it, I need to see her. I push open the door and head in.

I'm greeted by Laurel and Hardy once again. The big buff guy still glares at me like I'm about to pull a gun on him.

'Good evening sir,' the guy with the dodgy moustache says. I wonder if he ever stands up or does he just put up with the haemorrhoids. 'Ten pounds, please.'

'Do you know if Sarah...Bunny is working tonight?' I say, handing over the money.

'I don't know, check when you get in,' he replies, not looking up from his clipboard. I pay the money, wander past the big guy and make for the bar.

Deafening music echoes around the corridor as I walk inside, wondering if I'm doing the right thing. The bar bustles with people. At the far end, a bunch of guys are loudly shouting at one of the girls on the tables, looks like a stag do. To the left are four guys in tie-less suits chatting loudly to two other women, also in suits. I don't know why but seeing women in a strip club surprises me. I must be getting old. I scan the line-up of girls next to the stage. Bunny isn't one of them.

'Good evening sir.' A dark-haired, tanned, half-naked waitress stands next to me. She holds an empty tray in her hand.

'Hi, is Bunny working tonight?' I ask.

SEX LESSONS

'Uh, I'm not sure, I only just started. Take a seat, I'll see if she's here. Can I get you a drink?'

'Just a beer, thanks.' She nods and walks away. I wander over to a table and park myself. The girl on the pole moves slowly up and down, then spins around and pushes her arse into it, bending down slowly. The stag-do boys are raucous. It feels like I'm left waiting for ages. I keep checking my watch, uncomfortable being here on my own.

The waitress arrives with one of the strippers. She's got huge breasts under her swimsuit costume thing. Her hips wiggle as she walks and her long red hair almost reaches her arse.

'Hi, I'm Carla, you looking for Bunny?'

'Yeah, is she here?' The waitress places my drink on the table and walks away.

'She's not working today.'

'Oh.' Of course she's bloody not.

'You a regular?'

'Sort of,' I reply. Now what? I could call her I guess. Just feels like I need to talk to her in person.

'How about an alternative?' Carla says, sitting down next to me. I move away.

'Thanks but I need to see Bunny.'

'Okay. Can I give her a message?' I stand up.

'Tell her James Kennedy came by.' I go to walk away.

'You're James Kennedy?' I turn.

'Yeah,' I reply. Carla stares at me.

'Bunny told me about you.' My heart leaps to my throat.

'Yeah?'

'You're an idiot.'

'How's that?'

'You're too late.'

'I just need to talk to her.' Carla stares at me, mulling over what to make of me.

'Like I said, you're too late. She left.'

'What?'

'Quit, two days ago.' Carla stands to leave.

'Wait,' I take out my wallet and pull out a fifty, 'where can I find her?' She looks at the money then shakes her head.

'Sorry. Can't help you.' Carla walks back to the other girls. I stand, throw a tenner onto the table for the beer and leave.

SEX LESSONS

...TRY

I take a cab back to my apartment. I sit in the back, lost in a world of thought and analysis. She quit the club? What does that mean? I wander in and shut the door. I walk into the living room, open the French doors and look out at Canary Wharf. It's raining again. I pick up my mobile and find Sarah's number. I click 'Hide Own Number.' Then I dial her. It rings three times then a click. I hear her voice, sounds like I woke her.

'Hello?'
'Sarah.'
'Who's this?'
'It's James.'
'James? What time is it?' I glance at my watch.
'Ten to three,' I reply. She groans.
'What do you want?'
'I went to see you at the club. They said you quit.'
'Yeah.'
'Why?'
'What do you care?'

'Come on. I care.'

'James, I've got to be up early tomorrow. I've got tonnes of catching up to do.'

'Look, can we meet? There's a few things I want to say.'

'Say them now.'

'Please Sarah.'

'No, James I'm busy. You know, I can't keep dropping things because you suddenly decide you want to see me.'

'It's important.' There's a long wait on the end of the line.

'Where?'

'My place? Or Brown's?' I hear her sigh on the other end of the phone.

'What time?'

'One, tomorrow?'

'Okay, Brown's at One.' She hangs up. The time's set, now I'm nervous as hell.

SEX LESSONS

TRY AGAIN

I don't sleep at all. I stare at the ceiling. Waiting. I close my eyes, but they seem to have a mind of their own, flicking open again. The ceiling's still there. I run through what I'm going to say to Sarah, none of it works. Eventually I give up on sleep, get up and make myself some breakfast. It's strange, just waiting. Darkness outside, me sitting with a cup of coffee and a piece of toast. Waiting. Even thinking about Sarah makes my heart beat faster.

After what feels like an agonisingly long time, the cuckoo clock next door strikes noon. I leave my apartment and jump into a cab that smells of shoe polish. I wipe the build-up of condensation on the window with my hand and stare out, the rain patting against the glass. This is it. Note to self, must make her believe I want her and I'm not just trying to win her back because things with Lauren didn't work out. Anyway, let's cross that bridge when we come to it. *If* we come to it.

DANIEL GRANT

I arrive at Brown's at twelve-thirty. I'm early but I want to get a seat and work out a well-conceived plan of attack. Also I need at least one beer in me before we proceed. To oil the engine.

I go inside. It's busy but not as packed as last weekend. Good. I order a beer and find a table in the corner.

What do you think, do I small talk first then hit her with the whole 'I love you' thing? Or do I just come straight out with it?

Small talk first? Yeah, I think so too. Okay, that was an easy one to get us started. How about-

'James?' I look up to see a woman, about my age, standing opposite me. She's got long, slightly messy dark hair and is developing bags under her eyes. She wears a little too much makeup, as though out of practice. 'James Kennedy?'

'Hi,' I say, confused.

'You don't recognise me?' she says, her smile fading slightly. Oh man, come on. What now, did Sarah send her older sister or something?

'Uhhh...' is about all I can manage.

'It's Susie. Susie Green. Well, Susie McMillen now.' Oh my God. Paris Susie.

'Susie? How are you?' I stand and move to kiss her on the cheek.

'I'm good. I just saw you come in and I thought it was you. I've been standing over there wondering if I was going mad.'

'Yeah, it's me...you look, great.'

SEX LESSONS

'No I don't but it's nice of you to say. That's what three kids will do to you.'

'Three? Wow,' I reply. She looks worn out. Tired but happier than I remember. There's still something in her eyes.

'You here alone or...?' she asks.

'No I'm meeting someone but...'

'Oh well, I won't keep you. I just wanted to say hi.'

'Yeah.'

'You look good James.'

'Thanks, you too,' she smiles, as though I've made a joke that wasn't funny but felt she had to laugh anyway.

'Well, I'll let you get on. I doubt whoever this girl is will want me hanging around.'

'How'd you know it's a girl?' She thinks for a moment and frowns.

'I guess I don't. Is it?' I nod slowly.

'Yeah. It is.' We look at each other, it's not awkward but I can't think of anything to say.

'Well, I live in Clapham. In the phone book if you ever fancy catching up properly one day.'

'Sure, yeah. That would be nice,' I reply.

'Good to see you again James.'

'Good to see you too.' She nods then turns and disappears into the crowd. I watch her go. Susie Green. How random is that? She looks so different. But there's still some connection somewhere. My heart is pounding like drug dealer in a raid. I feel all sorts of strange and conflicting things, I want to talk to her, catch up. And yet at the same time, I don't. Maybe it's better she remains a part of my past. All the issues I have are partly because of her. So many of my hang-ups, my neurosis about sex, so much of it stems from my time and experiences with Susie. And yet, here she is. Just another woman in the crowd.

SEX LESSONS

...AND AGAIN

I check my watch. Five to one. Okay, not long now. The clock ticks down to the moment. I glance back towards where Susie had been but I don't see her. Okay good. Don't need that hanging over me. I take another sip of my beer. What am I saying here? 'I love you?' Come on James. No, okay. Not 'I love you.' I care for you a lot. Sounds a bit wanky. Fuck, I don't know what to say. Maybe I should have written out index cards or something. I glance around, everyone is laughing and chatting. Seemingly having a great time. I catch my reflection in the mirror behind the bar. I don't know what to make of the likeness staring back at me. This was a bad idea. I stand up and shove the chair into Sarah's legs.

'Excuse me...oh hi.'

'Going somewhere?' she asks.

'No, I was just...do you want a drink?'

'Why don't you tell me what you need to?' she says. I nod and signal for her to sit down.

'Have a seat.' I say. She pulls the chair out and sits, folding her arms. I need to find my words now. Come on James, seal the deal.

'The thing is...all this time we've been practising for when I would be with Lauren. And well, it was nice but there was something missing.' When she doesn't respond I carry on. 'With Lauren, I mean, there was something missing with her. She's beautiful and smart but... she's not, I mean...it's not comfortable with her.'

'Look James, I don't think I can do the lessons anymore.'

'I don't want you to.' She looks surprised at that.

'So...why am I here?'

'Sarah, when it's you and me I don't have to try to be someone I'm not. I don't have to tell you things I think you want to hear. It's easy and relaxed. It's weird because I was with Lauren and I suddenly realised that she isn't what I want.' Sarah's face still hasn't changed expression. I was hoping for a softening or something but she just keeps staring at me with a blank look. Maybe I'm boring her. I breathe out too fast, giving away my nervousness. 'Look, I think you're great and I know we've had our ups and downs but...what do you think?'

'About what?' Okay. Don't make it easy, I get it.

'About you and me? Being together?' There I said it. About as graceful as a rhinoceros at touch-typing lessons. I stare at her, trying to read every slight change in her expression. She frowns. Fuck, she's not going for this. Then her eyebrows rise slightly and she catches me staring straight at her. It's more than a little disconcerting. I look away.

'Are you being honest with me James? You sure it wasn't the fact that maybe Lauren dumped you and you can't stand being by yourself?'

'No. She didn't dump me.'

'But you didn't come to this conclusion all by yourself, did you?'

'I did actually. Last night we had our Christmas party and I saw Lauren with Johnny Dougan.'

'The singer?'

'Yeah. He's one of her ex's. I watched them together and they weren't kissing or doing anything but you could tell they were just…comfortable with one another. They were better suited. I realised that's what we have. I can be myself with you. And don't tell me you don't feel something for me because I know you do. I've seen it.' She nods slowly, taking in my words.

'I do. I liked you the first day we met. I didn't want to admit it but…it got harder and harder for me, the more we saw each other. I got so excited when you texted me. But every time you brought up Lauren, it just hurt. Especially our last conversation.'

'I know. I'm sorry. I'm sorry it took me so long to realise all this stuff. But if you feel the same then...we can do this, can't we?' She glances to the table then back to me.

'I don't know James.' She shakes her head and starts biting her thumbnail. 'I don't know.'

SEX LESSONS

THIRTY-EIGHT - ACCEPTANCE

I feel like I've been sitting on this seat for a week, my arse thinks it's a block of stone. It's a glorious summer day and I'm wearing a brand-new dark grey suit I bought especially for the occasion. My girl sits next to me, wearing a hat. She's smarter than me. I should have put sun cream on my neck though because it feels like I'm starting to burn. In front of me Mark plays with his iPhone as discreetly as he can. His skin is far more suited to this climate so he doesn't need to worry about the factor thirty. In the front row, I see Billy. He looks uncomfortable all dressed up. I can't believe he asked Karen to marry him. I can't believe she said no. Well, what she actually said was 'not yet.' But looking at them, sitting next to each other all giggling and smiling I guess it's only a matter of time. Weird seeing them all dressed to the nines like this. Not sure about that floral dress Karen's got on but whatever blows her hair back I guess. I look around at all the other people waiting, clapping, chatting. Man these things go on.

'Then I hear her name...' Have you guessed yet? Course you have, you've been way ahead of me through most of this. Pisses me off.

'Sarah Thornton,' says the fat man with the silly robes. He stands on the stage searching the crowd. I look to Sarah who glances at me, a big smile on her face. She flicks her eyebrows up. She's so pretty with that cute little smile of hers, just gets me every time.

'Guess this is me,' she says, standing. People start to clap. Her black robe flows around her ankles as she heads up towards the stage. She walks gracefully up the steps and stands next to the fat man who hands her a scroll. A quick flash from the professional photographer as she shakes hands with the Dean. Then a whisper of congratulations. I'm proud of her, she's worked so hard for this. I hold up my camera and snap some shots for the album.

'Go Sarah!' Mark shouts, clapping and whistling. She smiles with a slightly embarrassed face as she heads down the steps. I stare at her walking towards me, suddenly feeling nothing but total appreciation for all the silly moments that brought me here. All that worrying and vexing. How much time did I spend agonizing, failing and disappointing. Years, decades? Here's the girl who solved it. The girl who showed me the way, with grace and dignity. She's started to walk in slow motion now, her eyes remaining on me. A smile

SEX LESSONS

fixed on her beautiful face. A gust of wind catches her hat which she manages to grab in time, giggling as she clutches it. Her wonderful laugh filling the air around us. Sarah Thornton, the only girl to see the real me.

Sarah and I started seeing each other on the twenty-second of December. She never went back to the strip club. Instead she spent all her time studying.

Our sex life is staggering. I have never been so at ease and so ready to experiment than I am with her. I have lost my fear and habit of overanalysing which, in the end, was what it was all about. Allowing my fear of not performing to paralyse me. I'm not saying that it doesn't happen every so often. It does. But when it crops up I look at it in a completely different way, I'm not scared of it. I know that if I just enjoy the moment, enjoy being with the girl I love, my body will follow. I am so in love with her I can barely focus on anything else. I love where we are and how we got here. It's that delicious time when everything's new and exciting. I can't wait to get home everyday to be with her and it pains me to leave her behind in the mornings.

Lauren and Johnny didn't rekindle their old romance, she said she'd been there and done him. She's started dating some guy called Ollie. Says he's a great guy, journalist or something.

DANIEL GRANT

Personally I don't trust that fucker, but whatever she wants is cool I guess. Lauren and I are good friends, she talks to me about her personal stuff and I kinda like that.

Weirdly Mark ended up seeing Sarah's friend, Kate for three months after we introduced them at my birthday. But they split up and went their separate ways. He declared it was the best sex he ever had but that 'the bitch was getting too weird.'

I have to say, my life's pretty much perfect the way it is now. Sarah's already looking on the net for deals to Argentina. Always wondered what it would be like. I've heard so many brilliant things about the place.

And to you, thanks for constantly keeping me in check and making sure I wasn't being a pillock all the time. But listen, the whole sex problem thing, do me a favour. Don't tell anyone, okay? I know I've sorted it out but that doesn't mean I want the whole world knowing about it. It can be our little secret, okay? Thanks, I knew I could count on you.

ACKNOWLEDGMENTS

I wish to thank all the people who gave their precious time to read and review early drafts: Caz Coronel, Adrian Pinsent, Laura Kuenssberg, Charlotte Essex, Jo Smith, Toby Brown, Alexandra Vanotti and David Riseley.

Thank you to Alison, without whose support this book would never have happened.

And thank you to the readers of youwriteon.com for their constructive comments that have only made the book better.

Lightning Source UK Ltd.
Milton Keynes UK
UKOW050615140412

190719UK00001B/2/P